DEATH FOLLOWS HER

ALSO BY RACHEL DYLAN

Standalones

INCRIMINATING EVIDENCE

OUT OF HIDING

PICTURE PERFECT MURDER

Atlanta Justice

DEADLY PROOF

LONE WITNESS

BREACH OF TRUST

Danger in the Deep South

LETHAL ACTION

DEVOTED DEFENDER

Capital Intrigue Series

END GAME

BACKLASH

POWER PLAY

Windy Ridge Legal Thriller Series

TRIAL & TRIBULATIONS

FATAL ACCUSATION

SURROUNDED BY DARKNESS

FALSE PROPHET

DEATH FOLLOWS HER

A DEADLY JUSTICE NOVEL

RACHEL DYLAN

Death Follows Her
Copyright © 2025 by Rachel Dylan
Ebook ISBN: 9781641973366
Print POD ISBN: 9781641973427

NYLA Publishing
121 W 27th St, Suite 1201, NY 10001, New York.
http://www.nyliterary.com

1

"Shots fired. I repeat, shots fired." FBI Supervisory Special Agent Samira Haddad hit the ground hard using the black government issued SUV as cover while the cacophony of gunfire erupted around her. She popped up quickly to look for her partner, Jalen Smith, but didn't see him. They were following up on what was supposed to be a routine lead in southwest Atlanta. This was anything but routine. It was just the two of them on the scene as they waited for the backup that Jalen had called in.

"Samira," Jalen yelled. "Are you hit?"

"No. I'm good." Her pulse thumped quickly as she assessed the threat level. "Are you?"

"Yeah. I'm coming your way." Jalen sprinted over to her side of the vehicle and crouched down low beside her. "Our intel wasn't solid on this one."

No, it wasn't, and that infuriated her. "It was a trap." More gunshots rang out, but after another minute, backup arrived on the scene allowing her to let out a breath. Two agents ran toward them and took cover as more shots were fired in rapid succession.

They were still outnumbered and by the sounds of those

rounds, they were out weaponed as well. "We should wait on SWAT before we go in."

Agent Sparks shook his head. "No, we can handle it."

She fought to keep her expression neutral. Sparks was a hotshot, and it was because of reckless ego-driven men like him that people got killed. "No way, Sparks. I'm the senior agent on the ground, and I say we wait for SWAT."

Sparks rolled his light brown eyes at her but didn't say a word. Then after a moment, he muttered under his breath.

"Want to say that any louder, Sparks?" She'd heard him well enough. A few choice words that included calling her weak. That was the furthest thing from the truth, but she didn't care what he thought about her. She'd more than proven herself time and again to those that really mattered, and Sparks didn't fall into that category. She had no problem pulling rank on him.

"I'm good," he said.

She glanced over at Agent Miller who just gave her a small shrug. She felt sorry for Miller having to be paired with a man like Sparks. He ran all over his younger, female partner. It wasn't Samira's place to interfere with their partnership, but on days like these, she really wanted to. Miller wouldn't have a chance at succeeding under Sparks' iron fist.

With SWAT's arrival, they could finally move toward the abandoned warehouse and try to apprehend the suspects. Jalen was close by her side and the other two agents were right behind. She fell in line behind the SWAT team. "Be careful. We don't know what is really going on in there. We're assuming they're all hostiles, but we just don't know. Nothing about this has panned out as advertised." The last thing she wanted was innocent blood on their hands.

SWAT had the heavy artillery that she didn't. They evaded more gunfire but as they got closer to the building, movement caught her eye on the roof and her heart dropped when she saw it. "Grenade!" She yelled as she fell to the ground, bracing for the worst. The explosion threw her backwards hard, knocking the breath out of her. Acrid smoke filled the air and she tried to sit up. She could hear SWAT barking out orders as loud sirens blared indicating even more reinforcements.

Jalen crawled over to her. "Samira, you're bleeding."

Looking down, she saw the blood on her shoulder. Moving her shoulder, she winced, but it could've been worse. "I think I was hit by debris. Nothing major." She stood up and felt woozy but didn't say anything. Jalen grabbed her arm. "You're not going in. There are a million cops here now."

She sighed out of frustration because her partner was right. The scene was now swarming with both FBI and Atlanta PD. She trusted Jalen with her life, but what a mess this had been. The bad guys were probably long gone now, and their lead to the crime boss they were hunting had just evaporated.

Another FBI agent she didn't recognize ran over to her. "Are you Agent Haddad?"

"Yes." She looked at the short, stocky agent wearing an FBI jacket.

"I'm Agent Morris. You're needed back at the field office."

"Now? What could possibly be more important than this? Are you aware of what just happened here? We need to clear the building."

The agent lifted up his hand. "I'm just the messenger, and I was told to bring you back. It's urgent."

Jalen moved toward her. "Go ahead. I'll handle it here."

"Thanks." She started walking with the agent and her mind went into overdrive thinking about the possibilities of why she'd been pulled out of an ongoing operation.

Once back at the Atlanta field office, she was instructed by the agent to go upstairs to her boss's office. A sinking feeling formed at the pit of her stomach. Unannounced boss's visits were never good.

When she arrived at the office of Assistant Special Agent in Charge Myron King, she looked into her boss's light blue eyes. The fifty something year old ASAC was an FBI lifer. Divorced, fiercely devoted to his job, and sometimes part of the old boys' club although he was coming around. Samira had been working to convince Myron that people like her deserved a seat at the leadership table.

"Samira, there's blood on your shirt," Myron said. "Are you okay?"

"Yes, sir. Nothing major. Just collateral damage from the ambush. I'll be fine."

He didn't look fully convinced. "Sorry to pull you out of the field, but this is a hot one."

"They said this was important." She held her tongue from comparing this meeting to the crime scene she had just left.

"It is." His loud voice bellowed through the room. "I've got the higher ups breathing down my neck about this new case."

That didn't sound good. "What is it?"

Myron fiddled with his cufflinks. "Do you remember seeing the death of Russell Myers in the news a few months ago?"

She raised an eyebrow. "The plastics CEO?"

Myron nodded. "Yeah. He was CEO of Newton Plastics."

Samira snapped her fingers. "Hey, weren't they in a big trial this year over them dumping toxic waste in low-income neighborhoods?"

"Yes, and they won that case. The jury found no liability, and it was a huge victory for the company."

She still didn't understand how this involved her. She worked violent crimes. "What's the deal now?"

"The ME concluded it was a cocaine induced heart attack that killed Myers, but his family has been pushing the police to open up a criminal investigation because they believe it was foul play since they didn't think that Myers was a coke user. Because of the family's clout, Atlanta PD opened up a case, but still ruled the death a heart attack and found no evidence of murder."

"If that's all there is, seems a bit thin, don't you think? Just a rich and powerful family able to pull some strings because they don't want to face the hard truth about their loved one?" She understood all too well the pain of unexpected loss.

"But that isn't everything. The family wasn't deterred because since Myers' death, two other prominent CEOs have also died, including one just last week, and the Myers family is redoubling their efforts to try to get definitive answers. Answers that they want to hear. So, Atlanta PD is asking for our help and inviting us in. Local PD in Virginia has been looped in as well because one of the deaths occurred there. They need our expertise on this one."

She leaned in. "You've got my full attention now." As an experienced agent in the Criminal Investigative Division of the FBI, she'd seen and experienced a lot, and she wanted to hear more before casting any judgments.

"There's a common link between these CEOs that we know about. All three companies have been in big litigation recently, and they were represented by the same attorney."

"Are you bringing me into this because I went to law school?" There were many days when she wished she didn't have a legal background, and she was beginning to think this was going to be one of them.

"Honestly, that's part of it. You at least get the legal landscape better than most agents, but the main reason I want you on this case is because it's high profile. I need someone I can count on. You and Jalen are a formidable team. You're the senior agent here, so you'll be in charge of the investigation from the FBI side. We must have answers quickly and without making a mess. And even more importantly, we need to determine if there is an ongoing threat to CEOs and stop it."

"What do we know about the lawyer involved?"

"She's a well-known and highly regarded trial attorney representing big corporations, always on the defense side. For these cases we're talking about, she won them all."

Questions shot through her mind. "How did the other CEOs die?"

Myron opened up a folder and slid it in front of her. "That's where things start to get a bit tricky. Maxine French, car accident. Ran into a tree and had high blood alcohol levels. Then last week, Warren Cruz, prescription overdose that is being looked at as a suicide."

"So not the same cause of death."

"True, but there could still be a connection. Myers and Cruz at the very least have the drug commonality between them."

Taking a minute, she studied the documents in front of her. "Back up a minute. If there is a link between these deaths, and all three CEOs were actually murdered, are we thinking serial murder here? Someone with a vendetta against big company CEOs? Or maybe some radical anti-capitalist group?"

"Everything is on the table at this point, but Strickland has made it clear that this case was our top priority right now especially until we get a better handle on things."

She had some ideas about that. "Strickland just wants to make sure there isn't any fallout that comes down hard on him."

Myron had a strained relationship with his boss—the head of the Atlanta field office. Dominique Strickland was a gifted Special Agent in Charge, but Myron and Dom butted heads constantly. The two alpha males filled up any room they walked in, but Samira wasn't threatened by either of them and had to make sure both were supporters of her career. That required a lot of political finesse, but she had proven time and again she was up to the challenge.

She picked up the folder. "This could get messy. Big corporations have money and power which means they also have influence. I can see why Strickland is worried. How are we going to play this?"

Myron loosened his striped tie that appeared to be too tight around his neck. "Talk to Detective Perez with Atlanta PD. He's leading the charge, but the message was clear to me that they want to let the FBI run point on this. They are stretched thin and need our help. You and Jalen should review these files we have on the three CEOs, but if I were you, the first real move has to be to talk to this attorney. Lawyers always know where the skeletons are hidden because that's their job."

"Is she local?"

"Yes. A swanky Atlanta midtown firm."

She smiled. "This keeps getting better and better."

Myron stood and walked over to her. "This case could be a career maker."

It could also be a career killer.

2

That night Samira went over to Jalen's condo in Decatur. Her mind was still reeling from the events earlier in the day. What a way to start the week. First the ambush, and then the even bigger bombshell that her boss had dropped on her. This was a huge opportunity to advance and take the next step in her FBI career. They had told her she was one high-profile case away from a major promotion.

She'd been a prime target of intelligence agencies out of college—born in the U.S. of Lebanese descent, fluent in Arabic, and top grades from Georgetown. The CIA, NSA, DIA, they'd all come knocking at the government recruitment fairs on campus, but she'd had different ideas. Being an FBI agent was what she wanted to do.

Of course, the FBI made promises to her that they hadn't kept —namely that she'd get to start her career in the violent crimes division. They'd told her *after* she had accepted the job and soared through Quantico finishing at the top of her law school class that there wasn't an opening, and she'd been shipped off to counterterrorism over her strenuous objections. Most of her colleagues didn't trust her then because they never tried to get to know her. Her time in counterterrorism was a dark chapter in her life that she still hadn't fully come to grips with and prob-ably never would.

She knocked on Jalen's door. She hated showing up unan-nounced, but he hadn't answered his phone, and she didn't want to leave him a message about this.

After a minute, Jalen opened the door. His golden-brown skin glistened like he had either been working out or had just gotten out of the shower. "Are you alone?" she whispered.

Jalen laughed loudly. "Yeah, but it's not like you to show up without warning. What's going on?"

She eyed him again. "Put on a shirt. Let's go for a walk."

"Are you okay?" Concern showed in his big, brown eyes. They were tight and she considered Jalen family.

"Yeah. I'll explain."

"Come in. Just give me a minute."

She flopped down on his couch while he was in his bedroom changing. Jalen had been her partner for five years now. They'd both been a bit skeptical about the pairing at first, feeling like the FBI might be using them as tokenism for the next governmental diversity flyer, but they quickly put that concern aside and formed a bond that had only gotten stronger with each passing day. There was absolutely no one she trusted more than him.

Because they were so close, a lot of people wondered if they were a couple, but they had clear boundaries. Romance messed up a lot of things, especially partnerships. But she couldn't blame people for speculating. There was no doubt that Jalen was incredibly attractive and there was more fraternization between agents than most people realized. But to her, Jalen was the brother she never had. Not to mention she was still in love with her boyfriend who had died five years ago. No amount of therapy had been able to push her back out into the dating pool.

After a minute, Jalen returned in a red University of Georgia t-shirt and running shorts. "I'm ready. Talk to me."

"Let's walk and talk. I'm high-strung right now."

Jalen raised an eyebrow. "I can see that."

He'd sent her an email debriefing about what had happened earlier after she had been summoned to the office, but she wasn't here now to talk about that. Once outside of his condo, the early summer humidity hit her, and she could feel her naturally curly hair expanding by the minute. They walked down the sidewalk for a moment before he spoke.

"What's going on? What happened? Are we in trouble?"

Samira looked into her partner's eyes. "Not exactly, at least not yet. We're being brought into a big case."

Jalen grabbed onto her arm pulling her to a stop. "Hey, that's good news."

She took a moment and recounted what she'd been told earlier in the day.

Jalen let out a low whistle. "This could get messy. Corporations wield so much influence. If they think someone is killing their CEOs, there will be a lot of heat on the FBI to get a suspect apprehended ASAP."

"I had a good meeting with Detective Perez from Atlanta PD a few hours ago. They are drowning, and don't feel like they have the resources right now to put on this. They're leaning heavily on us to get the job done, so thankfully it doesn't seem like we're going to have any turf wars. I've reviewed everything, and I'll email you copies of what we have, but we need to go interview this attorney tomorrow."

"Tell me what you know."

"Her name is Quinn Kelly. Thirty-eight years old, works at Whitner & Stokes, which is a premier law firm in Atlanta that has offices across the country. She went to Emory for law school and undergrad and has spent her entire legal career at the firm. They specialize in defending big corporations—think banks, big Pharma, Fortune 500 types."

"This investigation may make you question whether you made the right decision by going to the FBI instead of practicing law."

She looked up at him. Something she was accustomed to

doing since he was a good foot taller than her. "I have no doubt I'm where I need to be. It might've taken me some time to get to the right part of the FBI, but once I got to violent crimes, I knew I'd found my place. Anyway, according to the research I did after I met with Myron, Quinn has an impeccable record as a trial attorney. She won these big cases we're dealing with here for this investigation and many more. She's only lost one case this past year."

"I'm looking forward to this one. We haven't had any investigation quite like this before. Who knows what we'll discover, and maybe you'll get that promotion to ASAC out of it."

She lifted up her hand. "We need to solve the case first. If we fail, the ramifications won't be good either."

Jalen squeezed her shoulder. "You know I've got your back. Let's do this thing."

3

The next day, they showed up unannounced at Whitner & Stokes. Unexpected visits from the FBI had a way of getting people's attention and that is exactly the effect that Samira wanted. She'd spent a long time last night internet surfing and digging into Quinn Kelly. There was a lot of fodder. Quinn dealt with the media regularly, and it seemed like all her cases were major ones. She definitely didn't shy away from the attention.

Samira respected someone like Quinn who could rise through the ranks of a big law firm. It wasn't easy. While she'd decided to go to the FBI instead of practicing law, she had many friends from law school who had gone to large firms—and some of them had crashed and burned big time. The pay was great, but the churn and burn twenty-four seven mentality wasn't something that everyone could handle. It took a special type of person, not only to survive, but thrive in that cutthroat, intense environment. And it looked like Quinn Kelly fit that bill.

They were ushered into a conference room by the receptionist and told that Quinn would be with them momentarily.

"Wanna place a bet on how long we'll be waiting?" Jalen asked.

"Quinn's probably racking her brain trying to figure out which one of her clients could be in trouble."

Jalen laughed. "Yeah. I guess that would be my first instinct as well if I were in her position."

They didn't have to wait long before the door opened, and Quinn strode in. They both rose to greet her. She walked with great confidence in heels that only accented her tall, lean frame. Her long red hair had been perfectly flat ironed, and her black power suit was most certainly tailor made. Freckles were scattered across her pale skin with rosy undertones.

Quinn flashed a smile. "Agents, I'm Quinn Kelly. Welcome."

"I'm Supervisory Special Agent Samira Haddad and this is my partner Special Agent Jalen Smith."

"Nice to meet you both. Please have a seat." Quinn motioned toward the large conference room table, and they took their seats.

"What can I help the FBI with today?" Quinn asked.

"We're here to talk about some of your clients," Samira said.

Quinn quirked an eyebrow. "Clients? What's going on?"

Samira glanced at Jalen and then he spoke. "What do you know about the death of Russell Myers?"

"He passed away of a heart attack a few months ago now," Quinn said softly.

"I'm sorry that this might be a difficult discussion for you." Samira didn't want to cause this woman pain, but there was a bigger picture here, and she feared the threat was still very much real.

After a moment, Quinn lifted her head. "It's okay, Agent Haddad. I understand that you have a job to do."

"When was the last time you saw Russell Myers?" Jalen asked.

"It was the week before he passed away," Quinn responded. "We were actually talking about me working with them again when the next lawsuit came in. The executives were very pleased with the results."

"And where were you on the night of March 3rd?" Jalen asked.

Quinn picked up her phone. "Let me look at my calendar." She scrolled for a moment. "I was at a legal conference in Orlando from March 2nd to March 5th."

Samira took down some notes. "I'm not sure if you're aware of the death of Warren Cruz?"

Sucking in a breath, Quinn's eyes grew wide. "Warren? No. What happened to Warren? I haven't heard anything about this."

Samira softened even further. "It just happened last week, and they've been trying to keep the news quiet given the circumstances."

Looking down for a moment, Quinn then reengaged eye contact. "What circumstances?"

"They're investigating his death as a drug overdose," Jalen said.

Quinn shook her head. "No way. Warren wouldn't have taken his own life. He was thriving both personally and professionally. He loved spending time with his grandkids and his business was booming. This doesn't even make sense. Agents, you're going to have to help me out here. What am I missing?"

Samira was far from done. "Unfortunately, there's more. Maxine French. Are you aware of her death?"

Frowning deeply, Quinn shifted in her chair. "Yes. It was a car accident. She was driving under the influence. Went to DC for a big lobbying event, had too much to drink, and then drove into a tree in the Virginia suburbs. She had actually invited me to attend, but I had a court appearance that conflicted. She was all about trying to support other women. I have wondered if I would've accepted her invitation if things could've ended up differently." Quinn tapped her perfectly manicured red nails on the conference room table. "You're starting to think that these deaths are not all accidental, aren't you?"

Samira wasn't surprised how quickly Quinn caught on. The woman was obviously brilliant or wouldn't be such a successful trial attorney. "That's what we're hoping you could help us with, Quinn. You're in the unique position of having been the attorney for all three of these CEOs."

Quinn lifted up her hand. "Technically, I wasn't their attorney in a personal capacity. I represent the various companies that they work for. My firm represents the company, not the individual."

"I get the legal distinction," Samira said. "But to the outside world, you litigated these cases and defended these three companies. Now all three CEOs are dead."

The room was silent for a moment before Quinn spoke. "What can I do to help?"

Jalen piped in. "We're going to need you to work with us to dig into those three cases, and importantly, we have to understand what you're currently working on."

"Why?" Quinn asked.

"Because if there is something sinister going on here, then those in your next lawsuit could be a target." Samira tried to remain patient.

Quinn's aqua blue eyes narrowed. "There are attorney client privilege issues here that I have to be acutely aware of. I can't just open up my ongoing case for you to ferret through. And for my past cases, we'd have to get the clients to sign off on anything as well. As you can imagine, most companies don't want the FBI rifling through their business."

The trial lawyer in Quinn had started to come out. Samira was surprised it had actually taken this long, and she had to hold back a smile. She appreciated this woman's tenacity. "Quinn, I don't think you understand the stakes here," Samira said. "People are dead. There's a chance that they were murdered and there could be more coming." She wanted to let Quinn know that she had no problem playing hardball too.

Silence filled the room before Quinn responded. "You're right. There has to be a way to reach both of our goals here. I'm still hoping that this is all just an awful, coincidental string of events."

"This could be nothing, but we don't know that yet, which is why we must investigate fully." Samira wanted her to understand that they weren't just going to go away.

"Even if I wanted to cooperate on the spot today, the firm simply wouldn't act under these circumstances without following all legal protocols exactly by the book. I'm sure you can appreciate that given the nature of what we do as a law firm." Quinn clasped her hands in her lap. "I will make the ask and explain the exigent circumstances involved. I'd also request that we have some sort of limitation on what is fair game. For instance, if during your search you find something totally unrelated, I want the FBI's agreement, in writing of course, that it cannot be used against my clients."

"We're investigating murders here, Quinn. We don't have an interest in these companies' business practices." Although she would've liked to have expanded the case, that wasn't her job, and protecting the lives of any future victims was her first priority.

"Good." Quinn gave a weak smile. "Then it seems like we're on the same page."

At least they were making some progress. "Thank you. Once you talk to your clients, we're going to need to do a more in-depth interview with you."

"I'll need a little time. We had today off because of a scheduling conflict with the judge but my closing argument is tomorrow."

"Fair enough," Samira said. "What about Friday? I know it's still quick, but unfortunately, we're racing against the clock here too."

Quinn nodded. "I can make that work. But as you can imagine, on some of this, I'll only be able to go as fast as my clients will go."

Samira also knew that Quinn would have a lot of control over the client's reactions and how much they would be willing to cooperate. "Understood. Your current case, the one you have the closing argument for tomorrow, can you please tell us about it."

"Sure. I'm defending Asbury Pharmaceuticals in a product liability class action. A typical Big Pharma case with no merit."

"Is the CEO involved in the litigation?" Jalen asked.

"Yes. He was a key witness, and he's the corporate representative at trial."

Jalen leaned in. "We should talk to him about the possible security threat here. Can you provide his information?"

Quinn grabbed one of the notepads from the conference room table and jotted something down. "Here's his info, but please let me talk to him first. Then you can do what you have to."

Jalen took the paper from Quinn. "Okay, but we need to have the conversation soon because there's an active threat."

"I'll call him as soon as you leave."

Quinn was basically telling them that their time was up for today. Samira wasn't ready to push. Not yet anyway. She gave Jalen a little nod.

"Thanks for your help today," Jalen said.

"I can have someone come back and escort you out."

"No need. We can see ourselves out." Jalen stood.

Quinn gave a bright smile that didn't seem authentic. "I look forward to speaking with you again soon."

Samira didn't believe that for a moment, but Quinn was good at playing the game. When they got outside, Samira turned to her partner. "She's the real deal."

"Yeah. Trial lawyer through and through."

"I would've done the same thing to protect my clients. She doesn't want us messing with her cases. Big companies don't like the FBI digging into their business, and I can't blame them. We both know there will be things they don't want the feds to know about if we start investigating."

Jalen looked at her. "We should go to the closing argument

tomorrow in Quinn's trial. It's possible that her current client could be a target, and we should have a face to face with him and level set his expectations."

"Agreed. We'll also get to see Quinn in action and find out what all the buzz is about. If today is any indication, then we're in for a show."

4

uinn took a deep, steadying breath as a bead of sweat rolled down her back. Even though the AC was blasting in the courtroom in typical southern fashion, it wasn't enough to cool her down. On the outside she had to show the jury ultimate confidence, but on the inside, she was worried about losing this case. Losing wasn't acceptable.

As one of the top trial attorneys in Atlanta, Quinn had a reputation for winning the most difficult cases. Her tactics were sometimes unorthodox, but she got the job done. Now she had to finish up the last lines of her closing argument with passion and without equivocation. And today she had an even stronger motivation—the two FBI agents who had visited her yesterday were in the audience. She loved nothing more than providing a star performance.

"Ladies and gentlemen of the jury, as I told you during my opening argument, and as I have shown you throughout the trial, the plaintiffs simply have no concrete evidence that would allow you to find in their favor in this vitally important case. Asbury Pharmaceuticals and their leadership including the CEO, Richard Hale, should not be held liable for the deaths of the plaintiffs. While our hearts go out to the families of the deceased, pinning the blame on a drug, when there is zero evidence to show that the drug was the cause of their deaths, is not justice. It is *injustice*. So, in closing, I implore you to follow the evidence, the science, not emotion. Justice systems built on emotion will always fail, and you must make decisions based on evidence and the legal standards put forward in front of you by this Court. Therefore, you should find in favor of my client, the defendant, Asbury Pharmaceuticals. I appreciate your time, and again thank you for your service."

Quinn walked back to counsel's table keeping her game face on and listened intently as the judge provided instructions to the jury. Now she would have to wait. Something she hated.

Her second chair, senior associate Allie Prince, gave her an approving nod. Allie had been at the firm seven years and was on her way to partnership if Quinn had anything to say about it. Allie worked tirelessly but would have to improve her political skills to handle the firm partners. The pretty, petite blonde had caught some of the partners' attention from day one but not for the right reasons. Quinn had immediately taken Allie under her wing to try to protect her from their leering eyes and prying hands.

"Quinn." Richard leaned over to her, his breath hot on her ear. "You did a great job out there. Now it's out of our hands, but at least we know we did everything possible to protect the company."

"Thank you, Richard. We have no way of knowing how long the jury will deliberate. We'll just have to take it one step at a time and try to remain calm."

Richard ran his hand through his thick salt-and-pepper hair. "You never seem to flinch, Quinn. You amaze me. I would never be able to do what you do."

If only he knew the half of it. "As I told you before, and as we've discussed with the board members, this is a tough case, but the settlement numbers are astronomical, so sometimes you just have to buckle up to go for a wild ride and hope that the chips fall in your favor."

Richard patted her shoulder and stood. "I know the risks involved in trying this case. You've done everything and more for us, Quinn. We won't forget that for future cases."

She glanced over her shoulder. "Those FBI agents I told you about are coming up here. They're going to want to talk to you."

Richard groaned. "I get it, but I don't like it."

"Let me do most of the talking, but remember, they're not investigating you. At this point, they're trying to protect you."

"Of course."

"Allie, we have some business to attend to on another matter with the FBI. I'll see you back at the office, and we can circle up on next steps."

"Sounds like a plan. You were great up there." Allie smiled widely. "I have a good feeling on this one."

She hoped Allie was right. She watched as the agents approached her. Samira Haddad, the senior of the two agents, had a petite frame but a big presence. There was something magnetic about her that interested Quinn. She wondered what her story was. Her long, wavy dark hair was pulled back in a low ponytail. She wore minimal makeup, just a little lipstick and mascara, and her olive skin was flawless. Quinn would've killed for that type of skin. Hers was full of freckles and got patchy red spots all too often. Wearing sunscreen was a must year-round.

Samira's partner, Jalen Smith, towered over her. Six three at least, with a smooth, shaved head, clean cut. Not to mention he was smoldering, but she wasn't looking for a fling with an FBI agent. She couldn't even begin to think what a bad idea that was.

"Agents, good to see you again." Of course, it wasn't that good to deal with the feds, but she was playing well in the sandbox right now because she wasn't sure where this investigation of theirs was going to lead. "This is my client Richard Hale, the CEO of Asbury Pharmaceuticals."

After some preliminary introductions, Samira stepped closer.

"There's actually an empty conference room down the hall that the bailiff said we could use to have some privacy."

Quinn looked around and saw Gemma Holland, the reporter for the Atlanta Legal Times. Privacy was probably a good idea. "Absolutely."

They started to make their way out of the courtroom and Gemma blocked her way. "Quinn, can I get a statement?"

"If you want to wait around, then yes. I have another matter to attend to right now."

Gemma eyed the FBI agents with great interest like a shark circling in bloodied water. "I'll be here when you get back."

Quinn had a love-hate relationship with Gemma. Sometimes Gemma was just what Quinn needed to further her ambitions and other times she was a real pain.

They made their way out of the courtroom and down the hall to the conference room. Once everyone had taken a seat around the table, Samira was the first to speak.

"Thank you for your time today, Mr. Hale," Samira said.

He gave a weak smile. "Please call me Richard."

Samira looked directly at Richard. "I'm not sure how much your counsel told you, but we're investigating the deaths of various CEOs—all of whom were represented by your counsel."

"Yes, Quinn told me that you're worried that I could be in danger too."

Samira shifted in her seat. "Potentially, yes. We're at the beginning stages of our investigation, but given what we know now, there is cause for concern—especially if you are victorious in this litigation."

"You think this guy is some sort of vigilante?" Quinn wanted to get as much information as possible to understand what she was dealing with.

"That's one possible theory," Jalen responded.

"What do you need me to do?" Richard asked.

Samira's dark brown eyes focused in on Richard. "It's ulti-mately up to you to decide what you're comfortable with, but if I were you, and had the resources to do it, I would hire some private security—at least until we get a better grip on the true nature of the threat."

Richard's face started to pale as he finally understood the ramifications of what the agents were suggesting. Last night when she'd talked to him, she had tried not to completely freak him out. She needed to keep him on her side. Let the FBI be the bearers of bad news. That was fine with her.

"I can talk to corporate security for the company," Richard muttered.

"That would be wise," Jalen said. "And if you start to notice anything out of the ordinary, please let us know immediately." Jalen offered his card. "This has all of my contact info. Call anytime."

Richard placed the card in his navy suit jacket. "Thank you."

"Is that it?" Quinn was ready to get back to work.

Samira nodded. "For now. But remember we're talking on Friday."

How could she forget? "Yes. Let's say ten o'clock at my office. If the jury is still out, then I'd be on call to return to the court."

"I understand," Samira responded.

Quinn took Richard by the arm and escorted him out. They walked back into the courtroom.

Richard grabbed onto her shoulders. "Tell it to me straight. How worried should I be?"

Quinn broke the contact between them. "We just don't know enough yet about the facts. Hopefully the FBI investigation will be able to determine quickly what is going on here. In the meantime, I do think taking extra precautions is a good thing."

"All right. Call me the moment you hear anything on the jury." He patted her shoulder. "Again, great job."

She started to pack up her things, and she saw that Gemma was still waiting for her.

Gemma was a tenacious young reporter. Smart as a whip with no fear, she figured that Gemma had her sights set on something bigger and better for her career in the future. Gemma definitely had a face for TV with sleek blonde hair and big hazel eyes. She decided it was time to deal with her, so she waved her over.

Gemma pulled out her phone. "I'd like to do a live video if that's okay with you so I can stream it to social."

Quinn wasn't that vain, but appearances were important, so she grabbed her lipstick out of her purse and reapplied before putting some powder on.

"You look great. I like the suit," Gemma said. "That royal blue blouse really brings out your eyes."

"Thanks." Quinn ran her hand through her silky red hair and faced Gemma. "I'm ready when you are." There was no room for being camera shy in her line of work.

"This is Gemma Holland, coming to you live from the Fulton County Courthouse in downtown Atlanta where closing arguments have just been completed in the case against Atlanta based drug company Asbury Pharmaceuticals. I'm standing here with Quinn Kelly who represents the defendant. Quinn, how do you feel like the trial went?"

Quinn flashed her best, confident smile. But not too confident. "We put on a vigorous defense of Asbury Pharmaceuticals because that's exactly what the company deserved. There is simply no evidence of their liability in this case. My heart truly breaks for the families involved but placing the blame on an innocent party isn't going to bring justice. And that's exactly what I always want no matter the circumstances, no matter the client." Quinn smiled broadly again. "Now you'll have to excuse me. I need to get back to work."

Gemma stopped recording. "That's all you're going to give me? Seriously?"

"While the jury is still deliberating, yes. It was a good sound bite. You should run with it."

"Well, it was streamed live, so we'll see what kind of reception it gets." Gemma put her phone in her pocket.

"I noticed that your follower count keeps growing." She'd kept close tabs on Gemma because it impacted her public image as well.

"And I work hard for each one of them." Gemma beamed. "I'm sure we'll be talking after the verdict."

"Of course."

"Hey, what were those FBI agents doing here?"

There was no way she was telling Gemma about that right now. "I'm sorry. I'm not at liberty to say."

"C'mon." Gemma pouted. "Give me something, Quinn."

"I just can't. It's not my place to say." That would be the quickest way to get on the FBI's bad side.

Gemma's nose scrunched up. "Interesting. Okay. I'll take that for now, but I'll be asking you again. You know I'm persistent."

And that she was.

Gemma turned and walked away, and Quinn finally had a moment to let out a breath and gather herself. She had eyed two of the jurors with skepticism. They seemed to hate Asbury Pharmaceuticals from day one—or maybe they didn't like her—or both. She hadn't lost a jury trial in the past ten months, and the thought of it happening now sickened her. The power had shifted to the jury and all she could do was wait.

5

That afternoon Samira looked across the conference room table at Jalen. They had a lot of work to do. "Let's start with the first known death and work our way from there."

Jalen lifted up his hand. "Hold up. You said first known death. You think there could be more."

It was something she'd given a lot of thought to. "First off, we don't know if Russell Myers was actually murdered, but for the sake of argument, let's say he was. My point is that he might not be the killer's first. It might just be the first one we know about."

"Always the eternal optimist," Jalen laughed. "Don't ever let me get as cynical as you. One of us in this partnership has to hold out hope."

He was right, but she wasn't changing. Cynicism was in her DNA. Jalen's optimism was what she needed to balance her out.

Jalen tapped his pen on the open folder in front of him. "Says here, Myers was CEO of Newton Plastics—a major corporation that was accused of mass environmental pollution. The plaintiffs were those from the neighborhood where they claim the toxic chemicals were dumped. A lot of kids got sick and two of them even died. Horrific stuff. Makes me sick."

"You're thinking one of the parents."

"I mean, if you thought someone was responsible for the death of your child, and they got off in a jury trial, maybe you'd take drastic action."

"It's a good theory. We will need to interview those families, focusing on the ones where the children passed away."

Jalen blew out his breath. "Those won't be pleasant."

"When is our job ever pleasant?"

"Good point. But we have to be careful. Those families have already been through so much. We can't go in accusing them of murder."

That's the last thing she wanted to do. "I have no intention of making that accusation, but we have to exhaust every avenue here, and they are a logical place to start."

Looking down, Jalen flipped through his notes. "What do you make of the cocaine being the cause of the heart attack that killed him? Could he have been given the coke by someone who wanted him dead? And would that alone have been enough to kill him?"

"Coke can cause heart attacks but if your goal was murder, don't you think you'd want to make more certain that you were killing him?"

"Yeah, and remember they were working this case not assuming any foul play. There could've been something else in the coke that wasn't looked for in the tox screen."

"We're limited to the information we have in the Myers file, so we may never have answers to that ultimate question."

He grabbed another folder from the desk. "Okay. Then victim number two. Maxine French. She was CEO of Crown Bank."

She studied her notes carefully. "The case against Crown Bank was a class action related to predatory lending practices. None of the plaintiffs were actually killed because of the actions of Crown Bank, but the economic impact could've been huge."

"And an economic hit could lead someone to depression, and they could've fallen into a deep and desperate hole. After the jury found Crown Bank wasn't liable, then maybe one of the customers took action into their own hands."

Samira thought for a moment. "Not as strong of a motive as your child dying but could still be motive nonetheless."

"Completely agree. But French getting drunk and driving into a tree might be more difficult to set up."

"Yeah. That would be tricky especially since there is no evidence of anything but alcohol in her system and they did run a thorough tox screen, so I think that rules out her being drugged with anything else. Says here in the file that there was also no evidence of any other car being involved, and no mechanical error with the vehicle. No forensic evidence showing anyone else in the vehicle with her."

Jalen shuffled the folders. "Even though there was no real evidence indicating another car being involved, it's still a possibility. What if she got forced off the road and there just wasn't anything left behind that the cops found?"

"We can't completely discount that possibility. Also, the killer would be crossing state lines. This happened in Virginia, so it's an outlier in that way as well."

"Also, something for us to consider is that French is female. We don't know if the gender of the victims will play a role in this."

She wrote that down to make sure to think about any patterns or deviations.

Jalen opened the next folder. "Then next we have Warren Cruz from Bentley Biologics. Class action case for a drug his company produced to treat various types of arthritis that the plaintiffs claimed caused cancer. Once again, the jury found Bentley Biologics was not liable. A number of the plaintiffs have died from cancer."

"I can say one thing. Quinn Kelly's record is impressive. This is a wide variety of cases, and she took them all on and won. I wonder if the CEOs were always present at the trial like Richard Hale was today."

"Their presence front and center at the trial only solidifies their taking responsibility for the actions of the company."

"The CEO point is a strong one, but we have a problem. We have identified separate motives for the plaintiffs in each case to kill the corresponding CEO, but what we don't have is any theory or explanation for the crossover, and that's what really bothers me."

"Everything bothers you, Samira." He paused. "Then we could have someone just taking out big company CEOs who they believe are bad actors, right?"

"Yes, but if that's true, how would we begin to narrow that suspect pool?"

Jalen drummed his fingers on his notepad. "What about jurors? What if one of the jurors got bullied into voting in favor of the corporation but then had second thoughts. So they try to make it right—only to find out they actually enjoy the vigilantism and decide to take it to the next level with other CEOs."

She bit her lip. "That's not a bad thought." Jalen was brilliant and had no problem thinking outside the box—just one of many reasons she enjoyed working with him. But she also felt something deep in her gut. A nagging feeling that they weren't seeing the truth, but she didn't have anything to go on. "We talked about the gender of the victims, but what about the killer? Vast percentages are in favor of a serial killer being male, but the manner of death could lend itself to the possibility of it being a woman."

"I think we have to keep all options open as far as the gender of the killer."

"Agreed."

"And now you're frowning."

"Yeah. Trying to put it together and I'm not liking what I'm seeing. Under any of these scenarios, we still have a murderer on the loose who will most likely keep killing."

Jalen groaned. "If there is a favorable verdict for Asbury Pharmaceuticals in this current trial, we need to push Hale harder on the security front. I know we didn't want to do that before a verdict was announced, but I don't see any other option."

"I agree with you. We'll see if Quinn convinced the jury once again of her client's innocence. What's your gut telling you? Bad coincidences or something more sinister?"

"Door number two."

"My fear exactly."

6

That evening Quinn sat on her sofa typing away on her laptop. In addition to all the work she did at the firm, she had a side gig that she didn't advertise—working pro bono for the women's domestic violence legal clinic.

Quinn did this work in the shadows because that's how she preferred it. She wanted to be the voice of other women who didn't have someone to fight for them. But the last thing she wanted was attention for her efforts. She tried to keep her involvement in public hearings to a minimum because she wasn't trying to get accolades for her work in this arena, but she was trying to get justice. Her driving force in life. To make sure justice was served.

She'd gone to work at a big law firm out of necessity. She had six figures of student loan debt from Emory Law and no family support of any kind. Initially, she'd only planned to stay as long as it took to get the debt manageable, but once she realized her gift for trying cases, she couldn't stop. It was like a drug for her. The high of standing in front of the jury against all odds. But that didn't prevent her from doing this important pro bono work that was close to her heart.

"What do you think?" She looked over as Felix, her large, orange tabby cat.

He let out a big yawn.

"Am I boring you?" She rubbed Felix's head and was grateful that he was the only man in her life. Felix wouldn't hurt her.

Unlike being in the background for her pro bono work, for her billable trial work, she thrived on being front and center. She spent more time than she cared to admit on social media and doing TV interviews. If she wanted to be known not just in the Atlanta market as a premier trial attorney, but the country, it would require putting herself out there.

A few years ago, she had decided to go all in on setting up the major social media accounts. She had thousands of followers, but that was only the beginning.

For content, she would often do short videos on hot legal issues and of course promote any big wins that she had. Because she was so accessible, she got her fair share of crazies who messaged her, but that was how social media worked. In the end, the extra effort would help elevate her profile which was really important for her long game.

It also gave her leverage with the firm because she was building her individual brand—not connected specifically to the firm. If the firm ever did anything stupid and she had to leave, she could take all of her followers with her.

Her cell rang. It was Richard. This couldn't be anything good at nearly ten o'clock at night. She had no choice but to answer it. Duty calls.

"This is Quinn," she answered.

"It's Richard," he said in an unsteady voice. "Sorry to call you so late."

Her stomach clenched. "Is everything okay?"

"I'm not sure. I feel like I heard a noise in my house."

She blew out a breath. "Are you worried someone is inside your home?"

"I thought I heard a crashing noise. I went downstairs, but I didn't see anything broken or out of place. Maybe I'm being paranoid, but I can't be sure, especially after what those FBI agents said."

She needed to think quickly on how to handle this. "You're right. You should call the police. Have them come and check it out."

"Do you think that's overkill?"

She sighed. "Richard, if you feel like someone is in your house, you should be calling the police, not calling me."

Richard groaned loudly. "Maybe I'm just on edge. I let those agents get in my head."

It was becoming clearer to her that Richard was crying wolf. "Where are you now?"

"I'm downstairs and I've turned on all the lights."

"Are you alone?"

"Yes. My wife is at our beach home."

"Don't you have a security system?"

"Yes, but I hadn't turned it on for the night yet."

That wasn't the smartest move, but she held her tongue. "Look, you need to do what you feel comfortable with. I get the hesitation on calling the cops, but are you going to be able to sleep tonight with it hanging over your head? Would you feel better if they came and looked around?"

Richard breathed heavily into the phone. "I'm just making another round."

She waited patiently. Once Richard had let the threat sink in, his mind had started playing tricks on him.

After a few minutes, he finally spoke again. "I've walked both floors of the house. I don't see anything. I guess I'm paranoid."

"No. You did the right thing by being cautious." She needed to keep his trust and the last thing she wanted to do was to make him think she took these threats lightly.

"I'm ready for this trial to be over. That way at least there will be some finality."

She felt the exact same way. "Maybe we'll get a verdict tomorrow. You never know how long it's going to take a jury." And whether justice would be served.

7

"What's taking them so long?" A red-faced Richard looked at Quinn as they sat beside each other at counsel's table. They'd been summoned that morning to the courtroom for the verdict. It was sooner than she had expected.

She patted his hand like he was a little puppy. "Richard, please take a deep breath. It actually hasn't been that long at all. You're working yourself up."

He let out a big breath. "You're right. Honestly, I'm not even sure what I'm more nervous about at this point. Winning and facing this unknown threat or losing and facing a very angry group of board members."

She fought to keep her composure because Richard was clearly not holding it together. She found it ironic that these big and powerful male CEOs were often the first to crumble under pressure. "Richard, this is a really tough case. I hope we won, but we'll have to see what the jury thinks. And as far as your personal security, the FBI is in the room right now. Nothing is going to happen to you."

His eyes lit up. "They are?" He craned his neck to search for them in the gallery. "Good. I see them. I do feel better. I never called the police last night, but I guess I should bring it up to the FBI if we talk to them afterwards."

"That sounds prudent." She'd spotted Samira and Jalen the moment they'd walked in. It didn't surprise her that they showed up. They were just doing their job.

The minutes seemed to drag on forever as she tried without success to make Richard shut up. At some point, she tuned him out as he droned on and on. Finally, the judge entered the courtroom and brought in the jury. She leaned over to Richard. "Stay strong. No matter what the verdict. Don't let them see you sweat, okay? This is important."

Richard nodded. "Yes. I understand."

Quinn had dealt with men like Richard her entire career. Privileged, wealthy, and never thinking that anything bad could ever happen to them—and if it did, there were always ways to fix it because money solved all problems. She'd seen the darkest side of humanity. Some days she didn't even believe there was much light left in the world, but she still kept fighting for the fledgling hope that she could make a small difference in her own small way. And that didn't include the work she did defending CEOs like Richard.

The judge started to go through some particulars before asking the jury for its verdict.

She waited patiently to see what those individuals had decided. Had she done enough? Was Asbury Pharmaceuticals liable? That was the multi-million dollar question.

Quinn sat with her head held high in the uncomfortable courtroom chair and waited to hear the words out of the mouth of the jury foreperson.

"We the jury find in favor of the defendant, Asbury Pharmaceuticals."

The courtroom was abuzz. Another victory. Oh, how sweet. Before she could do anything, Richard placed a slobbery kiss on her cheek.

"You did it, Quinn!" His eyes were wide with excitement as he grabbed onto her shoulders.

"Remember. Composure, Richard," she hissed. She didn't want the jury to see an overly exuberant Richard because sometimes that could make you look guilty even if you weren't. Appearances were everything, and while this jury's job was done, her reputation was something she was always cognizant of.

"Of course." He moved away from her, but she could tell he was about to burst. Guess it turned out after all that he was much more afraid of the board of directors than from a vague threat.

The next few minutes went by in a blur, but once the jury and judge had left the courtroom, she turned to Allie. "Great work on this case, Allie."

Richard nodded. "Quinn tells me how many hours you've put in and the company appreciates all you've done. I can't think of a better wing woman for Quinn."

Quinn was proud of her protégé. "Me either. You worked hard for this win, Allie."

"I'm learning so much from you, Quinn." Allie beamed. "I only hope that one day I'll be half the trial lawyer that you are."

She gave Allie a quick embrace. "You will."

Allie's light blue eyes met hers. "I'll get back to the office and check in with the Horizon Pharma team and see where we are on trial preparation."

There wouldn't be much turnaround time between the two trials. "Thank you, Allie."

Once alone, Richard turned back to her. "The Board will be ecstatic."

That also meant that she would most definitely be receiving the next big case that came in from Asbury Pharmaceuticals.

"I don't know what we would do without you. You won this case for us, Quinn. No doubt in my mind about that. If there's anything I could ever do to help you, just name it."

Before she could respond, the FBI agents popped up to rain on their parade. "Agents," she said. "I guess under the circumstances, I'm not surprised that you decided to pay us a visit."

Jalen moved in closer. "Congratulations on your victory, but now we have to consider that the threat against Mr. Hale has gone up."

Richard's mood shifted instantly, like a deflated balloon as reality was setting back in and he cleared his throat. "I was hoping you would tell me that there was no reason to be concerned anymore."

"Just the opposite," Samira responded. "This verdict, while great for your company, could be the inciting event for the killer."

"What am I supposed to do?" Richard asked. "I thought I heard someone in my house last night, but I never found anything or anyone."

Stepping forward, Samira placed her hands on her hips. "Why didn't you call us immediately? We gave you our contact info."

"I thought I was being paranoid."

She needed to jump in quickly. "Richard called me. I was on the phone the entire time as he checked out the house and then armed his security system. We discussed contacting the police, but Richard felt it wasn't necessary. Although, I see your point about the outcome of the case, and I'm sure Richard would like to hear your thoughts on his security situation." As would she.

Samira tapped her foot, clearly annoyed. "We are suggesting, as we did already, that Mr. Hale strongly consider getting private security. We don't have the FBI person power at this point to divert an agent given where we are in the investigation, but considering the many resources at Mr. Hale's disposal, I would think it prudent for him to act."

"I'm standing right here, you know," Richard piped up. "The company will provide me with what I need. How much security are you talking about here, agents? I just want to wrap my head around this."

"We're not talking about an army, are we here, agents?" Quinn wanted to level set expectations.

Jalen shook his head. "No. We'd even take one person, but two would be even better."

Richard's eyes darted back and forth. "Exactly how real do you think the threat is against me?"

"I'm not going to sugarcoat it, Mr. Hale." Samira wore a grim expression. "We believe there might be a pattern developing here. If we're right, and there is a killer intent on going after CEOs after they've won lawsuits, then it would be entirely reasonable to think that the threat against you is real. Having said that, we are still in the very early stages of this investigation. Things could change quickly, but we'd prefer you err on the side of caution."

She wasn't used to seeing Richard without words, but these agents had just rendered him speechless. She figured he'd had enough though. "Thank you for all the information, agents. Richard understands what is at stake here, but we were also just victorious in a major lawsuit, so we have some media commitments we need to handle now."

"Of course," Samira said. "Mr. Hale, please let us know if anything happens, no matter how small."

Richard nodded. "I will."

"Thank you both," Samira said.

Quinn took a deep breath. It was time to bask in the limelight for a bit and enjoy their victory. That meant speaking to the media who would be outside the courthouse. "Richard, we need to go now and talk to the press." Really, she would be the one doing the talking, but Richard would get the photo op as well. It was a win-win for them. It would also help Richard get his mind off of what the agents had told him.

Richard buttoned his suit jacket, and they walked out of the courtroom and down the long corridor that led to the front of the courthouse.

"What do you need from me?" Richard asked.

"Just nod and smile, but not overly so. We won and we should put our stake in the ground, but we need to do it in a classy way."

He placed his hand on her back. "I'll let you do your thing."

They stepped out of the courthouse and several Atlanta news crews were there to report on this huge case. It wasn't her first time in front of them, and it definitely wouldn't be the last. She had to admit, she actually enjoyed this part of the job. Another time to be in the spotlight. A place she thrived.

She noticed out of the corner of her eye that Samira and Jalen had decided to stick around. All the better that they understand how she handled the press.

"Quinn!" One of the reporters shouted. "How do you feel about the verdict?"

She took her own advice and gave a quick smile but then tampered her enthusiasm. "Today the jury got it right. We appreciate their hard work, and it's a great day when we see the justice system working."

Another overeager reporter stepped forward. One she recognized as young, ambitious, and most importantly, unfriendly. "What would you say to those that feel you distorted the facts for your client's gain? That you purposely confused the jury."

She stared the young man down without flinching. "I would say that type of statement doesn't do the jury justice and is condescending. The jury was a smart group of dedicated individuals who took time out of their lives to engage in their civic duty. They took the facts as presented and made their own decision."

The reporters peppered her for about five minutes, and that was her limit. Long enough to be relevant but careful not to overdo it. The balance with the media was a tough one she had to strike.

She was telling the reporters that she was finished when Richard spoke up.

"I'd like to say one thing."

Dear God, what was Richard doing? She'd told him to be quiet, but she couldn't exactly drag him away as that would look awful.

"I know you all are grilling Quinn, but I have to say there is no doubt in my mind after watching her in this trial that she is hands down the best trial lawyer in this town. Probably in the country. Asbury Pharmaceuticals is proud to have her as our counsel. Today the truth prevailed, and Asbury Pharmaceuticals can continue to do its vital lifesaving work."

"Liar!" Someone shouted. "Killer!" A young man emerged from the crowd of reporters and lunged toward Richard.

Instinctively, she stepped in front of Richard, shielding him, and took the brunt of the hit. Thrown backward, she landed on the courthouse steps hard with the man directly on top of her. The weight of his male body sent her to a dark place. Panic struck her. Struggling for breath, she screamed without even realizing it and pushed against him, trying to get separation between their bodies, but he felt like a huge elephant pressing down on her even though he wasn't even that big of a guy.

Still unable to take in a full breath, the world started to close in around her. The man's eyes widened when he realized he had landed on top of her and not his intended target. She feared she might black out, but then Jalen ran over and quickly grabbed him off of her.

The camera flashes were intense, and the news crews got much more action than they had bargained for. Her heartbeat was racing, and she was trying to put on a face of calm in front of all the reporters. Finally, she was able to take a deep breath.

Samira squatted down beside her. "Are you okay?"

Quinn realized she was still flat out on the steps. "Yeah." She started to stand, and Samira gave her a hand easily lifting her up from the ground. Samira was much stronger than she looked.

Richard stood pale faced. "What just happened?"

"We'll figure it out." Samira turned toward the media. "That's it for now. No more questions."

Quinn knew that was the right move.

Samira faced her. "We'll take this man in for questioning. I'm assuming you'd like to press charges."

Quinn's stomach clenched. "Whatever you think is best." She didn't know if this guy was really a threat, but he had acted in a rash and dangerous way.

Richard took a deep breath. "Could that be the man who you're looking for?"

"We won't know anything until we question him. We will keep you both updated. I need to go now." Samira ran to catch up with Jalen and the mystery protestor.

Taking her arm, Richard guided her down the steps.

She tried to take a few deep breaths and pull herself together.

"Quinn, you shouldn't have stepped in front of me. Are you sure you're okay?"

She'd had many worse beatings in her life. Faced much more pain. It had taken her completely off guard, but she wouldn't let this derail her or the sweetness of this verdict. "I promise I'm fine. I'm sorry that what should've been a victory lap turned into a circus."

He squeezed her hand. "There's nothing you could've done about that. We know we have enemies as a company. I can respect protesting, but physical violence is taking it too far. Someone could've really gotten hurt."

That someone could've been her. "Let's see what the FBI can find out." She paused. "Also, you didn't have to say that back there about me."

"I wanted to go on record, and I did. We would've lost this case without you, but I know better than to have said that. Let's go debrief everyone and then have a glass of champagne."

One glass wasn't going to be enough.

8

Samira looked across the table into the eyes of Connor Savoy, a twenty-one year old college student from Georgia State.

"I know my legal rights. I took criminal procedure." Connor crossed his arms in front of him in defiance.

Clearing his throat, Jalen squared off. "Connor, I don't think you realize the severity of the charges you're facing here."

Connor gave an exaggerated eye roll. "Why don't you tell me then."

This kid was trying her patience, but she was having a hard time imagining that this young activist was a serial killer. "For starters, assault. You attacked someone today."

"I didn't mean to hurt the lady lawyer. I was going after that dirty CEO. Do you realize what that company does? Their drugs kill people and meanwhile, the company and its executives line their pockets with blood money."

Jalen cleared his throat. "Connor, I can tell this matters a lot to you. So much so that maybe you decided to take matters into your own hands."

"That's exactly what I had to do today. I had to speak. Exercise my first amendment rights. Go out and protest."

"You did a lot more than speak, Connor. That's the problem." She didn't think he realized there was a much bigger picture.

"I did what was necessary. I didn't want to let that pig stand there and gloat. Now the news will carry the real story. That was my goal. To expose the company for what they really are."

"This isn't the first time you hurt someone to reach that goal though, is it?" Jalen asked.

Biting his bottom lip, Connor leaned in. "I'm not sure what you mean. Today was actually the first time I ever touched anyone in a protest. Like I said though, I didn't mean to hurt that woman. She's complicit in this, but it's the CEO who really has to be held accountable."

"With their lives?" She watched him intently.

"The CEO is alive and well."

"What about the other CEOs?" Jalen's eyes narrowed.

"I don't know what you're talking about."

She needed to see his reaction. "Russell Myers of Newton Plastics, Maxine French from Crown Bank, and Warren Cruz from Bentley Biologics. Did you kill them, Connor?"

"What?" His voice went up an octave. "I didn't kill anyone." The color drained from his puffy cheeks. "Do I need a lawyer? I promise I didn't do anything."

His youth was beginning to really show. They had to push him though because they couldn't afford to be fooled. "It's your right to have an attorney, but if you want to make some sort of deal, it will be much easier now."

Tears started to well up in his light, blue eyes. "I didn't kill anyone. I swear. When did they die? You can dig into my life, and you'll see I'm innocent."

Jalen took a moment and asked for his alibis. Connor gave the name of two different friends who he claimed to have been with on the relevant dates.

"Are you going to arrest me?" Connor's eyes were wide with fear.

She took a deep breath. "Ms. Kelly is deciding whether she

wants to press charges. We won't hold you today, but we will be following up with you about those alibis and depending on where that leads, you could expect a search warrant to be served."

Connor ran his hand through his hair. "I just wanted to do something, you know? To make a difference. I swear I didn't kill anyone. I'm not a murderer. I want to make the world a better place, not a worse one."

Jalen looked over at her. She gave him a little nod. They'd probably put the kid through enough misery for the day. She hoped his alibis would check out and they could move on.

"You're free to go, an agent outside will escort you down. But if Ms. Kelly presses charges, you'll be paid a visit by the Atlanta police."

Connor hung his head. "I understand."

Once Connor had left the room, Jalen turned to her.

"There's no way that's our guy, Samira. He's just a kid who got in over his head being too overzealous. Nothing about him fits the serial killer profile."

"You're right, but given the media circus that this involves, we have to make sure we're buttoned up even if it makes the kid uncomfortable. I don't think Quinn will press charges. She seems to be the type who would support a healthy protest. Connor just went to the extreme. Hopefully, he learned a valuable lesson today, but we'll check out his alibis and make sure everything is tied off."

"At least the kid cares. Wrong methods, but it's good to see someone who is passionate about important issues."

She agreed. "We've still got big problems though. We got sidetracked with Connor." She looked at her watch. "Let's hit the road."

9

ate that afternoon, Samira and Jalen walked up the raggedy steps to the front door of Marilee Nix's mobile home. Her daughter was dead, and the lawsuit had alleged that Newton Plastics was to blame. They'd made the drive and ended up in a rural area in the town of Cordele which was about two hours south of Atlanta.

"Are you dreading this as much as I am?" Samira asked him.

"Probably more. Remember, we go in super easy here. The last thing I want is to cause this family more pain."

"I'm with you." When she'd made the call to Marilee Nix, and that was hard enough, she hadn't wanted to discuss details. Marilee graciously had agreed to meet even without her providing specifics.

Jalen knocked on the door and after a minute, a woman answered. Probably in her low thirties, her blonde hair tied up in a messy bun. But it was Marilee's light blue eyes that got her. The grief was still flowing off of her in waves. She didn't believe she was looking at a killer, but they had to do their due diligence.

"Y'all must be the FBI agents. Please come on in."

They walked inside.

"Please have a seat."

It was small but impeccably clean and organized. They took a seat on the sofa. "Thank you for seeing us."

"Do you want any sweet tea?"

"No, Ms. Nix. We're fine," Jalen said. "Thank you for offering."

"Are you here about my baby? Are you investigating Newton Plastics?" Her eyes lit up just a bit.

Samira's heart broke, but there was no easy way to have this conversation. "Ms. Nix, not exactly. Are you aware that Russell Myers, the CEO of Newton Plastics, has passed away?"

Marilee's eyes narrowed. "Yes. I saw it on the local news when it happened. Heart attack." She sucked in a breath. "I'm a God-fearing woman, but I have to tell y'all, when I heard the news, I rejoiced. That man was responsible for the death of my baby and for another family's child plus countless others who are still sick and struggling." She took another breath before she kept talking. "They thought they could dump here in this trailer park area because we're poor. White trash is what they called us. That was even in an email they showed at trial. Can you believe that? I may be poor, ma'am, but I'm not trash. And my baby was definitely not trash—she was a treasure. A gift from God, and that evil company took her away from me. She was all I had and cared about in this world." The tears started to flow freely down Marilee's face.

Jalen pulled a tissue out of his jacket pocket and offered it to Marilee.

This woman was clearly in pain. Was she in enough pain to do something as drastic as murder? And even more, to go on a killing spree? She had serious doubts. Thankfully, Jalen spoke up.

"Ms. Nix, I can't even begin to imagine your pain and what you've been through. Can you tell us a little bit about why you think the jury found in favor of Newton Plastics?"

Marilee let out a big sigh. "Honestly, we got out lawyered.

That savvy redheaded attorney, Quinn Kelly. She was something. Our attorney was good, but not *that* good. I wish she would've been on our side instead of theirs. She had a way of twisting things, and by the end, the jury was eating out of her hands. I don't know how that woman lives with herself, but I'll leave it up to God to judge her."

She thought Jalen was best suited to continue the discussion, so she kept quiet and waited for him.

Jalen looked directly at Marilee. "Vengeance is mine, says the Lord."

Jalen's faith was a huge part of who he was. He was also much more comfortable verbalizing his faith than she was. She tended to keep her beliefs to herself.

"I remind myself of that verse often," Marilee said softly. "What are y'all doing here if you aren't investigating Newton Plastics?"

Jalen glanced at her and then spoke. "We may have reason to believe that Russell Myers's death was not of natural causes."

Marilee sucked in a breath. "Really?"

"Yes," Samira responded. "We're talking to everyone involved to get a better sense of what could've happened to him." She was doing a delicate dance, but it was the best she would do.

"And you think I killed him?" Marilee let out a laugh.

It hadn't taken her long to ferret out their real reason for the visit.

"We're not saying that," Jalen said. "We're just asking questions."

Marilee sat quietly for a moment before speaking again. "I didn't kill that man, and the Lord may strike me down right here and now, but if given the opportunity to do so, I would've killed him. He took away the most precious and innocent child. But I didn't see him after that day. He went back to his fancy life in a swanky Atlanta suburb, and I came back here, to this lonely home. Men like him don't have time for women like me."

She hated to push but they'd come this far. "Do you know of anyone else who could've had reason to hurt Mr. Myers."

"I'm sure all the parents involved in my lawsuit didn't shed one tear over his death, let's put it that way."

Shifting gears was her next move. "Do you know a Warren Cruz or Maxine French?"

"No." Marilee frowned. "Don't sound familiar to me. Who are they?"

"Other CEOs who are now dead."

Marilee placed her hand over her heart. "I don't know anything about them. All I know is that Russell Myers was an evil man who deserved to die."

Samira understood her thirst for revenge all too well. "Thank you for your time, Ms. Nix."

"I'll say one last thing and you probably don't want to hear it. If someone is out there killing these evil CEOs, then I pray to God that y'all never find them."

10

There truly was no rest for the weary in her line of work. Quinn sat in Richard's living room in his Buckhead mansion in full babysitting mode. Richard had reveled in the victory from the lawsuit for most of the day taking calls—of course Quinn stuck close by his side to make sure she got the much needed credit that she deserved, but then once evening came, he was now in panic mode again.

"What if they come and kill me?" Richard paced around the expansive living room almost making Quinn dizzy as she watched. He was quickly becoming unhinged.

"We don't even know if there is a *they*, Richard. The FBI is just taking extra precautions, and remember you have those two security guys right outside the door. With guns! No one can get in. Shouldn't that ease your concerns?"

Richard turned to her. "It's not your life that's on the line here, Quinn."

It was imperative that she stayed in his good graces, so she would have to suck it up and cater to his whims at the moment.

He grabbed onto her hand. "I'm sorry. That was stupid for me to say especially after you took the hit today from that protestor. Did you hear anything else about him from the FBI while I was tied up?"

"They're checking his alibis, but they don't think he's the guy. Just an overly exuberant college student who thinks he's saving the world from the evil Big Pharma empire. I'm not going to press charges." That would be just one more headache that she didn't need.

"I figured as much."

"You shouldn't sit in fear while in your own home. You have top-notch security guards on duty. They are not going to let a soul into this place. It's fortified. You're safe."

He let out an exaggerated sigh. "Maybe for now, but you know how you get that feeling of something bad coming?"

Oh yeah, she did. "Yes."

"That's what I can't shake."

She walked over to him and gave him a friendly pat on the shoulder. "It's natural to be on edge. It's not every day that FBI agents tell you that you might be the target of a deranged serial killer, but you're doing everything right."

"I'll feel a lot better when there's some closure."

She agreed. Having loose ends annoyed her. "Hopefully, you'll get closure quicker than you think. The FBI seems to be on top of things." Both agents had impressed her, but she wondered if they had any real idea what they were dealing with, but she was going to keep that thought to herself. There was no need to rile Richard up any more than he already was.

"I'm glad they're competent. I just don't get people. Why would someone kill over the result of a lawsuit?" Richard asked.

"Maybe they feel like they were wronged by a big company and want to get revenge. Today was a poignant reminder of the bad blood that is out there against drug companies."

Richard huffed. "There's different levels of revenge—murder seems like an extreme option to me. I can't even wrap my head around it. There's so much evil out there. I didn't do anything to deserve this."

"It was a long day for you. Why don't you try to get some rest? You should be able to sleep comfortably knowing that you have security right outside. Nothing is going to happen to you tonight." She felt pretty confident of that.

Walking over to her, Richard took her hands. "Quinn, I can't thank you enough. You've not only been the best attorney we could ask for, but you've also been a trusted confidant for me during this difficult time."

"I'm just doing my job."

"It's above and beyond and everyone at the company knows the vital role you play."

She broke contact and took a step back. "I'll check on you tomorrow."

"Thanks, Quinn. You should try to get some rest too. You deserve it."

Quinn made her way out of Richard's house, saying goodbye to the security guards, anxious to get out of there. Richard was right. It had been a long day for her too, but she felt like her work was never done.

Sleep never came easy. She often did her best and most important work at night. Deciding she needed to clear her head, she just started driving around in her Jeep as she wasn't quite ready to go home yet. She still had to face the inquisition of the FBI about her cases. She wasn't convinced that they really had a solid theory yet, but she would listen to them carefully and take it all in. Her work was everything to her, and she couldn't have the FBI meddling. She would have to run interference with her clients to make sure the FBI didn't annoy them personally. Everything would need to go through her and that was just the way it had to be.

The jury was still out on the FBI agents. They both seemed smart, capable, and discerning, but trust wasn't something that came easily to her. They had their angle, their agenda, and she was pretty certain it didn't align with her own. She'd play nice for now and see if she could get them off her back so she could get her job done.

11

First thing Friday morning, Quinn had been summoned to Sterling Ward III's office. Sterling was the managing partner of the firm, and every bit as pretentious as his name sounded. They had an intense dislike for each other on a personal level, but Sterling loved what Quinn brought to the table—both financially and reputationally, and Quinn enjoyed the practically unlimited firm resources at her disposal. It was one of the reasons she put up with his utter nonsense.

She walked into his corner office, the best in the firm, and prepared herself for a paternalistic lecture as she took a seat. Sterling was in his fifties with gray hair and beady brown eyes. He was a self-proclaimed southern gentleman, but she knew better.

"Quinn, what in the world is happening? I saw the news reports. Talk about taking one for your client. Are you okay?"

He didn't really care that much about her but more about optics. "Yes, just a little bruised but fine."

Sterling leaned forward. "I talked to Mitch about the FBI investigation, but I wanted to hear it from you. What's the latest?"

She had initially gone to Mitch, who was the number two in

firm management, after the first visit with the FBI. Mitch was much more tolerable than Sterling, but now that she was here, she had to face the music. "The FBI is concerned that there may, and I repeat, may be a serial killer out there who has some type of vendetta against CEOs—especially those who are victorious in their cases."

Sterling frowned. "Having clients get murdered is not a good look for us."

She bit her tongue. Of course it would all be about perception for Sterling. He could not care less about the actual well-being of the CEOs. "I know this is difficult, but the FBI is working the case, and I'm hopeful they will find answers."

"I'm worried about the fact that this killer seems to be targeting only CEOs *you* are defending Quinn. Is there something you're not telling me?"

The nerve of this guy. She would love to dethrone him and kick him to the curb, but now wasn't the right time for that. She had to be patient. "No. I'm cooperating with the FBI, and I'm working with Richard as are the FBI to make sure that he remains safe. In fact, the FBI are going to be here later this morning for a follow up meeting."

Sterling rose from his seat. "Good. I don't want this to get out of hand. We could have a PR nightmare brewing. Right now, all the media buzz is positive over you diving in front of Richard, but we all know how fast things can turn."

She also stood and walked over closer to him, enjoying the fact that she was able to look down at him. "I told you I have it under control. The FBI is doing their job. I'm doing mine—which is winning cases. I plan to win my next trial too."

He crossed his arms. "Remember, Quinn. No matter how high you are, the fall can come quickly."

"And you would love nothing more than that, wouldn't you, Sterling?" She'd had enough.

"Regardless of what you may believe, I hold you as a very valuable asset to this firm."

"Asset, meaning money maker. That's okay. We all have our roles here, but let me be clear. When I finish this year with all of these big wins, I'm going to get an increase in partnership units. No excuses this time." Units were how they were compensated, and she felt she needed an even bigger piece of the pie.

"You know the compensation committee makes that decision," he shot back.

"A committee in which you are a powerful member. If this firm values me as much as you say they do, then that will be the proof. I always have attractive offers from various suitors— including our key competitors."

Sterling moved toward her. "I don't like to be threatened."

"Then leave me alone and let me do my job. I'll get the results you and the firm want, but I don't need to be micromanaged, especially about media matters."

"I understand you like your autonomy. I'm just warning you that someday you may get in over your head."

She walked to the door and looked over her shoulder. "Today is not that day."

12

L ater that morning, Samira and Jalen waited in a fancy conference room at Whitner & Stokes for Quinn's arrival.

Jalen stood and looked out the large window with amazing views of Midtown Atlanta. "I don't know about you, but I can't stop thinking about our conversation with Ms. Nix."

"Yeah. I don't think she's responsible, but I do believe she's living a nightmare right now."

Jalen nodded. "I can't even imagine how much pain she's going through. It's heartbreaking. And listening to her talk, and seeing her raw emotion, it does make you wonder whether she would've killed Myers if she had the chance. But I agree, I don't think she's good for this. She definitely doesn't strike me as the type of person to go on a killing spree."

Samira had tossed and turned last night, not able to sleep, trying to go through everything in her head.

"Good morning, agents." Quinn gave a bright and cheery smile as she walked into the room.

Quinn probably wasn't enthused about this meeting so she would try to smooth things over the best she could. "Thank you again for your time. I know you're extremely busy with multiple pressing cases."

Quinn looked at her and then Jalen. "You both made it perfectly clear that there wasn't really much of an option. Let's get right to it. I have a ton of work today."

"No time to enjoy your victory from yesterday?" Jalen asked.

Quinn shook her head. "No. There's always the next case. Any further updates on the college student?"

"Yeah. His alibis were solid," Jalen said.

"I'm not surprised. I don't want to mess up his life with pressing charges. Let's just move on. And speaking of that, I have a huge case coming up."

Samira hoped to get a lot of information today. "Well, we're going to want to talk about that, but before we get to your upcoming cases, we need to go back through your old litigation. Why don't we start with Newton Plastics."

Quinn fiddled with the sapphire ring on her right hand. "All right. What can I tell you??

Everything. But she couldn't say that. She had to be narrower, or they would get nowhere. "Let's start with the CEO Russell Myers."

After a moment, Quinn spoke. "Russell was a difficult client. He ran a tight ship."

Jalen leaned forward. "What do you mean by difficult?"

"Russell believed he always knew best. Eventually he saw it my way and realized I was the legal expert with a vast range of experience, and he wasn't. But we fought along the way on many strategic issues. Almost to the point that I didn't want the case anymore, but I saw it as a challenge and didn't want to back down. I've dealt with plenty of men like him before."

Samira could relate. "How did you manage to get a defense verdict in favor of Newton Plastics?"

"I can see you've done your homework, but let me explain. The plaintiffs had a great story, but that's exactly what it was—a story. Their lawyer tugged on your heartstrings, but it takes more than that to convince a jury. It requires evidence and the facts to back up the claims. And, fortunately for us, the evidence was on our side. There is nothing linking the actions of the company to any of the resulting illnesses or death. Overall, it was a pretty weak case from their side. Even though it did have a lot of emotional appeal. I won't deny that."

Samira wasn't sure if she believed that. Maybe Quinn was trying to make it seem easier than it was. "We talked to Ms. Nix. Seems like a pretty awful situation."

Quinn sighed. "I'm not saying that it wasn't awful. My heart broke for them. All of those impacted. They simply had no evidence linking my client to the harm. There were a million other casualties involved. And since you're FBI agents, you know you can't just go on feeling. That's not how our justice system works. There has to be cold, hard facts. We have the rule of law for a reason."

She was still trying to figure out Quinn's angle in all of this. If she was truly a crusader of justice, why was she defending the companies? Why wasn't she a prosecutor or plaintiff's lawyer? But it wasn't her job right now to psychoanalyze Quinn's career choices. It was her job to figure out what the killer's next move would be. "Did Russell or the company receive any threats during the lawsuit?"

Quinn shook her head. "Nothing directed to them that I'm aware of. Obviously, there was a lot of media coverage. Gemma Holland was going live every day." She paused. "Gemma's the big legal reporter in town. Always looking for her next big story. You might have noticed her hovering around in the courtroom. Young, pretty, blonde. And very persistent."

Usually, Samira would stay far away from the media when working a case, but maybe they needed to talk to Gemma in this instance.

Quinn looked at her. "I didn't think much about it at the time, but I have received some threatening messages and general hate mail. Not the old school kind of mail, but things on social media. I get a lot of ridiculous comments on my posts and videos, but I also get tons of positive feedback. I don't take the negative comments that seriously because I know how the internet is and people will say anything on there, but I did get some more disturbing threats over the past few months."

"What kind of threats?" Jalen asked.

"Criticizing the companies I defend. Saying that I would pay for supporting them. Some of them were particularly violent. But I took them with a grain of salt. I never really thought anyone would act on them." She paused. "That is until now."

Samira's pulse quickened. "We'll take a close look at your social media presence. What if someone believes that by killing your clients, they're actually hurting you. Your reputation could take a big hit. The firm's reputation too. And think broadly. The killer could be a man or a woman. At this point, we're casting a wide net."

"Do you think I'm in real danger?" Quinn's voice wavered.

"We can't be sure, so you need to be on guard," Samira said.

"I'll be more careful."

The more Samira learned, the worse she felt. "If you think of anyone in your life who is a potential threat you need to let us know."

"I will."

"Let's get back to your cases. What about the case against Crown Bank?"

"Plaintiffs claimed predatory lending practices. We had the better side of the argument. The case wasn't as sexy as the Newton Plastics case. Lots of boring financial information that had the jurors less engaged. I think that helped me."

Jalen cleared his throat. "And Maxine French. Tell us about her."

"Maxine was the real deal. It's hard to rise up the ranks in the big-time financial sector as a woman, but she did it. Very tough. Maxine never showed one ounce of emotion. Ever. Even when we won, she didn't crack a smile." Quinn laughed. "And they claim women are overly emotional. Richard could barely handle himself after our verdict."

Samira was detecting a pretty clear undercurrent with Quinn, and it had to do with men. She really couldn't blame her. Samira felt the pressures of being a woman in the FBI and knew that Quinn had to deal with a lot of sexism in her profession as well. But she couldn't shake the feeling that it was more personal with Quinn. That it ran a bit deeper than just professional issues.

Jalen pulled out a folder from his bag and looked down at his notes. "Were you surprised when you heard what happened to Maxine?"

"Not exactly. I knew Maxine drank too much, but that wasn't my business. Thankfully she didn't hurt anyone else with her reckless behavior. She easily could've hired a driver. I'm not sure why she would've even driven to the event."

That was a good point. "Although sometimes powerful people think they are superhuman. That they can handle anything."

"Very true. At some point, they all find out that everyone has their limits. Some things are just going to be out of your hands no matter how much money and power you have."

"Sounds like you speak from experience," Jalen said.

"I don't lose much, but I have lost, and my clients aren't happy when they're found responsible, and their financials are hit. Then of course, someone has to take the fall which means their head is on the chopping block. But it's not life and death. It's just money."

Jalen frowned. "Unfortunately, what we're dealing with is life and death in this case."

Quinn looked down. "I'm not trying to be difficult here."

"How long ago was the case you lost?"

"About ten months," Quinn said. "That one stung. I hate losing."

"And the CEO was present at the trial?"

"Yes. Lew O'Malley. He was a big witness. I don't think the

jury liked him. That was part of my problem. But really the biggest issue was some of the damning documents. There was nothing I could do to overcome it once it was introduced into evidence and shown to the jury."

Samira jotted down Lew's name.

"I hesitate to bring this up initially because the last thing I want to do is point the finger at someone and be wrong, but given the stakes here, I feel like I should say it."

Now they were getting somewhere. "We're listening."

Quinn stared out the large window for a moment before continuing. "There was a member of the jury in the Newton Plastics case. Juror number five. Kevin Trask. He was a marketing manager and IT geek. I don't have any hard evidence on this, but I always felt like there was something off with him."

"Like what?" Jalen asked.

"He looked at me the entire time. Sometimes I felt like he was making strange faces. Even when others were speaking, he was focused on me."

"You're right to tell us this." Samira knew Quinn had been holding back. This might not be anything, but it was worth following up on for sure.

"Okay. I know you won't jump to any conclusions without evidence."

"We won't," Jalen said.

"Why don't we shift gears and talk about your current litigation." Samira could tell Quinn wasn't comfortable talking more about juror number five.

"I represent a drug company called Horizon Pharma. They produced a birth control device that the plaintiffs allege caused numerous harmful side effects."

"Can you be more specific?" Jalen asked.

"Yes, the plaintiffs claim that women who used the Horizon Pharma IUD suffered from internal bleeding and inflammatory disease with the worst-case scenarios leading to infertility and death."

Jalen grimaced. "Those are some serious allegations."

Quinn nodded. "No doubt, but once again, it's hard for the plaintiffs to prove that the IUD is the cause of the harm. I won't lie and say this is an easy case. Far from it, but I don't back down from a challenge."

Samira wondered how Quinn could defend these big companies that in most instances were guilty of the conduct of which they were accused. Quinn must be much better at compartmentalization than she was, because there's no way she could handle it. "Although sometimes when there's smoke, there's fire."

"There's still legal standards of proof."

Jalen smiled. "Samira understands your legal speak. She went to law school."

Quinn raised an eyebrow. "Really. I had no idea. You decided to be an FBI agent instead of an attorney then."

"Yes. It all worked out for the best, but Jalen is right. You don't need to dumb any of this down for us. We get it."

A smile spread across Quinn's face. "Duly noted. If you want to dig into the medical studies, you are more than welcome. I'm just trying to save you some time and effort."

Jalen's cell rang and he looked down. "Sorry. Excuse me for a moment." Jalen walked out of the conference room.

Now it was just her and Quinn, and she took a moment to think about her next move.

"You can ask me, you know," Quinn said.

"Ask you what?"

"How can I defend these companies? You don't have a great poker face, Agent Haddad. I can tell that you disapprove."

Was she really that transparent? "You can call me Samira. And it's not my job to judge your decisions as a lawyer. It's my job to find out if there's a killer out there."

Quinn leaned in closer. "You seem like a straight shooter, and I get the whole due diligence thing and all of that. But do you really think that there's a serial killer running loose wanting to murder CEOs?"

Samira looked into Quinn's bright blue eyes. "I can't say for certain, but that's why you need to be vigilant. Back to your Horizon Pharma case, who is the CEO?"

"John Rossi."

"You should tell him what's going on, so he isn't caught off guard."

"I can do that."

"Tell me about Mr. Rossi."

"Extremely smart. Bordering on brilliant with a smooth and easy way about him. He will present well to the jury."

"Another male CEO."

"The way of the world, as I'm sure you're well aware. For every one woman CEO I defend, there are twenty male CEOs."

"Yeah, and it has to have been hard for you to get to the top of the legal profession."

"Hard work, a little bit of luck, and being willing to make the big moves. So many women are content in their position at work. They don't like change. It brings too much uncertainty. But I've embraced it. And once I started winning, I got power that not even the old male partners could take away from me because clients insisted that they wanted *me* as their first chair trial counsel. I've ruffled some male feathers along the way, but it's all been worth it."

"I've found that the things that matter the most are worth fighting for."

"And sometimes you might have to compromise because of the bigger picture, right?"

Samira thought for a second back on her career. "Yes. I agree with that."

Quinn looked down at her smart watch. "Is there anything else at the moment? I need to get back to work."

"That's it for now, but we'll be in touch." Samira walked out of the conference room to track down Jalen. She was building a rapport with Quinn that would hopefully come in handy. Quinn might be the key to getting out ahead of this thing.

13

That afternoon, Quinn was finishing up a meeting with Allie before her client's arrival.

"Where are we on the exhibit list?" Quinn asked.

Allie glanced at her legal pad. "We're making progress. There are still a couple of video deposition disputes I'm dealing with opposing counsel on, but since most of our witnesses will be live, it isn't a big deal."

"Good. You've been running around the clock managing the junior associates on a lot of different projects. It hasn't gone unnoticed."

"You know how much I want to become a partner here. I'll do whatever it takes."

She had to keep Allie in check. It was a fine balance to strike. "You have to know when to draw that line though, Allie. Sometimes you have to stand on principle."

"And other times you have to push the limits."

Quinn laughed. "Are you quoting me now?"

A smile spread across Allie's face. "I am. You say it enough." Allie paused. "Without your mentorship, I know I wouldn't be as far along as I am on the partner path. I started this firm as a timid, young associate, too afraid to speak up. I appreciate the fact that you saw something in me and were willing to take a chance."

Allie had been very rough around the edges, but her work ethic and strong intellect set her apart from her peers. Quinn appreciated both of those things and made it her mission to be her advocate. And her protector.

"Do you want me in the meeting with John?" Allie asked.

"No." She looked at the time. "He'll be here soon, but one more thing I need to loop you in on."

"What?"

Quinn had wanted to shield Allie from the FBI investigation, but it was going to become impossible, so she needed to make sure Allie was informed. She took a few minutes and told her what the FBI had shared so far.

"Wow. That is intense, Quinn. Is Richard worried?"

"Yes, but he's got security. He'll be fine."

Allie raised an eyebrow. "You need to be careful, Quinn. If there is some psychopathic killer out there, you could be in danger too."

"You've read too many thrillers. I'm not in danger."

"Maybe not yet, but I am concerned." She paused. "Given my involvement, should I be worried too?"

Quinn shook her head. "No. But if it makes you feel better just be a bit more cautious, okay? There is no need to change your life though. The FBI is getting on top of it."

"Thanks for trusting me enough to tell me."

"Of course. You know I have your back. Now get out of here before John arrives."

Allie hung her head. "I still wonder if I overreacted to how he treated me."

She saw red thinking back to the things that John had said to Allie. Thankfully, Allie had immediately confided in her and since then, she wouldn't let them in the same room if she could avoid it. "No, you did not. His comments crossed the line, and while I have to deal with him, I will not subject you to his tactics."

Allie gave a weak smile. "Thanks for having my back. If you need me, I'll be in my office."

Once Allie left, she took a deep breath as she waited for John Rossi. She felt more comfortable in the spacious conference room than in her office alone with him. He'd given her the creeps from day one, but he was her client, so she was stuck with him.

She'd been telling the FBI the truth—a jury would love John. Good looking, smooth as silk, with a dazzling smile and a disarming way about him. But that was all an act. A complete lie. A play for the crowd. When he was in small group settings or one on one, the real devil came out of him. She'd seen it in one of their first meetings and it had taken her off guard. But now she was prepared, having dealt with him for the past nine months on this case. She'd bitten her tongue more times than she could count, but today's meeting was going to prove to be especially challenging. John wasn't going to like what she had to tell him about the threat and some stuff about the litigation.

John entered the room a few minutes later and engaged in some fake niceties including a kiss on the cheek she could've done without. Wearing a fine designer navy suit and purple tie, he was completely put together from head to toe including his fancy gold watch. He was a vain man who worked out obsessively. His size and strength only made her more nervous to be alone with him because no matter how much training she had done, she could never take him in hand-to-hand combat.

"You look tired, Quinn."

Hello to you too. "I've had a lot on my plate."

His dark eyes bore through her. "Including another victory. I will expect nothing less in our case, as do our shareholders. Don't screw me on this."

She bit the inside of her cheek and counted to five to try to contain her response. "I always put forth my best in court regardless of what I think of the merits of the case." She paused. "Or the client."

"You better."

They had butted heads over the case multiple times. She believed that there was a lot of exposure to the company, but none of the executives or the Board wanted to talk settlement, so that's where she came in and had to pull off the impossible. She had not told the FBI any of that because in her mind it was most certainly protected by the attorney client privilege.

Now she had to get this conversation over with. "We need to talk about a few things today."

John smirked. "Let's get this over with. I have much more important things to do than to be hassled with this legal mess."

It took all the strength she had not to walk out of the conference room, but she was ready for a battle, and this was going to be one. "It's come to my attention from our IT people that you deleted documents from your computer. What were you thinking? Do you realize how big of a deal this is? What if you get caught? If we get caught?"

John reached over and patted her hand. "Come on, Quinn. Take a breath. We aren't going to get caught. No one knows about those documents but me. I gave you the best chance to win this case. If those documents would have ever come out, we would have been toast. And you're my lawyer, so there's nothing you can do about it. You have to look out for the best interest of the company. I was also doing that. Don't get all high and mighty now. It doesn't look good on you."

She had to know. "What exactly were in those documents, John?"

"Don't you prefer to have plausible deniability? Isn't that a thing? All you need to know is what I did, I did for the company. And I would do it all over again. I don't need you breathing down my neck and quacking in my ear. We're talking millions and millions of dollars here. The future of the company."

She took another deep breath. "I can assure you that the

plaintiffs would not see it that way. In fact, the women who are now infertile or who died don't have a voice in the matter. And now you've taken away their opportunity to prove Horizon Pharma was responsible because you destroyed evidence. How can you live with yourself?"

John laughed. "I sleep pretty well at night actually. And don't for one second think that you're going to blow this case because all of a sudden you developed a moral compass. I'm not buying it for one minute. You and I are more alike than you're willing to admit. You're in this for yourself, to get richer, and to get more famous. I know your goals. That you want to be the top trial lawyer, not only in the state, but in the country. You're going to go out there and you're going to win this case and do what you do. And let me do what I do. Do we have an understanding?"

Oh, they did. "You're crystal clear, but there's something else we have to talk about that's unrelated to this specific issue."

"What is it?"

In a sick way, she was going to enjoy telling him this. "The FBI paid me a visit. They've actually paid me a few visits because it seems that CEOs I've represented are turning up dead, and they're beginning to think that it might be foul play."

John's mouth dropped open, and he didn't immediately speak.

Good. Let that sink in for a minute.

"Wait a minute. You're saying that someone is killing your clients?"

She nodded. "More specifically, the CEOs of companies I represented and won cases for. As you know, I just got the favorable verdict yesterday, and the CEO has hired private security to protect him. That's at least until the FBI gets a better understanding of the investigation. But they refuse to believe in coincidences and there's three CEO deaths that they know of. Which brings me to you, because if there is a connection, and there is a killer out there, then you could also now be a target."

John stood up and started pacing. "You've gotta be kidding me."

"Unfortunately, I'm not. The FBI is all over this. They are also asking questions about this case and you. You'll be happy to know that I told them you were a completely charming guy, and that I thought you would do well in front of the jury. So well that we had a good chance of winning. They are concerned about you. Your safety. They need to talk to you, but I wanted to break the news to you first." And she was so glad she did. After all he had put her through, this was so worth it. She loved seeing him squirm. It was something he rarely did.

"What do you think I should do?" His voice was no longer steady and in control.

So now he wanted her help. "You need to be careful. If a killer is out there, you could be the next victim, but that hinges on the fact of us winning. Because for whatever reason, it appears the killer is going after cases in which I won. As you may recall I lost a case earlier this year. That CEO is still very much alive and well today."

John ran his hand through his hair. He muttered something unintelligible.

"What?"

"You're telling me that if we win this case, that some psycho serial killer is going to come after me?"

She held back a smile. "It's very possible. But don't worry. It won't impact my performance at all. I'm still going to go out there and try to win this case. I'm sure the company will pay for security for you, so it really shouldn't be an issue, should it?"

"Quinn, you are enjoying this way too much."

She had to keep herself in check. "No, I'm not. I wouldn't wish any harm on anyone. Which is why I'm upset about what you did with those documents, but that's beside the point now. We have to deal with the situation we're under and face those facts. Which means I have to prepare to win the trial, and you have to stay safe. It's just that simple."

He took a seat and moved close to her. Way too close and placed his hand on her shoulder. "You're going to have to get over the documents. I did what I had to. Now it's your turn to win this case. Let me worry about this wild serial killer theory." When he moved an inch closer, she'd had enough and stood up.

But he met her and grabbed onto her wrist tightly, getting right in her face. "Are you sure you're in this to win?"

"Absolutely." Failure wasn't an option.

14

"I hope we don't regret this," Jalen mumbled.

They sat in the Midtown Atlanta coffee shop waiting for the meeting. Talking to the reporter, Gemma Holland, wouldn't have normally ever been on her to-do list, but given the unique circumstances at hand, and the fact that Gemma covered all the trials extensively, Samira thought it best to have the meeting.

"You know she's going to want something in return," Jalen said.

"Always." She understood how reporters worked. "But maybe it'll be worth it. And look at me actually being the optimistic one this afternoon."

He laughed. "I'll give you that."

She looked at the coffee shop door and saw the young blonde reporter walk in. "She's here." Samira waved and caught Gemma's attention.

Gemma rushed over—her face flushed. Her light blonde hair was pulled back in a low ponytail. "So sorry I'm late. Traffic. You know how that is."

Jalen smiled. "All too well."

Gemma gave him a wide grin and she had to fight back her

own. She couldn't say she was surprised that Gemma seemed instantly smitten by Jalen. He had that effect on women.

They took a moment and did introductions and Gemma grabbed a coffee before returning to the table. Given it was midafternoon, the coffee shop wasn't too crowded. They'd chosen a table in the back corner to give them some privacy.

"Thanks for meeting us," Jalen said.

"It's not every day that I get called by the FBI." Her hazel eyes were wide with excitement. "You have definitely piqued my interest."

She wanted to say, slow your roll, but she didn't. She needed Gemma's cooperation, so she took a different tack. "We need this discussion to be off the record."

"Seriously?" Gemma groaned. "You've got to give me something. That's not how this works. It's a two-way street and you both know that."

Jalen shot her a knowing look before jumping in. "And we understand all of that, but we need to have an open dialogue first. How does that sound?"

"Okay." Gemma pulled out her notebook.

"No notes," Samira said. "Just listen for now."

Gemma frowned but put down her pen. "I guess I'm not in a position to negotiate if I want to hear what you have to say."

Samira ignored that comment. "We want to know about your experiences covering a few cases."

Gemma raised an eyebrow. "Which ones?"

Best to get right to it. "Cases with the following defendants, Newton Plastics, Crown Bank, and Bentley Biologics."

Gemma picked back up her pen and tapped it on her note pad. "Yes. I covered those cases. All wins for Whitner & Stokes, more specifically for Quinn Kelly, but I'm guessing you already knew that. You were at the trial for Asbury Pharmaceuticals too. So, what gives?"

Samira shook her head. "First, we need to hear about your experience in the coverage of these cases."

"All right." Gemma took a deep breath. "Why don't we take them one at a time. Newton Plastics was a very emotional case. I would say out of all three cases, it was the one where the verdict surprised me the most. Granted, I'm not poring over the evidence in the jury deliberation room, and from my understanding, there was lack of causality—I think that's the correct legal term. But man, what happened to those families. Those kids who died, and the ones who are still sick. There were jurors visibly shaken by the testimony, but I guess at the end of the day emotional appeal doesn't always win big cases. That's one thing I'm learning by watching Quinn in action. She has this amazing ability to take all that emotion and somehow turn it around to her advantage. And she does it by not appealing to emotion." Gemma sighed. "I'm probably not explaining it that well, it's just that she's a very gifted attorney."

"How long have you been doing legal reporting?" Jalen asked.

"Right out of college, so it's been about five years. A lot of people wonder why I haven't gone to law school, but that's not my interest. My real driving force is getting the story. The real story. And I have to say that covering Quinn's cases is good for my business. My follower count has grown exponentially over the past year or so."

"Is there anything else you remember about the Newton Plastics case? Anything about the jury? The CEO?"

Gemma perked up. "The CEO was mild mannered on the witness stand, but I couldn't help but wonder if it was authentic. I'm probably a bit distrustful of everyone in general. Goes with the territory, but I couldn't help but feel like he was hiding something. As far as the jury, no one person stood out. Like I said before, there were some intense emotional moments. I would've loved to have been in that deliberation room and seen how they came to the determination to find in favor of the company."

"What about the Crown Bank case?" Jalen asked.

Gemma picked up her coffee cup. "Now that case was

straight up boring. I had to fight to stay awake. Quinn did her best to make it as dry as possible to downplay the human angle, and the plaintiff's lawyer just wasn't that good."

"Nothing stands out to you? Were you surprised about the verdict?" Samira wanted to keep digging. There had to be something they could use.

"Not really. I saw one of the jurors fall asleep at one point. I think the case had the potential to turn out differently, but based on what I saw, it wasn't really close."

"And the CEO?" Jalen asked.

"She seemed very on top of things. Exactly what you would think of someone running a bank. Completely buttoned down without a hair out of place. To the point. Direct. And very dry." Gemma paused. "Why all the interest in the CEOs? When are you going to tell me what's going on here?"

Samira had to finish this line of questioning. "Before we get there, what about the Bentley Biologics case?"

Gemma looked down. "Another tough one. A drug used to treat things like rheumatoid arthritis was alleged to have caused cancer. I found it similar to the Newton Plastics case. Very emotional but Quinn out lawyered everyone and the hard evidence wasn't there. And before you ask, the CEO seemed like the nicest of the bunch. Or at least he presented that way. Very calm and disarming. The jury once again seemed highly disturbed by the allegations but at the end of the day that wasn't enough." Gemma shifted in her seat. "Okay. That's all I'm saying until you tell me what's going on."

Gemma must have finally sensed that she might have some leverage. "We need your off the record commitment."

"I already told you that you had it," she said. "I can handle it."

Samira glanced over at Jalen before speaking. "Were you aware that all three of the CEOs we just talked about are dead?"

"No. I wasn't. How did they die? What happened?"

Samira could tell that Gemma's wheels were spinning.

"That's what we're trying to figure out. The official record right now has Myers dying of a heart attack, French driving under influence and hitting a tree, and Cruz overdosing."

Gemma leaned in, brimming with excitement. "You think it's foul play. This could be huge. Are we talking murder here? Multiple? Meaning serial killer?" Her voice squeaked.

Jalen held up his hand. "We don't know that. All we know is that we have three CEOs dead in a relatively short time period, and there are some family members who aren't buying their current cause of deaths."

"You have to have more than that. Don't you?"

Samira wished they did. "We told you it's early on in the investigation. There is no solid evidence yet to support the theory, but we have to examine all avenues."

Gemma snapped her fingers. "Wait a minute. If you're right, then Richard Hale could be in danger. Is that why you were in the courtroom? To provide him protection?"

She shouldn't be surprised that Gemma was just trying to do her job, but it made Samira's job even more difficult. "We're obviously not going to be able to answer all these questions about a sensitive, ongoing investigation."

"You gotta work with me here," Gemma said. "This story could be a career maker for me."

At least she was being honest. That was refreshing. "And I appreciate that, but we've got safety concerns to be aware of and frankly, we really don't want the killer to know that we're onto them. We're going to need you to sit on this until we tell you otherwise. Then we will give you an exclusive interview. How does that sound?"

"I guess I'll take it," Gemma said reluctantly.

"Good." She felt that Gemma would keep her word because burning two FBI agents wasn't going to help her career. But this story could end up being big. Samira hoped it was all nothing, but she feared otherwise. "I should tell you something about Quinn."

"What?" Jalen asked.

"She had some creep that wouldn't leave her alone. Did she tell you about him?"

"No." Why had Quinn not told them about this guy? "What do you know?"

"I saw him in the courtroom a few times, and he never looked at anyone but Quinn. Then one day he followed her out into the parking garage. I saw what was happening, so I tailed them."

"Really?" Jalen asked.

"I *am* a reporter. But in this instance, I didn't think Quinn realized anything, and I wanted to make sure she was okay. It's not always about the story for me."

"What happened?" She was almost afraid to ask.

"I caught up to them in the parking garage. The guy was getting way too close to Quinn backing her toward her SUV. That's when I yelled really loud and started running toward them, and the guy fled."

"Did you ever see him again?" Jalen asked.

"Yeah. I've seen him in the courtroom gallery multiple times, but I didn't see him with Quinn again."

Jalen picked up his pen. "Can you give a description?"

"White, probably mid-thirties. Short blond hair. Tall and thin."

Samira wanted to know one more thing. "Did you talk to Quinn about it?"

"She just thought he was a random creep, and tried to play it off, but it still seemed scary to me."

"Thanks for telling us that." They had more secrets to uncover. "One more thing. Do you ever pay attention to the jurors?"

"Sure. I like watching to see how they are reacting, and sometimes after the case I interview them."

"Do you remember juror number five in the Newton Plastics case, a Kevin Trask."

"Oh yeah. That dude was a bit strange. He was always staring at Quinn and squinting. He may have had the hots for her."

"Did you ever interview him?" Jalen asked.

She shook her head. "No. He didn't want to talk, but that's not too unusual with jurors."

"But he's definitely not the man you saw in the garage?" Jalen asked.

"No way. I'm certain of that."

Jalen closed his notebook. "We're good for now."

"All right. I'll be waiting for the exclusive."

"Thank you for your time. We'll be in touch." They had a few leads to track down.

15

"Thanks for coming over," Richard said. "I hope the security guys out front were nice to you."

Quinn smiled. "Of course they were. Highly professional and they seem like they have you pretty locked down. You said it was important. Has something happened? Do we need to call the FBI?"

Richard put his hand on her arm. "Please have a seat."

She sat while Richard went to the kitchen and returned with two cups of coffee.

"What's on your mind, Richard?" As an attorney she was used to not only being legal counsel, but also psychological counsel to many clients. Richard was no different and unfortunately this situation only made things much more stressful for all of them.

He took a sip of his coffee and turned toward her. "I might be losing it."

She could already tell this was going to be a taxing evening. "Why do you say that?"

"I keep feeling like I'm hearing things at night. I know the security guys are out there, but I just can't shake it. There's this sense that someone is watching me when I go out."

She found it hard to believe that someone was watching him, but she had to ask the questions. "Have you seen anyone?"

Richard shook his head. "No. But I can feel it. I promise you that. Someone is out there."

She gripped her coffee cup tightly. "You're probably just overthinking this whole thing." But was he? Richard was many things, but paranoid wasn't one of them. Was there something she was missing here?

He groaned. "But it's like I'm sleeping with one eye open. I can't fully relax no matter how much wine I drink, so now I've given up and stay caffeinated."

She had to ask. "Are you feeling any guilt over the outcome of the lawsuit?" They'd had many conversations protected by the attorney client privilege where Richard had revealed that he in fact did believe that the initial version of Asbury Pharmaceuticals wonder drug did bring about severe and even deadly side effects. But Richard was convinced that the good outweighed the bad and that the newer formulations were completely safe. He feared a loss in court would undo all the good work that the company did do, so he refused to back down.

Richard averted his eyes. "I probably should, but is it bad to admit that I don't?"

She wasn't surprised. He was more worried about his own personal safety because Richard was ultimately selfish. "You've got a lot on your plate."

His eyes met hers. "But I must admit to having a one-track mind now. I can't even focus on my work. It's just like I wake up and wonder if today will be the day that I die. Am I delusional?"

"Hardly." She took another sip of coffee. "If the FBI is right about the threat, then you have every reason to be worried, but you're also doing everything right. You're not being reckless. You have your security. No one is going to get through those guys."

Richard reached out and touched her cheek softly. She tried

not to cringe. The last thing she wanted was for him to think that he was going to take her to bed tonight.

"Quinn, will you stay with me?" he whispered. "Please. I need you."

Ugh. Now what was she going to do? Yeah, she'd flirted with him at the beginning of their relationship in a moment of really bad judgment, but she was *not* going to make that mistake again.

"Did I overstep?" he asked.

"I don't think that's a good idea." How much would he push her?

"Okay. Honestly, I just want the company. I don't want to be alone right now. Can you understand that?"

"And your wife?" The words had come out of her mouth before she could take them back.

He laughed loudly. "Melanie is still at our beach house. She doesn't want anything to do with me. She's sleeping with her personal trainer, and frankly I can't blame her. It's not like I'm ever going to win the husband of the year award."

She didn't understand marriage at all. It was one of the reasons why it would never work for her. "I can stay for another cup of coffee, but I will be going home. How does that sound?"

"Perfect." His eyes sparkled.

She had to keep her head in the game and focus on her ultimate goal. That would make all of this worth it.

16

Samira sat beside Jalen at his place as they continued to work and devour their Thai takeout. They'd tracked down Kevin Trask and interviewed him. He had airtight alibis for all the murders, and while he was a bit odd, it appeared he wasn't a threat. It turned out that he'd broken his only pair of glasses the first day of trial and according to him, he focused on the redheaded blob that was Quinn to make it seem that he was engaged. His story was consistent with Gemma noticing him squinting, and since his alibis were solid, they felt they were at a dead end where he was concerned.

"Since we now know the Trask lead was a bust, we need to confront Quinn about this random guy. What if she has a stalker? What if the stalker saw these CEOs as some sort of a threat and decided to act on it?"

"Even Maxine?" Jalen asked.

"Maxine might be the odd woman out here. When you combine the nature of the lawsuit and the manner of death, she might not be part of this puzzle."

Jalen picked up his spicy noodle bowl. "It would make things tidier. Then at least we're dealing with two male victims. Heart attack and overdose both could be manipulated and involve drugs."

"Hear me out. What if Quinn has this stalker. He doesn't like the men in her life. Once she wins the lawsuits, the CEOs seem even more powerful. The imagery in the news shows the victorious CEOs with Quinn. That could conjure up a lot of jealousy as it relates to his fixation."

"Why not take out the CEO who lost the lawsuit?"

"Maybe in the stalker's mind, the lawsuit makes him less of a threat. Less of a man. Impotent even."

"You're going there? You think this is sexually motivated?"

"Possibly. I'm not wedded to the theory yet, but we have to talk to Quinn about this guy. She certainly didn't volunteer the information, and I'd like to know why."

"In her defense, we didn't ask that direct question."

"True." She paused. "Are you starting to have a soft spot for our leading lawyer?"

Jalen laughed. "She is a force of nature. I would love to hear what they say in those stuffy partner's meetings when she's not around."

She had an idea. "Probably nothing good. Those guys are threatened by her success. They have to tolerate her because she's a winner. A mover and a shaker, but if she started losing a lot of cases, they would try to force her out so quickly it would make your head spin."

"And I thought the FBI was tough," he muttered.

"It is, but I think maybe law firms are worse because you're not only dealing with power but exorbitant amounts of money. So much power centered around a few central partners. Most of whom are white men. They have the relationships with the big clients. It is getting better, but change is slow. We know that from the FBI."

Jalen squeezed her shoulder. "I still give you so much credit for sticking around when they sent you into counterterrorism as your first job after you had been perfectly clear that you didn't want to do that."

Sometimes she was surprised that she had managed to push through and overcome.

His brown eyes softened. "Five years of our partnership and you still rarely talk about those days. You didn't have to stay. You had a law degree and were at the top of your class and didn't need the FBI. They are the ones who needed you."

She rested her head on the sofa for a moment before responding. Jalen was a safe space for her. He related to her experience in ways others couldn't even begin to because he'd had his own challenges in life. Things that she couldn't fully comprehend, but there was a level of empathy between them that made their partnership bond unbreakable. "I didn't want to be a lawyer. I wanted to go to law school to learn how to think. How to advocate and analyze. How to argue my points. I thought it would make me a better FBI agent and it did. It's one of the things that helped me get through the dark times." She could still remember it like it was yesterday.

"I'm sorry you had to go through that."

Taking a deep breath, she decided to open up further. "We've never talked about this, but growing up, I felt very isolated. Like I never fit in anywhere. It goes far beyond what box I was supposed to check on the forms. Based on my name alone, I was viewed differently, but I was struggling with who I really was and who I wanted to be. One of the reasons I got my undergrad degree in Arab Studies at Georgetown is because I wanted to fill that void in my life. At that point especially, I was longing to understand my identity, my history. I wanted to know more about my heritage. My father has always been so closed off about everything in his past including our extended family. He was insistent that I should try to be as Americanized as possible, and I never understood his reluctance to fully embrace Lebanese culture. Losing my mom to cancer without ever really knowing her forever left a hole in my heart. And while my grandmother was amazing, there was only so much we got to talk about on a deep level since I was just a teenager when she passed away."

"They would've been proud of you, Samira." Jalen paused. "And don't ever feel like you can't share this stuff with me. I know I'm coming at things from a different angle, but I do get a lot of what you're saying. You were put in a box whether you wanted to be or not. Whether you were even capable of processing how to act in that box. Expectations were placed upon you that you weren't necessarily in a position to handle."

"Given those struggles, it only made my stint in counterterrorism even harder." She'd held onto these things for years. "I knew I would never fit in—at least not with that current group of agents in counterterrorism. But from that point on, I realized that I had to make a stand and claim my voice because no one else would. Yes, I wanted to fight those terrorists who attacked our country, but I desperately wanted to show that the actions of a few didn't define an entire group. It was an uphill battle. I think I convinced some, but others to this day, if I cross paths with them, it's always tense."

"That was one of the main reasons that you left HQ, wasn't it? You didn't want to be in DC."

She hung her head. "Yeah. There were too many painful memories there." Both professionally and personally.

He grabbed her hand and squeezed it tightly. "You're a fighter, Samira. I hope one day I can be half the agent that you are."

His kind words warmed her heart, but he was selling himself short. "Jalen, you're already the best agent I've ever worked with."

He lightly punched her arm. "Isn't this a love fest?"

She smiled. "Enough of all of that. Why don't we get back to this case."

"I checked in with Richard Hale's security team today. They said all's been super quiet."

"I'll take that." Quiet was better than the alternative.

"But they did tell me off the record that Richard is a mess."

"I hope we didn't push it too far. Living in fear is no way to live. If he has the security, he should feel pretty confident. We're not dealing with organized crime or gang violence here. There isn't going to be a drive by. It will be much more surgical than that."

"Do you think we need to bring in someone from the behavioral team?"

"I asked Myron about that this morning, but he said it was too premature. The BAU is really strapped for resources right now. They are booked up with cases they know for certain they can help with. This one is still a bit of an unknown."

"Unknown until it's not. Myron's already putting the heat on us to get somewhere, but we're hamstrung with our resources."

"The two of us can do a lot."

"I know, but hopefully we can get additional help if this thing implodes."

She groaned. "Give me your best gut instinct on this. Serial killer or no?"

Jalen sat quietly and looked at her.

"If you're thinking that long, I'm not sure how to take it."

"I don't have a strong sense on this one. What do you think?"

She also took a moment to gather her thoughts. "I'm not sure about a serial killer, but something isn't right. I'm not sure what it is, but I just have a feeling."

"Hey, I trust your instincts. They are usually spot on especially with this kind of thing."

"I guess time will tell. Speaking of time. Can you pull up the timeline again? Remind me how long it was between the verdict and death of the CEO?"

"Sure thing." Jalen typed on his laptop. "For Myers, the time was just two weeks. For French, it was three months. For Cruz it was three weeks."

"That's another piece of the puzzle to argue against French's inclusion. And if this is a pattern, our killer should strike within the next three weeks."

Jalen rubbed his chin. "Hopefully, our friend Richard can last that long."

"Doesn't it just show how powerful people can become incredibly uncomfortable when the power is taken away from them and everything is out of their control?"

"You don't like that guy, do you?"

"I don't dislike him. I just think a man like him hasn't really dealt with true adversity in his life. Think, Jalen. These CEOs we're dealing with here, aren't just rich. They're super rich. They are getting bonus payments of fifty mil. And that's in a so-so year."

"Yeah, that type of money doesn't even compute in my head."

She laughed. "Me either. Which is why these guys are just built differently. And woman for that matter, French was loaded too."

"But you don't look at her the same way since she was a woman?"

"I don't. That doesn't mean that she wasn't similar in some ways to these guys, but I bet you her pay wasn't close to equal, even if it was exorbitant."

"I can tell you're really not sold on her being in the mix."

"I'm not. I keep getting the feeling about a man who is threatened in some way by these other men. Maybe Quinn is part of the optic—maybe not."

"Or, what if we are dealing with someone on an anti-corporate mission? Not necessarily revenge from the families impacted, but someone with a larger social viewpoint? Someone like Connor but much more dangerous."

She'd given that a lot of thought but wasn't sold. "Doesn't it feel more personal than that?"

"How so?" Jalen asked.

"If this was just someone randomly killing these CEOs out of a deranged notion of moral principles, then why go to such lengths to cover it up. To make it seem like a heart attack and an overdose. Wouldn't you want your cause to be known? At least at some point so you could take credit and get publicity? This seems to be the work of someone who doesn't want to get caught and plans to keep on going."

"You might be right."

"Which brings us back to the families or someone connected to them or possibly connected to Quinn, like this stalker guy."

"Or maybe an overzealous reporter?" Jalen said.

"I think Gemma is an unlikely suspect, but she knows even more than what she told us. She's holding back to try to get more, and that's her job, so I get it."

"Oh, I did an initial review of Quinn's social media accounts. She was right. The comments ran the gamut from loving and glowing, to hateful and deranged. Some were really violent like she said. Men and women but the ones that were most disturbing were from men."

"We should have an analyst get us a short list of people we should examine further—focus on those with the most violent comments that post regularly."

"I'm on it."

"It would be pretty brazen for the killer to be blasting Quinn on social media for all the world to see, but at this point nothing surprises me."

17

As Quinn started her drive home from Richard's, she noticed the taillights that appeared behind her in the darkness. She was still in a residential area near his house and gripped the wheel tightly because the car seemed too close. She even thought about turning around and going back to Richard's but that was silly. Taking it slow and deliberate, she wanted to see if she was imagining things. Was Richard wearing off on her?

Once she got out on the main road, she decided not to get on the interstate, because she needed to know if she was really being followed or if all of this was all in her head. Her pulse quickened, and her hands felt clammy on the wheel.

Nothing is going to happen to you. She tried to calm herself by taking deep breaths, but she couldn't shake the fact that someone was coming after her. But why? Could this be the same person that Richard thought was watching him? Her mind raced as she sorted through the possibilities.

After a few turns, she proceeded down a busy road off the interstate, and the car still pursued. Not super close, but close enough. She took a few random turns and the tail continued. The more she drove, the anger started to build and bubble up inside of her. She'd dealt with too much fear and pain in her life. She refused to cower to this unknown threat, but she had to play this smart. There was no way she was going to her house until she lost this tail.

She floored her Jeep and weaved her way through the Piedmont area until the interstate was in sight. Hopping on 85 north, she waited to see what happened. She noticed the lights of the car did not follow her onto I-85. Someone had been watching her. They knew she was at Richard's. But who?

By the time she got home, it was well after midnight. She was drained from babysitting Richard and dealing with the mysterious tail. Who had been coming after her? She hated being in the dark.

Earlier she thought Richard was her biggest problem, but at least he had respected her wishes and didn't push her. That was something that couldn't be said for all men.

"Oh, Felix. I'm glad I have you." The tabby purred loudly as she rubbed his ears.

She double checked her alarm system and all the locks. Not wanting to take any chances, she pulled her gun out of the safe and had it at the ready. She didn't really like firearms, but she was trained, and would use them if necessary. How had things gotten out of hand so quickly?

Even though it was late, she wasn't sleepy. Her insomnia was basically a way of life and that had only been amplified by the events of the evening. She'd been told by Dr. Lane, her psychologist, that insomnia was a coping mechanism she had developed as a child. That if she stayed awake, she had better odds of fending off her abusers.

Those thoughts stirred painful memories even today. It was a demon she could never get rid of. She closed her eyes for a minute and went back to that dark place. Slumping down onto the floor, she curled up in a tight ball on the kitchen floor as her breathing grew heavier.

That college student hadn't been targeting her, but the heavy weight of his male body pressing down on hers brought it all back. She was a little girl again. Defenseless. And the man who should've been her protector was her betrayer.

Her father hit her a lot. Beat her down. Yelled at her. Called her a worthless piece of trash. Her mother had died in childbirth, and it had sent her father into a tailspin, but she honestly believed he had been evil long before that. She'd wondered if her mother had to have been too smitten by him to notice the darkness behind his eyes. He carried it with him all the time, even when he wore a fake smile. But she noticed it. One of her earliest memories was looking into his eyes and feeling fear.

Having a daughter was like a curse to her father. He was a monster. And as she started to get a little older, he had no problem letting his buddies into her bedroom. If she fell asleep, she stood no chance against them. They were older, much stronger. But if she was awake, at least she could fight. Fighting meant she was still alive. That she had some small measure of control even if she was ultimately beaten into submission and her young body ravaged by monsters.

She would often know when it would be one of those awful nights. One of the only things that had gotten her through those horrific times was her ballerina music box. She would open the box and let it play when she thought she might have unwelcome guests in her bedroom. Focusing in on the melody helped her escape from the present darkness that surrounded her.

Taking a moment, she replayed the melody in her head. There were so many things she still wanted to say to her father. To confront him about the abuse. About his actions. But she couldn't do that because he was dead. He'd taken so much from her in life and now in death. He'd been gone for ten years, but in a way, it seemed like just yesterday that she'd gotten the phone call. One of his drinking buddies had found him dead at home.

Her body shook as the fresh tears poured down her face. A wave of sadness and anger washed over her.

She opened her eyes. "Enough." She hated giving her father

any time even now in her thoughts. That was one of the reasons she enjoyed her work so much for domestic violence victims because she could actually *do something* about their situation even if she couldn't change her own past. Inaction drove her nuts. She liked to make things right.

Wiping her eyes, she got off the floor and went to her bedroom to change clothes before heading down to the basement to get on the treadmill. A couple of miles would make her feel a lot better. She ran a lot at night. It was one of her best coping mechanisms, especially if paired with some kickboxing. She might not have been able to defend herself when she was young, but she could now after having been taught self-defense by one of the best instructors in Atlanta. She'd taken those classes just as seriously as any of her cases, because in her mind, it could be the difference between life or death. She'd have trouble fighting off most men given the size and strength difference, but she wouldn't make it easy on them.

Tonight had been a stark reminder about how fragile a position she was in. She wasn't quite sure yet what to make of what had happened, but it unsettled her, nonetheless. And it would just keep coming because dealing with John next week might kill her. The man was beyond reprehensible. The way he looked at her struck fear in her heart. Not only was she worried about him on a personal level. It was professional too. She'd had clients do shady things before, but straight up destruction of evidence and doing it so boldly, was even new for her. There's no way she'd give him the satisfaction of seeing her lose the case though because he would make sure that the blame would be squarely placed on her shoulders. No, she was going to win this one. No matter what it took.

18

'm guessing Quinn isn't going to like this unexpected Saturday morning visit to her house." Jalen joined her as they walked up the steps to Quinn's place.

Samira shrugged. "We can't cater to her. We have a case to run. And it's almost eleven, so she must be awake even if she is the type to sleep in, which I highly doubt." Samira thought Quinn was more likely the type to be up at six a.m. even on the weekends. The overachieving, never resting, and very hard on themselves type. She knew it well because she was one of them

Jalen rang the doorbell and they waited. The big two-story home was on a nice piece of property in an exclusive Buckhead community. Immaculate landscaping and bright, colorful flowers adorned the garden out front.

When the door opened, Quinn's eyes widened. "Agents, what's going on?"

Quinn looked completely different today. Her red hair was pulled up in a high ponytail. She was fresh faced and wore a black t-shirt and orange polka dot yoga pants.

"Can we come in?" Jalen asked.

Stepping back, Quinn ushered them inside. "Please come in and have a seat."

They followed her to a sunny and airy living room. The main floor was open concept, and the design was bright white, clean and modern—fitting Quinn perfectly. Colorful artwork adorned the walls.

Quinn turned to face them. "Can I get you anything? I have coffee, tea, water."

"No, thank you," Samira took a seat.

"Then please tell me what's going on." Quinn stood with her hands on her hips.

Samira decided there was no point in playing games. "Why didn't you tell us about your stalker?"

"My what?" Quinn sat down in the large chair.

"The man who was stalking you at court?" She wasn't going to go easy on Quinn. This was too important.

"That guy?" Quinn sighed loudly. "I would hardly call him a stalker. He might have had some mental issues. I only talked to him once in the parking garage. Wait. Did Gemma tell you about this?"

"Yes," Jalen responded. "But you should have."

Quinn tightened her ponytail. "Honestly, it didn't even cross my mind. I thought the guy was totally harmless. He said he'd been watching me in court and wanted to get to know me better. Once I told him I wasn't interested, he backed off. I didn't hear from him again."

"Did you get his name?" Samira asked.

"He just said his name was Luke." Quinn paused. "You don't think that he had anything to do with this, do you?"

"We don't know, but the possibility of you having a stalker is definitely something you should've brought up to us. That makes us wonder what else you're holding back." Samira was pushing a bit today, but her frustration level was high.

"I'm not holding anything back. That guy just didn't even come on my radar for me to tell you about. I'm sorry."

Jalen leaned in. "And you're saying that you haven't seen this Luke guy since that day in the garage? Are you sure?"

"No." Quinn looked down. "I'm not saying that. I saw him during this trial, but he didn't make any effort to talk to me."

A large, furry orange tabby cat walked into the living room and started rubbing against Jalen's legs. Samira watched in amusement as Jalen squirmed. He was not the biggest fan of cats. To his credit, he didn't say anything, and the cat soon jumped onto Quinn's lap.

"Quinn, this man clearly has an unhealthy interest in you." Jalen's voice was firm as he was playing a bit of the bad cop role. Maybe the cat had set him off. "That's an important piece of information that we will need to investigate. You need to think long and hard right now about whether there's anything else you have been keeping from us."

Quinn ran her fingers down the cat's back. "As I told you before, I wasn't hiding anything. I still don't think any of this is about me. It's about these companies. Why would anyone care about me? I'm just the lawyer."

Samira looked at her. "You're right in the middle of this whether you want to be or not. And you are the face and representative of these companies in court. You're all over social media and the news. That visibility means something."

"I realize that, but I'm not quite sure what you want me to do about it."

The tension in the room had gone up too much. She needed to defuse things. "It's not your job to do anything about it. All I'm asking is that you tell us the truth."

"I am." Quinn stood. "I should tell you something in the spirit of transparency."

Samira's stomach clenched. This couldn't be good. "What?"

"Last night I was over at Richard's. He's been really stressed and worried over all of this and wanted company. This threat has him completely on edge and he's having difficulty coping, so I tried to talk him down. When I left his place, someone started following me."

"Are you sure?" Jalen asked.

"Of course I can't be certain, but I did some pretty nonsensical turns and they tailed me the entire way."

"Since when did you learn evasive maneuvers?" Jalen asked.

"It was instinct. I felt like I was being chased and I wanted to shake them. It wasn't anything I'd ever been taught. I wasn't going to go home so I wove around the neighborhood, then went down Piedmont and eventually got on the interstate. That's when they stopped following me."

Samira didn't like the sound of any of this. "Could you get a look at them? What kind of car?"

"I couldn't see who was in the car. It looked like a dark SUV of some type, but that's all I could make out."

Samira had more questions. "So someone knew you were at Richard's. Did you notice anyone on your way there?"

Quinn shook her head. "No, I didn't."

"Have you felt like you were being followed at any other time besides last night?" Samira feared this might not be the first time.

"No."

Jalen cleared his throat. "Maybe they were waiting at Richard's when you arrived."

"But why? This doesn't make sense." Quinn's pale cheeks were beginning to turn red.

She had some troubling ideas. "They didn't stay at Richard's. They followed you which makes me think *you* were the target. This is all the more reason to check out this Luke guy. You said yourself that he was at the trial. He saw you with Richard. Maybe Richard was easier to track down, so he sat on his house and hoped that you would eventually show up."

"Do you realize how sketchy that sounds?" Quinn asked.

"I do. Which is why you need to take this all very seriously." Samira wanted Quinn to realize that the stakes had just gone up a few notches.

"I'm just trying to take this all in." Quinn stood with her hands on her hips.

"We're going to get right on tracking down Luke." Jalen cleared his throat. "In the meantime, you need to be careful. We also have to consider that whoever was following you wasn't Luke."

"Whoever it is, has gotten my attention. I won't be caught off guard again."

The message appeared to have been received. "Good. And call us immediately if there are any issues.

Quinn put the cat down gently on the floor. "I will."

Samira stood and Jalen followed suit. "Lock up after we leave. Even during the day make sure you're locked in."

"You don't have to worry about that." She took a deep breath. "And I should tell you that I have a firearm and am trained to use it. If a man breaks into my house, I will not hesitate to shoot."

Samira saw something she hadn't seen from Quinn before. Fear.

19

On Saturday night, Quinn sat down to dinner with Mimi Hicks, one of the public interest attorneys who ran the Atlanta Domestic Violence legal clinic. After everything that had happened, Quinn had wanted to bail, but she refused to let some creep make her live each day in fear. She'd had too much of that in her life already.

Mimi lifted up her glass. "Cheers to another victory for the best trial lawyer in town."

"Thank you. I was worried I wouldn't be able to pull it out, but I'm not going to complain that I did. Enough about me. How are things at the clinic?" She cared much more about that topic.

Mimi tucked a strand of curly brown hair behind her ear. "Way too busy. Just when I feel like we're catching up, the floodgates open again. And while normally it would be good for attorneys to be busy, as you know that doesn't hold true in my line of work. More cases meant more women and children who have been hurt and abused."

"I don't know how you do it day in and day out. It has to take an emotional toll on you." The limited amount of work Quinn did was hard enough. She couldn't imagine doing it twenty four seven like Mimi did. She admired Mimi's tenacity and commitment. She would do everything in her power to help the cause.

Mimi set down her glass. "But you know it's worth it. Our work is vital. These women have nowhere else to turn. Thank you again for taking on that extra case last week. Your oversight helping our younger attorneys is invaluable. There are never enough experienced lawyers to do the work, but we make do the best we can thanks to people like you."

Quinn considered for a moment whether she was going to open up to Mimi. She knew that Mimi would understand. "I may have a stalker." She blurted it out instead of easing into it.

Mimi's light brown eyes widened. "What? Why do you think that?"

The concern was evident on Mimi's face. She hated laying this on Mimi, but she needed a friend right now. She didn't have many in her life, and Mimi had earned her trust. "I don't want to worry you, but I know you understand all of this."

Reaching out, Mimi grabbed onto her hand. "Of course I do. Have you talked to the police?"

"More like the FBI."

"Okay. Now you're starting to scare me. What is happening?"

Quinn took a few minutes and told Mimi everything she knew.

Mimi blew out a breath. "I know you can't help it because of your work, but being so visible in the public eye comes with challenges. I saw your last video you posted on social. It had thousands of hits, Quinn. Your face is everywhere."

It was important to her career that she be high profile, and she wasn't going to let this stalker dictate how she lived. "But there's good that goes with that too. It's not all bad to be out there, and for the content I post, I get to control the message. That's important to me."

"I hear you, but it just means sometimes you're going to have to deal with unfortunate situations like this one. I know how trained in self-defense you are, but if I were you, I still wouldn't be going out alone right now. Not until they really know who this guy is and what he wants. Sometimes stalkers can be creepy but harmless. Other times, Quinn, I hate to say this, but they can be deadly."

A chill went down her back. "I know."

"I've dealt with a few very scary stalking cases in my career, and unfortunately none of them had happy endings. They got really messy. Do you think you should ask your firm to hire you some private security?"

Quinn huffed. "I would never do that. It would just give them one more thing to hang over my head. And they would use it against me. To try to show that I'm weak in some way. No. I have to handle this myself."

"You have the money to hire security yourself. I know you do."

Quinn didn't like the idea of random men encroaching on her life, even if they were doing their job to protect her. "I'm not very comfortable with that concept."

"Okay. I get it. You can still do things to protect yourself. Don't do anything foolish to try to prove a point. Or worse, I know you well, Quinn, you might think you can rationalize with the guy. Win him over like you do a jury, but it doesn't work like that. You don't know what his mental state is."

Quinn bit the inside of her cheek. She didn't like all of these unknowns. Especially when it came to her own personal safety. "I know I can't track this guy down and confront him, but I would really like to."

Mimi squeezed her arm. "Please promise me you won't try to do that."

"I'll let the FBI deal with it." But she wasn't going to stand by and be victimized again. She'd endured enough of that in her life. "I'm sorry I put a downer on our dinner."

"You can always talk to me about anything, and if there's anything I can do, just name it."

"Thanks for being there for me, Mimi. You have no idea how much I appreciate it. I really needed this night out."

Mimi leaned back. "You work way too hard. I get that our jobs are stressful and all consuming, but I worry that you don't take any time out for you. It's always about your clients."

That wasn't entirely true. "I care about my career."

"As you should, but you should also care about you as a whole person."

She wasn't sure she'd ever be a whole person again. Not after everything she'd been through. She was doing her best to make a difference in her own way. "I'm just taking it one day at a time."

"We've been working together for five years. I know that you have suffered trauma, but we've never talked about any of the details. If you ever change your mind and want to have a safe place to work through anything, my door is always open."

"I appreciate that. I still go to a psychologist, although not as frequently as I used to."

"That's good. Maybe given all this stalker stuff you should make an appointment. I'm sure it's bound to stir up latent feelings."

Mimi had a point. She hadn't visited Dr. Lane in months. "Thanks. I think you're right." She looked down at her watch. "I know it's getting late. I don't want you to burn your babysitter."

Mimi laughed. "Yeah. A good babysitter is worth her weight in gold."

"Have you talked to Clark lately?" Clark was Mimi's worthless ex.

"No. He's still AWOL. I've come to the realization that I'm going to be doing this thing alone. And I've accepted that. We don't need him in our lives."

"Don't let him worm his way back in if he decides to show up and beg for forgiveness. He hurt you too badly."

"I won't."

"Good. I've got the check. You can get out of here."

Mimi leaned in. "No way. I'm going to make sure you get to your car safely."

"Deal, but I've still got the check."

Mimi didn't fight that. And after a few minutes they were walking to the parking garage that was across the street from the restaurant.

They walked up to her Jeep. "See. All good. Hop in and I'll drive you to your car."

"Thanks. I'm one level up."

She dropped Mimi off and then headed out of the garage. On high alert, she didn't notice anyone behind her as she pulled out of the garage. Maybe this was all in her head. What if no one had been following her and now she had all this unwanted FBI attention on her? Getting inside of her own head was the last thing she needed to do. What she had to focus on was staying rational and alert. If there was someone out there who wanted to hurt her, she would be ready. If not, then all of this was just going down a useless rabbit hole. Unless there could still be some good no matter what the outcome.

Once she got home, she went to unlock her front door and saw it was already slightly ajar. She let out a scream before it even registered. Someone had been inside her home and had trashed it.

"Felix!" She yelled his name as she began running around looking for him. It hadn't even occurred to her that the intruder could still be inside until she ran upstairs. She grabbed her gun from the lockbox in her nightstand. "Felix!"

Her pulse raced as she thought about the fate of her faithful friend, and at the same time why someone would've done this to her.

"If you're still here, come out now!" She gripped the gun tightly in her hands, ready to use it if necessary. She would not hesitate to pull the trigger.

There was a chilling silence that seemed to go on forever until Felix rushed toward her meowing loudly. She let out a sigh seeing him unharmed. She grabbed him with her left hand, holding him close to her, and he started purring in the safety of her arms. She kept the gun in her right hand. There was no way she was letting down her guard. "Are you okay? Who was here?" She had no trouble talking to Felix even if he couldn't answer her back.

She put Felix on the bed for a moment. Fear bubbling inside her quickly turned to red hot rage. Her home had been invaded. She pulled out her cell and scrolled to Samira's contact info.

Dialing, she waited for an answer, trying to steady her breathing.

"Quinn, are you okay?" Samira didn't even say hello.

"Not exactly. I just got home from dinner and my place is trashed."

"Do you think you're alone now? That they've already come and gone?"

She took another deep breath. "I think so. I've looked around, and I don't think anyone is still here. But they were here, and they made a big mess."

"Okay. Lock back up and stay put. Don't try to clean up anything. We'll have a forensics team that needs to document everything. I'll be over in a few minutes along with backup. Do you want me to stay on the line with you?"

She thought for a moment and that seemed like overkill. She had her cat and her gun. That's all she needed. "Thanks, but I should be okay. See you soon." Quinn couldn't believe this. Why was someone inside her house? What were they looking for? Something for one of her cases? Or was this more personal?

Those thoughts left her unsettled. She liked to be in control of all aspects of her life, and right now, she felt like she was riding a wave that was threatening to take her out to sea.

She hated leaving everything in disarray, but Samira had been perfectly clear in her instruction. It wasn't that long before a throng of Atlanta police and FBI agents descended on her home. She wasn't prepared for the intrusion, but tonight it seemed that anyone and everyone was a guest in her house—wanted and unwanted.

She sat at the kitchen table with Felix on her lap. They both needed each other's company right now. Jalen and Samira were also there with her.

"What do you think is going on here?" She wanted answers. Needed answers.

"It's looking more like you do have a stalker," Samira said. "What we don't know yet is whether the stalker is also the one who killed the CEOs."

They were probably going to push that link because she had to admit it made a lot of sense. "Why trash my place?"

Jalen looked at her. "Could be a power play. Trying to mess with your head."

"I agree," Samira said. "Or, what if this is related to one of your cases and they thought you had some important information here at your house."

She blew out a breath. "I don't keep any paper files here. Everything is on my laptop. I checked and it wasn't taken."

Samira frowned. "That is weird. Do you notice anything gone? No matter how small."

She shook her head. "No. Not that I can tell. Just one big mess they left for me."

"Maybe they just wanted to send a clear message that they know how to get to you," Samira said. "Did you set the alarm when you left?"

"I may have forgotten." That had been a dumb move on her part, but she was running late, and it slipped her mind. "What do I do now?"

"We need to see what the team finds, if anything. Do you have some place you can stay tonight?"

"I'll take Felix and get a hotel room near the office."

"That's good. Jalen, why don't you stay here and supervise the team. I'll take Quinn to the hotel and make sure she's settled in."

Quinn almost rebuffed the offer but then thought better of it. If someone was out there trying to get her, she would appreciate the protection of a federal agent. She hated being dependent on anyone else, but in this instance, she wasn't turning down the help. "Thanks. I'll just need a few minutes to get my things and get Felix's stuff." She kept Felix close to her as she walked up the steps to her bedroom and quickly packed a bag with far too much stuff for one night, but she feared it could be longer. Felix wouldn't like the new environment, but she had to keep him safe, and this was the way she knew she could assure it.

She pulled out her cell and called the Ritz Carlton downtown. If she was being kicked out of her place, she was going to live comfortably. Money wasn't a concern for her, so she booked a suite and went back down to meet Samira.

"We'll go in my car," Samira said. "I can have one of the agents drop yours off later at the hotel."

"Sounds good." She grabbed Felix's carrier and put him in the trunk of the SUV as he meowed loudly in protest. "Sorry, I have to warn you, he's going to whine at us the whole way."

Samira smiled. "Doesn't bother me. I like cats. Even mouthy ones."

Quinn appreciated that Samira was trying to act like everything was okay, but she couldn't get over what was happening. "I can't believe someone was in my house rifling through my things. It feels so invasive."

Samira glanced over at her. "That was his point. And I know we don't know for certain that it's a man, even if it's not Luke, but I'd put all my money on it." She paused. "Where are we headed?"

"Ritz Carlton, downtown."

Samira shot her a look. "Guess I should've known you weren't a budget hotel kind of girl."

She laughed. "You're funny."

"I'm not exactly known for my humor."

"Me either." She thought for a moment. "I think we have a lot in common. I realize it may not seem that way on the surface, but it's deeper than that."

"I could never be in the spotlight like you and thrive though. I do my best work in the background."

She thought she did too, but she didn't admit that to Samira. "The spotlight has its pros and cons. I really don't have an exciting life. I'm fine being a homebody when I'm not at work or otherwise entangled in some sort of event that I have to show up at."

"You ever consider flipping and becoming a US Attorney or prosecutor?"

Quinn sighed. "I always thought I would be a prosecutor until the law school debt piled up to be something insurmountable. I don't come from money, so I was on the hook for all my loans for undergrad and law school and had to pay for everything myself. Working at a big firm let me have the freedom to be able to pay off those debts. It took years, but I did. By then I was so deeply entrenched into my litigation practice, defending big companies, that there really wasn't any other path I could imagine."

"I guess you do some pro bono work though. Isn't that expected in big firms these days?" Samira drummed her fingers on the steering wheel.

She thought about how much to tell Samira and whether opening up could be beneficial in some way. "I do, but I do it quietly. I work for the domestic violence clinic."

"I hope I'm not overstepping, but did you choose that because of your own experiences?"

Quinn took a deep breath. "Is it that obvious?" She needed to be more careful. It was important for her to stay in control of her own narrative.

Samira shook her head. "Absolutely not. I've been told I'm much more perceptive than most people."

"Well, yeah I had a difficult childhood. My mother died in

childbirth and my father was abusive." That was putting it lightly.

"Quinn, I'm so sorry."

"There's no need to pity me. I'm stronger now for it."

"That's an amazing way to look at it. Is your father still alive?"

"Thankfully not."

Samira winced. "I get it. My family is messed up too. My mom died of cancer when I was only two. I was pretty much raised by my grandmother."

"And your father?"

"My father is in international business. As a child, he was an absent father. Always working. On the road constantly. He didn't really know what to do with me. He'd always wanted a son, but that didn't happen. Then once I went to college, he spent most of his time overseas for work."

"Family is complicated. Sometimes it's easier the less that we have. Please don't mention anything about my work at the clinic. The last thing my clients need is attention. That's why I fly under the radar when working with the clinic."

"I respect you for that."

"Honestly, I believe it's much more important than the work I do at the firm. These women need advocates, and that's where I come in."

"They're very fortunate to have someone as committed as you."

"Thank you." She never liked to let any of them down.

"Quinn, are you sure you've told us everything? I feel like there may be something you're keeping to yourself, and you might think you have a good reason for doing it, but I fear it could cause you to end up getting hurt."

"I'm not stonewalling. You know what I know. I really don't have any further info on that Luke guy, and my initial thought was that he was harmless. I like to think I have good instincts, but in this case, I might have been wrong." And that scared her the most. Her ability to read people was key to everything she did.

"Remember, we're tracking him down, but it's possible there is someone else."

"And you believe that any of those options could lead you to the killer of the CEOs?"

"There has to be a connection. You seem to be a critical piece in all of this, whether you want to be or not. Before tonight, I still could've made a case for other theories, but the attention on you at the moment makes me believe that it's all connected."

"Oh, I don't want to be at the center of this. I want to be left alone and focus on winning my cases." That would enable her to keep doing her vital work.

"I've learned the hard way that we don't always get to choose our paths."

"Wait, I thought you wanted to be an FBI agent and you chose it over being a practicing lawyer."

"Oh, I wanted to be in the FBI, but I started out in counterterrorism. Something I most definitely did not want."

"But you did it anyway. You worked in counterterrorism?" This was an interesting tidbit to learn. She watched as Samira gripped the wheel tightly. This was obviously a difficult subject for her.

"Yeah. I put in my time, but I told them I wouldn't go back. I'm in the right place now working violent crimes."

"Do you enjoy trying to get into their heads? These killers?"

Samira didn't immediately answer. "I wouldn't say enjoy, but I'm good at it. I see things that others don't."

"Like you knowing why I wanted to do the domestic violence work."

"Exactly. I also like putting pieces together in a complex puzzle. And often, even with all that, at the end of the day, the most simple explanation is the one that wins the day. For example, I'm sure you've heard that if a woman is killed, it's most likely by her husband or boyfriend. Someone close. It's much more likely to be that than the random stranger on the street."

"And what are you getting from this killer you think is taking out the CEOs?" They stopped at a red light.

"This one feels like they have a purpose. This isn't random. This is strategic. Initially, they appeared to be trying to cover their tracks, but assuming the killer and the stalker are one in the same, they have come out of hiding now. They are acting more directly. They have a message. At some point they may even communicate with us and tell us what that message is."

"What do you mean by communicate?"

Samira glanced over at her quickly. "I don't mean it in a literal sense necessarily. Although it could be. I'm thinking more of the next victim and how they are killed. That would be a start. Once again, assuming the killer and stalker are one in the same, they probably now know we're onto them at this point. The killer is calculating and intelligent. Cool and collected. These aren't crimes of passion even if they may have a passionate reason behind them. They're highly driven by a purpose, and I believe you're tied into that. Does that make sense?"

"I have to admit, I'm impressed. I would've never gathered all of that from what we know."

"Well, I'd never be up in front of that jury like you. So we each have our places we operate." Samira looked in the rearview mirror.

"Is everything okay?" Quinn's heart started to beat faster fearing that someone was following them.

"Yes. I don't think we've been tailed. I took a few extra detours along the way just in case, but we're ready to pull into the hotel now. I'll make sure you get safely into your room."

"Thank you." She wasn't normally rattled this easily and that was almost bothering her more than the fact that someone was stalking her.

Once they got up to her room, Samira insisted on going in first. "Stay behind me."

"I highly doubt someone could be in there. I just made the reservation."

"I know. Just want to check it out."

Quinn swiped the key card and let Samira walk ahead of her. She had Felix in his carrier and sat it down once they got inside.

Samira whistled. "Now this is a room."

It really wasn't a room at all but a suite. And one that Quinn had zero guilt for booking. "Yeah. I figured if I had to be held up in here, I wanted something nice."

"I don't blame you."

Quinn could hardly believe that. Samira seemed like a practical woman who lived on a budget. Quinn didn't even need to budget because at this point in her life, she had more money than she could spend. After rising to the top of the firm a couple of years ago, her earnings had been substantial by any standard, but she was fighting for more of the profits based on principle, not on need.

Felix started meowing to get out of his carrier. She wanted him to start exploring to get comfortable with his surroundings, so she opened the carrier door. "So what now?"

"I'd like you to stay put tonight for sure. We'll have an agent bring over your car and leave the keys with the valet, but please don't leave tonight. Tomorrow we'll determine next steps."

"I can handle that."

Samira touched her shoulder. "It's going to be okay, Quinn. We're gonna catch this guy. I promise you."

Quinn wasn't so sure.

20

On Sunday, Samira and Jalen walked up the steps to his mother's house. "Hopefully we can put work out of our minds for a bit." They both needed to do a much better job at that.

"Mama will be so happy to see you." Jalen smiled.

It had been a few months since she'd visited Cherise Smith. Jalen's mom had welcomed her with open arms from day one with a standing Sunday dinner invitation. But Samira made sure not to accept too frequently because she knew how sacred that family time was for them. She had never experienced anything like it in her life.

They walked inside and Cherise made a beeline for her. "Samira! It's been too long." Cherise gave her a huge hug. Something she rarely got from anyone.

"Thank you, Mrs. Smith, as always for having me."

Cherise squeezed her shoulder. "I've told you a million times, you call me Cherise. Or Jalen's Mama. I'll always take that one." She laughed and gave her son a huge hug and kiss on the cheek.

"Mama, you act like you haven't seen me in years, and we just saw each other this morning in church."

Cherise grinned widely. "I'm just so glad you both could

make it. Your sister Jada is at home with little Rose. She has an earache, so it's just us."

Jalen's oldest sister, Anisa, lived in Florida with her husband and two kids. Jalen had grown up as the man of the house because his dad died of a heart attack when he was only seven.

"Come on in and have a seat. You two must be starving. Samira, I know you don't eat real home cooking that often."

"You're right." Her stomach growled just thinking of Cherise's southern cooking. Samira was raised in the Detroit area where sweet tea wasn't even a thing.

Jalen stepped forward. "Mama, how can I help you?"

"Son, will you go fix those lights in the upstairs bathroom? Samira will give me a hand in the kitchen, won't you?"

"Of course." Spending time with Cherise was bittersweet given her family situation with her mother dying before she even knew her. It had been Sitti, her grandmother, who had helped make her the woman she was today, and the pain of her loss still stung.

Cherise peeked inside of the oven and pulled out the green bean casserole and placed it on top of the stove. "Tell me what's new with you. Jalen says you're working on a stressful case."

She realized quickly that Cherise didn't intend to have her help. She only wanted to talk. "It's going to be a bad one, but that's what we do. We're used to the pressure."

"And how is my son doing?"

"Great." That question took her off guard. "Are you worried about something?"

Cherise sighed. "A mother always worries."

"Well on that front, you should rest easy. Jalen is a rock. I love working with him. He'll go far at the FBI and beyond if that is what he wants."

"And what about you?"

"What do you mean?"

"Aren't you looking to move up the FBI ladder too?"

"Yes. My job is everything to me."

Cherise touched her shoulder. "I know I have no right to say this to you, but over the past few years you've been working with my son, I do feel like I've gotten to know you, and I have to say that there's more to life than work. I tell Jalen the same thing, but I don't know if there's anyone telling you that."

She'd confided in Cherise about her family life, and she knew Cherise was coming from a place of love. "You sound a lot like your son."

"I raised him right." She laughed. "Seriously though. Just think about it. You can still reach your goals at work and also have a broader, more full life."

She wasn't surprised to hear this, but she simply wasn't interested. All she could do was say thank you and move on.

"Let me pull the chicken and bread out of the oven and we'll be ready. Go get Jalen if he's not back downstairs yet."

She walked into the dining room where Jalen was already sitting at the table. "I hope she didn't badger you too much."

"Just the usual." She had to admit that it was nice to have people in her life who cared. After Sitti had passed away when she was just sixteen, she had lost her family. Her father worked all the time, and it wasn't like he had ever been a real support system for her anyway. She'd only gotten that love and support from Sitti.

Cherise walked in carrying a platter of baked chicken. "Jalen, please grab the rest."

Jalen returned with the bread and green bean casserole, and they all sat down at the table.

"Jalen, please say grace for us."

Samira was used to this custom. She respectfully closed her eyes as Jalen prayed. She'd learned early on that his family was a strong family of faith. Another stark difference between their upbringings.

"All right, eat up," Cherise said. "I don't want a lot of left-overs so whatever you don't finish, you'll take home with you."

She took a sip of sweet tea. This was the only place she

would allow herself to indulge in such a decadent luxury. She had no idea how people drank sweet tea every day.

"It's wonderful, Mama, as always." Jalen patted his mom's hand.

There was no doubt in her mind Jalen would make a wonderful husband and father someday, and she would be so happy to see it. "Yes, it's delicious. You both know my cooking skills are limited to take out and delivery."

Everyone laughed and by the time they were finishing up, she felt more relaxed than she had in weeks. She was so glad she hadn't turned down the invite this time.

Jalen looked at her. "I haven't seen you smile this much in forever."

"Your mother is a good influence on me."

Cherise beamed. "Well, I'll come out and say it. I've held my tongue on the topic for too many years."

Jalen gave her a nervous glance.

What was going on?

"Mama, maybe you should keep holding your tongue."

Cherise shook her head. "No. I have to get this off of my chest."

"What is it?" Samira asked.

"I can see the way the two of you look at each other. It's obvious you care very much about the other."

"We're partners, Mama. Which means Samira is family."

"Yes. There isn't anything I wouldn't do for Jalen."

His mother's dark eyes lit up. "That's exactly my point. You would fit in quite nicely with this family and the two of you would have such beautiful children."

She choked on her tea.

"Mama!" Jalen said. "You're gonna run Samira off talking like that, and she'll never come to Sunday dinner again."

A sheepish grin spread across Cherise's face. "I'm just putting it out there."

She didn't even know what to say as she looked over at Jalen.

"Samira is like another sister to me."

Thank you, she mouthed. She didn't want to offend Jalen's mother, but there was simply no chance of the two of them getting together. Ever.

Cherise lifted up her hands. "I surrender, you two. I won't bring it up again. Let me go get the peach cobbler."

Jalen laughed. "And I thought we would make it through dinner without any fireworks."

Samira knew better.

21

On Monday afternoon, Samira and Jalen sat across from Luke Mullen in the field office. They'd been able to track him down from footage surrounding the courthouse.

"What's going on here?" Luke's blue eyes were bloodshot.

She wasn't sure if he was using or if he was just exhausted. "We need to ask you some questions about Quinn Kelly."

"What about her?"

"Do you know her?" Jalen asked.

"Not exactly," Luke mumbled. "I've seen her in court."

She leaned in toward him. "Why were you in her house Saturday night?"

Luke straightened up in his seat. "Wait a minute now. I wasn't in her house."

Samira had to determine how much to push this guy. In his late twenties, currently doing gig work, the man in front of her wasn't screaming violent stalker, but there was something off with him. "Well, someone was, and we think it was you."

"No. No. No." Luke shook his head. "It had to be him."

"Him who?" Jalen asked.

"There's been a man following Quinn. I wanted to tell her

about him so she would know and be on the lookout. That's why I tried to talk to her after court in the parking garage, but I never got to explain because the reporter rushed in, and I didn't want to cause a scene."

Samira found this tale unlikely at the moment. "Luke, right now, it seems like *you're* the one who has been following Quinn. If that's the case, it will be much easier for you if you come clean and we can try to work this out."

"I'm telling you. I would never hurt Quinn. I love her."

Uh oh. This guy was clearly obsessed. The big question was whether he was dangerous. "You love her so much that you want her to yourself, right?"

Luke's shoulders slumped. "I know she won't ever go for a guy like me, but I could show her how much I loved her by keeping that creep away."

Was this guy delusional? Maybe they needed to have him see a psychiatrist. She wasn't trained for this. They needed an expert.

Jalen cleared his throat. "Tell us about this guy you saw."

Luke's eyes lit up. "He's a white dude. Average height. Probably just under six feet. Dark brown hair."

"And why do you think he was following Quinn?" Samira needed a lot more answers.

"Because I saw him do it. Not just in the courthouse." His voice got louder as he spoke. "I saw him outside of her law firm too."

Could Quinn potentially have two stalkers at once? Or was this a troubled man who had come up with this delusion in his head? She knew better than to discount his story though because there was a chance he was telling the truth.

"Wait," Luke said. "I took a picture of him. It's not great, but it's something." He pulled out his phone and after a moment handed it over to her.

She looked down at the grainy picture that he had taken from a distance down the street near Quinn's law firm. Yeah, there was a guy fitting the description Luke had given, but there probably wasn't enough for any type of positive ID given the image quality. "This could be any man going to work in those offices in midtown."

Luke slammed the table with his fist. "I'm telling you. He's not just any man. He's after Quinn. This wasn't a one-time thing. He's been watching her."

His outburst confirmed her theory that at the very least he had some emotional, and more likely more severe mental issues at play. Nothing about this seemed right to her. "For how long?"

"For the past couple of months."

"Luke, what exactly do you want from Quinn?" Jalen asked.

"Nothing. Like I said, I know she's way out of my league. But I love watching her in court."

"Have you ever been to Quinn's house?" she asked.

"Yes, but I've never been inside."

"Where were you Saturday night?"

"I was playing piano at Del's Steakhouse. I was there from about five thirty to eleven thirty. You can ask anyone who works there."

"We will." Samira feared that his alibi would check out and that would mean that while he was not stable, someone else had broken into Quinn's house.

Jalen stood. "We're going to need to hold you here while we check on a few things. Also, we're going to need everything you have on that phone. All the photos."

Luke gripped tightly onto the phone. "You aren't going to delete them, are you?"

"No, we won't delete anything." Samira wanted to get this guy some help.

She and Jalen left the room and made arrangements for Luke to be seen by a psychiatrist while he was in holding.

Once she and Jalen were alone, she turned to him. "We've got big problems."

Jalen huffed. "You think? We've got someone in there who

has some serious mental issues, but I'll tell you right now he's not our killer, and I think his alibi will check out and we'll find out he isn't the man who broke into Quinn's house."

"Don't you think the best theory we have going is that the killer is the one who was at Quinn's?"

"Best theory, yes. Only theory, no. We underestimated Quinn's star power. I fear she's picked up some unwanted fans along the way. Luke did show some violent tendencies when pushed. We've got to keep him out of this and away from her, but the bigger issue is, what now? Luke thinks that guy was following Quinn, and as wild as it sounds, I don't think we can discount it."

"I don't either. Luke may be unstable, but he seems fiercely devoted to Quinn, and he was definitely following her for who knows how long."

"What are we going to do with her in the meantime?"

"Quinn wanted to stay in the hotel the rest of the week and that's the right play. She can afford it. Maybe we'll be able to get some clarity in the meantime."

"Do you think we should post someone on her?"

"She pushed hard against that. I get that she still wants her freedom, and we don't have anything concrete to go on, but if anything changes, we'll adjust—whether she wants it or not. What's the latest on Richard?"

"I talked to him again last night. Nothing to report on his end, and man, he is getting antsy. I told him that we suggested he keep the security going. Not sure if he will listen."

"Okay. Let's assume the killer is the person who broke into Quinn's house. What was the angle? To shake her up?"

"To say, I'm watching, and I can get inside your home any time I want." Jalen frowned. "If Luke is right, then this guy has been watching Quinn for a while."

"Why break the pattern and go into her home now though?"

Jalen groaned. "We have far too many questions and little

answers here, and I can't help but feel like the other shoe is going to drop soon."

Samira feared Jalen was right. "I touched base with one of the junior agents we had screening the men and women from Quinn's social media account. It's a dead end. A whole lot of hot air. All of them alibied out."

"Too many dead ends."

"I'll go to Quinn's office and let her know about the latest."

"She isn't going to like it."

"Oh, I know."

"I'll deal with Luke while you're talking to Quinn."

It didn't take long for Samira to make her way to Quinn's office, and Quinn didn't look too happy to see her. "You can't be here for anything good."

"I'm afraid you're right."

"Did you find Luke?"

"We did, and Quinn, I believe he has some mental issues, but is definitely obsessed with you. Although at the moment, it's not Luke that I'm the most worried about."

Quinn raised an eyebrow. "What do you mean?"

"I don't want to freak you out because we are still investigating this."

"Just spit it out."

"Luke claims that there is another man who has been following you. He says that's why he confronted you in the parking garage to try to warn you, but he never got the chance."

Quinn lifted up her hand. "What man?"

"We don't have his identity yet. Frankly, we don't know if he exists or is just a creation of Luke's mind."

"Do you think Luke could be the killer?"

Samira wanted to answer honestly. "It's possible but my gut is saying no. He seems much more interested in you than in anybody else, and while troubled, I don't picture him as having what it takes to be a serial killer."

"And what's the deal with this other man?"

Samira filled Quinn in on his description and where Luke claimed he had seen him. Including near Quinn's house.

"Are you telling me that there is a possibility that two different men have been stalking me?"

"I know it's a lot to take in and we're still trying to verify Luke's information."

Quinn looked down. "I haven't noticed anyone else besides Luke, and I most certainly didn't see anyone around my house."

"I realize this is disturbing, and we're going to do everything we can to track down this other man and get answers."

"Are you now thinking that this unknown guy could be the killer?"

"It's an option on the table."

"I'm not quite sure what I'm supposed to be doing here."

"I get that you're frustrated, and you have every right to be. Right now, all I can do is ask for your patience and vigilance."

"That's asking a lot given the circumstances."

"I know." Samira felt for Quinn, but she was limited in how she could fix this. The only thing she could do is work hard at solving this case.

"I also have this other trial that is about to happen." Quinn stood and started pacing. "I have to be at the top of my game, and all of this is a bad distraction I don't need."

Samira needed to make a point. "I appreciate that, but your life is more important than any trial."

Quinn let out a little laugh. "If you haven't noticed yet, Samira, my life is my work. Without it, I am nothing."

Samira was married to the job, but Quinn's words held even more significance to her. Quinn seemed truly sad today for the first time, as all of this was starting to take its toll. "You can focus on your case knowing that we are working on everything else. If we assess that there is a real and present danger to your life, though, we will have to make additional security arrangements."

"I'm hopeful that won't be necessary."

Samira couldn't help it and reached out to take Quinn's hand.

"I don't like your privacy being invaded either. After what we talked about before, I could see how you would be sensitive to that. But know that I have your best interests in mind." Samira wanted to protect Quinn. Yeah, she lived a privileged life that Samira couldn't imagine, but it appeared that Quinn had earned it all. Nothing had been given to her. And Samira respected that.

"I appreciate your kindness, Samira." Quinn gave a weak smile.

"I'm just doing my job."

"No. You're doing a lot more than that, and I know it."

22

Quinn sat in her office trying to fight off a horrendously bad mood and pounding headache after Samira's visit. And what's more, how could she have been so oblivious to the fact that she was being watched? She felt that Luke was pretty harmless—and he still might be. But this other mystery man that Samira had dropped on her, that made her nervous. She hadn't sensed that she was being watched or followed until the other night. Had he been waiting in the wings? And how long had he been there? Did he know all of her comings and goings?

She picked up a stapler and threw it hard across the room and it crashed into the wall and dropped with a thud to the floor. She began to pace back and forth. It was so unlike her to lose her cool, but she didn't like being the object of some man's obsession. She'd been burned so many times and now this?

Racking her brain, she thought about the physical description of the man. Could it be her ex, Felipe? That seemed hard to comprehend. He did fit the general description, but he was the one who broke it off almost two years ago. Saying that she couldn't handle real commitment and feelings. So why would he be after her now? Surely, he'd moved on to a nice, stable woman.

Someone who could give him all the things that she couldn't. And Felipe never seemed like the obsessive or jealous type. In fact, he had been pretty perfect if she hadn't been so messed up. No, it simply couldn't be Felipe. It had to be someone else.

Yes, she was front and center on social media and the news because of her job. Her career was defending these companies at any cost. But that didn't mean it should be open season on her as a person, did it?

A sick feeling formed in the pit of her stomach, and she leaned against the desk as she started to become lightheaded.

She grabbed her cell from the desk and pushed Richard's contact.

After a few rings he answered. "Quinn, how are you?"

"I've been better." She took a moment and explained what had transpired today. It was good to be able to tell someone who at least had some frame of reference for this discussion.

"Quinn, I talked to Jalen last night, but this new information is really troubling. Honestly, I'm planning on getting out of town this weekend. Want to come to my place in the North Georgia mountains? We can hold up there. You can work remotely."

She considered his offer for a moment. "I'm not so sure that's the best idea."

"If you change your mind, or if you just want to get away for a night or two, the offer is open."

"Are you bringing your security with you?"

"Maybe just one guy. Seems a bit excessive at this point. I hate to say it, Quinn, but you're the one that seems to be in the crosshairs right now from what I can tell. Not me. Are you going to ask the firm to get you security?"

Asking the firm for help was completely off the table. "I don't want that. I'll be fine. I'm staying at the Ritz. I feel safe there."

"When will you go back home?"

That was a good question. "I'm not sure." The idea of being back there unsettled her, and she had so much to do.

"Why don't you come over tonight and we can talk about it?

Unwind a bit. It's not like anyone else can really understand what we're going through here."

For a moment, she considered his offer and decided it might be nice not to be alone tonight. "Yes. I'll see you tonight." She hoped she wasn't making another mistake.

23

ate the next night, Samira was awakened by the shrill ring of her phone. She sat up quickly and picked it up, knowing it was bad news.

"It's me," Jalen said.

"Who's dead?" It had to be someone.

"Richard Hale."

"How?" She ran her hand through her hair and tried to shake off the cobwebs.

"I don't know a lot. Detective Perez called me. One of Richard's security guards found him. Looks like maybe some kind of drug related incident. I'm on my way to get you so we can head over there."

"I'll be ready." She hopped out of bed, threw her unruly hair up in a bun, there was no time to wash it, and took a five-minute shower. It was almost three in the morning, and her mind was starting to process what Jalen had told her.

It wasn't long before she was headed out the door and got into Jalen's SUV.

She didn't waste any time airing out her thoughts. "This could be the same MO as Cruz if we're talking overdose."

"Yeah. Suicide seems unlikely with these circumstances."

"The tox screen will be key. In the Cruz case, he did take an exorbitant number of pills. I'll be interested to see what shows up here."

"And what did the security guards see," Jalen said.

"So many unanswered questions. Given this latest development, we have to put an FBI detail on Quinn."

"Yeah."

She took a moment and made some calls to get someone over to the hotel. "I hate to contact her at this time of the night or morning or whatever it is, but she would want to know, especially since an agent is on the way over."

Jalen nodded. "I'd make the call."

Samira took a deep breath. She hated doing this, but there was no other option. She dialed Quinn's number and waited, but not long, as Quinn answered on the second ring.

"Samira?"

"Yes, it's me. Quinn, I'm so sorry to call you at this hour, but I have some bad news."

"Oh no," Quinn's voice caught. "What happened?"

There was no way to sugarcoat this, and Quinn deserved the truth quickly. "Richard is dead."

"Are you sure?" her voice cracked.

"Yes. We're on our way over to his place now, and I've got an agent on his way to the Ritz. Things have kicked up a notch. We have to take extra precautions."

"I understand," she said softly. "I just saw Richard on Monday night."

"How was he?"

"Frustrated. On edge. He was getting ready to go to his place in the North Georgia mountains."

"Did he seem like he was in a place where he could've considered taking his own life?"

There was silence.

"I don't think so. Yes, he was tired of all of this, but that was more anger at the situation. He had a lot of life left to live." Her voice shook.

"I'm so sorry, Quinn. I know you were close to him. We'll do everything we can to catch this guy and bring him to justice."

"Please do," Quinn whispered.

"The agent will knock when he gets there and identify himself and show his badge. Don't open the door for anyone else, okay?"

"I understand."

"I'll check on you later." She ended the call and looked over at Jalen. "She's a strong woman, but this is even beginning to take its toll on her."

Jalen nodded. "It would on anyone. We're behind on this one, Samira. Way behind."

"I know." They rode in silence the rest of the way to Richard's house.

Once they arrived, the place was swarming with Atlanta PD. She noticed Detective Perez immediately and walked over to him. His dark eyes were filled with concern. "What's the status?"

"I had my people secure the scene but that's it. We knew you wanted to go in first."

"Thanks. Please keep a secure perimeter, our FBI forensics team will be here any minute. Where are the security guards?"

Perez pointed to his left. "There was only one guard here at the time. He's freaked out. Didn't want to stay in the house, so he's sitting in the back of my car. He said the body is in the bedroom. I'll stay out here and make sure the FBI team gets in and that we keep the perimeter secure."

"We appreciate it." She put on her gloves and followed Jalen into the house. Everything looked immaculate and the design was chic and refreshing. She steeled herself for what they might find in the bedroom. As many dead bodies as she had dealt with in her career, it never got easy for her, but that was probably a good thing.

The primary bedroom was upstairs, and that's where they found Richard's body in the bed. Out of an abundance of caution, she checked for a pulse on the off chance that the security guard could've been mistaken. But she could tell once she touched his neck that he was most definitely dead—and probably had been for a few hours.

Jalen walked around to the other side of the bed. "I know we said suicide doesn't make sense, but what about accidental overdose? He's mad at life and wants an escape. He has more to drink than he realizes, and then pops some pills not understanding how much he was taking and how it would all interact with each other."

She surveyed the room as she considered Jalen's suggestion. "Possible. But I would think a man like Richard would know his limits."

"But he's never faced anything like this before. Maybe he just pushed it too far."

"If this were an isolated incident, then it might make more sense, but we have to view the totality of the facts."

"Wine glass and liquor highball on the nightstand." Jalen squatted down by the nightstand. "And, Samira, look at this."

She walked over and saw a few specks of white powder on the nightstand. "Could be remnants of coke."

"Just like Myers. We'll have them run it and the tox screen will also show if that's what this is." Jalen got a text. "ME is on her way in."

"Good. All of our speculation can only get us so far. I want to see what the science tells us. We'll get out of her way and let her work. I want to look around the rest of the house, but I do want to check out the bathroom and see what's in the medicine cabinet."

She walked into the bathroom followed by Jalen. Opening up the cabinet, she saw a multitude of pill bottles.

Jalen let out a low whistle. "Well, maybe he was taking more drugs than we predicted."

She picked up a bottle. "This is for high blood pressure." She pulled out another. "Cholesterol meds. Vicodin. Some other muscle relaxers and pain killers."

"Showing off your pharmaceutical knowledge."

"I worked a case years ago right before we became partners that caused me to get up on a lot of different prescription drugs"

Jalen picked up one of the bottles. "If he was used to taking these though, then he should've been aware of his limits. Kinda like your point earlier."

"Let's go talk to the security guard."

They went downstairs and headed outside to find the guard smoking a cigarette outside of Perez's vehicle.

"Mr. Wallace, can we have a word?"

"Please call me Scott."

Samira hated to start all over, but she needed to hear it directly from Scott. It wasn't that she didn't trust the young agent who had arrived first on scene, but she wanted to see how Scott handled himself because as much as she hated to admit it, they had to rule him out as a suspect given the close proximity.

"Scott, I'm Agent Haddad and this is Agent Smith. I know you've covered this information before, but we're lead investigators on this case, so I'd like to hear everything that happened."

Scott took another drag off his cigarette. "Starting on Monday, Richard decided to cut down security to one guy per shift. Things had been so quiet, and he was preparing to leave for the mountains this weekend, so we worked out a one guard per shift schedule."

"What time did your shift start?" Jalen asked.

"Six p.m. I relieved M&Ms. That's what we call him. His real name is Manny Morris."

Jalen took down some notes. "And had Manny reported anything suspicious on his watch?"

Scott shook his head. "Quiet as a mouse."

"Any visitors yesterday?" she asked.

"Mr. Hale had three men from the company over for happy hour. According to Manny they got here around five, so they were already inside when my shift started. They left around seven p.m. I watched them all leave. Then Mr. Hale ordered delivery for me. I took the food from the guy. He didn't go inside."

Samira perked up. "Are you sure about that?"

"Yeah, I think so. I mean I saw him drive away."

"Do you do delivery often?" Jalen asked.

"Yeah. Mr. Hale feeds us every day. He was really good like that."

"Do you have the names of the men who were here last night?" Samira had to close off all possibilities.

Scott pulled out his phone. "We've got a shared log we use to track everything. I can send you the names right now." A few taps on his phone and then he looked back up. "Sent."

"Thank you. Did anyone else go into the house?" Jalen asked.

"Just the cleaning ladies early yesterday morning."

"And before that?" she asked

"His lawyer was here on Monday. Stayed pretty late. Isn't the first time. Probably isn't my place to say, but there might be more going on there than just a client attorney relationship. But that's none of my business."

Samira found it hard to believe that Quinn would be sleeping with Richard, but anything was possible.

"How did you find out something was wrong?" Samira asked.

"Richard always texts right before he goes to bed. Sometimes he goes to bed really late, but he always texts. When it got to be one o'clock, and I hadn't heard anything, I decided to check on him." Scott sighed loudly. "I went inside and looked around and didn't see him. I thought maybe he'd had too much wine with his friends. When I went to his room though, I saw him, and he didn't look right. I couldn't see him breathing. That's when I started freaking out a bit. I checked for a pulse and when I didn't get one, I got out of there and called Agent Smith per the protocol we'd been given."

"You did the right thing by calling," Jalen said. "When was the last time you saw Richard?"

"At shift change. All was good at that point. He and his friends were having a good time. Having drinks and smoking cigars." Scott looked down. "Do you think he did this to himself?"

"What do you think?" Jalen asked.

"I obviously don't know him that well, but if he did, it would surprise me. But I guess you never know about what's going on in someone's head. I know he was ready to get out of town and try to get away from all of this."

"Have you noticed anyone around the house at all who shouldn't have been?"

Scott shook his head. "No. I'm telling you this has been one of the most tame jobs I've ever had. Literally nothing happens. And then tonight all of that changed."

"If you think of anything else, please call us," Jalen said.

"Can I go home now?"

Jalen nodded. "Yes. We'll let you know if we need anything else."

"Thank you." Scott walked away.

Jalen turned to her. "I just sent the three names to the analysts to do background checks on, and we can visit them tomorrow."

"We need to talk to Quinn. If she and Richard had a thing, that could've provided even more motivation for the killer to take him out, right?"

"Yes. This is stacking up to possibly be about her and her stalker. If that's true, our theory about the French case being an accident is also likely right. He would be going after other powerful men who he sees as threats. That syncs up with our prior theories about not needing to take out the losing CEO."

Her phone went off and she looked at the text. "The agent is stationed at the hotel. All good there."

"At least that's one positive thing. We can't afford another dead body."

"No, we can't. Myron isn't going to be happy."

"You get to be the one to tell him." Jalen laughed.

"Thanks, partner."

24

The next morning, Quinn had an FBI escort to the office and was instructed not to leave the office without one. She was dreading the meeting that was about to take place with Samira because she had a sinking feeling about what topic would come up.

"You don't look so good," Quinn said.

"That's what happens when you're called to a scene at three a.m., but I'm not worried about me. Have you slept?"

"I don't sleep well in the best of times, so no, I didn't sleep much last night. Especially after we talked."

Samira reached out across the desk and placed her hand on Quinn's forearm. "Again, I'm sorry for your loss."

"Thank you."

"But I do need to ask you some questions."

Here it comes. "I figured as much."

"Let's just get this out of the way. Were you romantically involved with Richard?"

Quinn bit the inside of her cheek. She'd thought about how to handle this and ultimately the truth seemed like the best option. "No, but not for his lack of trying."

"Did he force himself on you?" Samira asked softly.

Not Richard. At least she could say that for him. "No. He didn't."

Samira's dark eyes narrowed. "You can tell me if he did."

"I would tell you. There was some harmless flirtation that I entertained, but then I put a stop to it. It's not good for business. He's tried a couple of times and I've said no, and that was that."

"What do you know about his use of prescription drugs?"

Quinn drummed her fingers on her desk. "Not much. He once offered me some muscle relaxers, but I stay far away from that stuff."

"Can you tell me about what happened the last night you saw Richard."

"Yes. He invited me over. He was still trying to talk me into going up to the mountains. He has a nice place up there. He was pretty persuasive, but I can't run away from my problems. My cases need me here. We had some dinner he had delivered."

"How did he seem to you?"

"Ready for a vacation. He was also concerned about me. About the stalkers. God, even saying that, I can't wrap my head around possibly having two stalkers and one of them being a killer."

"As I told you before, this killer, although normally calm and put together, has gotten a bit bolder in his actions. He's on a mission to get to you—his ultimate fixation."

"Are you trying to frighten me?" It sure sounded that way.

"No. I'm being straight up with you. Initially, I believed the killer might be someone either from one of the plaintiffs' groups or someone with an ax to grind against corporate America. But now, there have been too many things pointing to you as the driving force."

"Are you saying I'm responsible?"

Samira shook her head. "Of course not, but this guy is focused on you and is probably still trying to watch you closely because he can't help himself. Now that you're limiting your activity, that might cause him to react. In fact, maybe he killed

Richard because he was acting out. Maybe he knew you were at Richard's on Monday night. He's obscenely jealous."

She placed her hand on her chest. "I hate to think that Richard's death is because of me."

"Stop saying that. It's not, but it is related to you. We have to make sure that your next client is not a target. I wonder if the killer knows about John Rossi."

"Gemma has written about the case."

"We'll talk to Mr. Rossi again and reiterate that the threat level has gone up and he should act accordingly."

"I'm assuming given everything, staying at the hotel is better than going home."

"It's up to you. Now that you have a protective detail agent with you it would be fine for you to go back home if you would prefer."

She still couldn't believe her home had been violated by this stalker, but she refused to hide out in that hotel room any longer. She was going to take back her life, and that meant she needed to find this guy before he found her.

25

The next morning Samira walked into the FBI conference room and found Jalen surrounded by documents. "I just got a phone call from Myron."

"Uh oh." Jalen set down his coffee.

Myron had been pretty fired up after hearing about Richard's murder and wanted to be more aggressive. "There's an SSA from the BAU that should be here any minute."

Jalen's eyes grew wide. "Are they taking the case?"

"No. He closed a case yesterday in Florida, and Myron thought he might be able to give us a fresh perspective. He flies back to DC later today, so it's a quick in and out."

Before she could say anything else, Supervisory Special Agent Wyatt Turner walked into the conference room.

"I'm Wyatt Turner from the BAU." He looked at her first and then at Jalen. "Am I in the right place?"

She rose to greet him. "Yes. I'm Samira Haddad and this is Jalen Smith." No need to focus on titles at this point, but she did take a moment to size Wyatt up. He had some of the most striking blue eyes she'd ever seen which contrasted against his tan skin and full head of dark brown hair. He was almost Jalen's height with a lean, muscular build.

Wyatt shook their hands. "Nice to meet you both. I'm here to help the best way I can. Nothing is too small, but I don't want to distract you from your work. I'm all yours in any way you need me."

Jalen shot her a glance. "Thanks, Wyatt. Unfortunately, we've just had another murder."

"I did hear about that, and I conducted a highly preliminary review of the case files I could get my hands on last night, so I'm eager to jump in. I've got some initial thoughts but let's hear what you have first."

"Great." She took a breath. "Have a seat. We were about to get started."

Wyatt sat down and pulled out his laptop and a notepad.

"All right." Jalen stood. "I just got off the phone with the ME's office."

"They found something, didn't they?" Her pulse started to kick up. Maybe this would finally be the news that they needed.

Jalen looked at her. "Oh yeah. Richard Hale didn't just take pills. We were right. He was doing coke."

A much needed connection. "Just like Myers. That cannot be a coincidence. Did the mixture of the pills and coke kill him?"

"No," Jalen responded. "The cutting agent in the coke did."

She hadn't expected that. "Fentanyl?"

Jalen nodded.

"Dirty coke," Wyatt jumped in.

"Looks that way," Jalen said.

She was trying to put the pieces together. "Let's think this through. The killer has to be connected to the coke in some way. Maybe he was the one who sold it to Richard?"

"Yeah." Jalen started typing. "We should check Richard's online activity. Sometimes these types of deals all happen over the net. The product gets delivered and there's never any face to face exchange."

"Good point. Although, wouldn't the killer have had to seek out Richard to make it work?" she asked.

"Yeah, and that could get tricky, but we'll have to see what we can find." Jalen looked up from his computer. "Why am I not surprised that this guy was using prescription drugs and street drugs?"

On the outside Richard seemed put together. He didn't seem like the type of man with a drug addiction, but these things could be hidden. Functioning addiction was a real thing. "It's possible that he wasn't regularly using, but this investigation sent him over the edge. He decided to escape by any means he could get his hands on."

Wyatt typed quickly on his laptop.

"I don't think he was planning for his death though," Jalen said.

Jalen was right. "Me either. Given all the circumstances, we have to treat this as a homicide."

"How is Quinn dealing with this?" Jalen asked.

"About how you would expect," she responded. "I also asked her about their relationship. She says that Richard was interested in her, but that nothing happened between them."

Jalen looked at Wyatt and then her. "Our killer doesn't know that. All he knows is that Quinn was over at Richard's late at night multiple times."

Wyatt stopped typing notes. "I think you two are onto something here. Based on my preliminary review, I believe this killer to be extremely mission driven. He has a reason for acting this way. It's not just pure rage and hate. It's planned and calculated." Wyatt looked at her. "Samira, I read your notes describing the killer as passionate. I one hundred percent agree with you. I also agree that the stalker and killer are one in the same."

"Would make our lives a lot easier if it's true," Jalen said.

Wyatt nodded. "But you have to be prepared to be wrong about that, but for now, that's the most fruitful avenue to explore, especially focusing on Quinn's life. I believe there's a man out there who is living and breathing Quinn Kelly right now."

A chill shot down her back. "That's scary."

"It is," Wyatt said. "You're doing all the right things by keeping a close eye on her. Eventually, this guy will want to reach his ultimate goal and fixation. And right now, the best theory is that it's Quinn Kelly. I would like to take some time today to dig further into the files as I was only able to do a cursory review last night."

"Sure," Samira said. "We are about to go speak to John Rossi to make sure he is taking his security seriously, but you're welcome to stay here and go through anything and everything."

Wyatt gave her a smile. "That would be great. Then we can circle up again when you get back before I return to DC. Like I said. I just want to help, not get in your way."

Jalen looked down at his watch. "We should head over to Horizon Pharma. We don't want to be late and who knows how bad the traffic will be."

She agreed and they left Wyatt in the conference room to drive over to Marietta where the Horizon Pharma offices were located.

"Okay, Samira, you know I'm going to say something," Jalen said.

"What are you talking about?" She looked straight ahead at the road.

Jalen laughed. "Don't play dumb. The moment you saw that guy, your whole demeanor changed."

She swatted her hand at him. "No way, Jalen. You're out of it."

He smiled. "I'm not. And it looked to be mutual to me. Maybe you should ask him to dinner."

"Absolutely not." She turned and looked at him. "I told you I'm not interested in dating."

"I know what you said, but I saw your eyes when you looked at Wyatt, and those big, brown eyes of yours, don't lie. Especially not to me. I can read you like a book."

She sighed. "Yes, Wyatt is attractive, but that doesn't mean anything. He's here for work today only, and I'm not interested in entanglements."

"Maybe an entanglement is just what you need."

Her cheeks flushed. "I'm fine on my own. So if we could just focus on the case. That would be great."

He lifted up his hand from the steering wheel. "Whatever you say. You're only lying to yourself."

She'd had enough of his armchair psychology for one day and let it go. They had an appointment with John Rossi and needed to explain to him the gravity of the situation. This would be their first in person meeting as the other conversations had happened by phone—mainly due to his extremely busy schedule as his assistant had put it. But it was time to talk to him face to face and make sure he was fully apprised.

They walked up to the non-descript white office building.

Jalen opened up the door for her. "I hate being so behind the eight ball here. Doesn't make us look good."

She walked through the main entrance. "I know but we can't worry about what we look like at the moment."

They spoke to the receptionist and were escorted up to the fifth floor and put in a conference room. After a few minutes, the door opened, and John Rossi walked in. Tall, very muscular and his presence filled up the room. He was quite handsome, with wavy dark hair and intense brown eyes.

"Agents, it's nice to finally meet you in person."

The words rolled easily off his lips, but she wasn't buying it. "Thank you for taking the meeting. We know how busy you are." She hated kissing up but right now it was necessary. She wanted to start the meeting on the right foot.

John gave a friendly smile. "Please sit and tell me what I can do to help you."

She took another moment to size him up. He looked a few years younger than the other CEOs. His gray suit was perfectly tailored, and his gold watch was no doubt worth a good chunk of her yearly salary.

"Mr. Rossi, things have gotten more serious since we spoke on the phone," Jalen said.

"How so?"

Jalen glanced over at her before turning his attention back to John. "It hasn't hit the news yet but will today. Richard Hale is dead."

John's dark eyes narrowed. "How did he die?"

"We're investigating it as a homicide, but I can't get into further details at the moment," Jalen said.

John nodded. "I see. And you think now I'm the next on the chopping block."

She had to walk a fine line. "We have to count that as a serious option. None of the other murders happened until after the trial, but this killer is getting bolder, so it's possible he may break his pattern."

A deep frown appeared on John's face. "Hearing this, I believe I will get my own private security. What else can I do to protect myself?"

"Be careful about those who you surround yourself with," Jalen said. "Keep your circle tight to only those people you really know and trust."

She didn't want to reveal too much, but she had to say something else. "You need to be extremely careful with taking any substances, such as drugs—street or prescription."

John raised an eyebrow. "Well, Agent Haddad, now you have really intrigued me, but you can rest easy. I don't take any drugs —prescription or otherwise, but I can read between the lines here. I've got your message loud and clear."

She wasn't so sure that John was as squeaky clean as he claimed, but they had done their part warning him on that topic. "Your trial is also coming up next week."

John groaned. "There's no need to remind me. A complete pain in my ass. Those people are just out for my company's money."

"No sympathy for the victims?" How would he react to a reality check?

He looked at her as if she had three heads for making that suggestion. "Not when they're wrongfully trying to steal what is mine."

This man's flippant attitude toward the victims disturbed her.

Jalen shot her a look that let her know she had probably taken that line of questioning far enough.

"Tell me this. Why do you think this guy is killing CEOs?" John asked.

"We're trying to determine that," Jalen said. "Do you have any ideas?"

John fiddled with his cufflink. "CEOs, especially those of drug companies like mine get a bad rap. We do so much good work, but the people only focus on the negative. Maybe there's some vigilante out there who has an ax to grind. I saw on the news that kid jump on Quinn trying to get to Richard. There are plenty more of his types out there. I'm not sure why they would be so focused on CEOs that Quinn has defended, which, I'm not an FBI agent, but I would assume she has some role in this. Maybe someone is trying to come after her."

"We're considering that as well." She wasn't going to tell John about the stalker because that really wasn't any of his business. They'd warned him of the threat.

"Do you work well with Quinn?" Jalen asked.

John laughed. "We don't always see eye to eye, but I recognize that she's good at her job. She can be a bit grating on the nerves at times, but I appreciate that she has a high stress job and people like me tend to make her life pretty miserable."

"Have you worked with her on any other cases before?" she asked.

"This is actually the first case my company has hired her for. We saw the results she was getting for other corporations, and decided it was time for a change because our last counsel had a couple of bad losses. And I'm not the type of guy that takes losing well. Especially when it impacts my bottom line."

"Who was your formal counsel?" she asked.

"A fellow named Rhett McGee."

A thought struck her. "With large companies like yours, does firing your counsel happen often?

"If they aren't getting results, then yeah. There are other reasons you may fire your lawyer besides performance. For instance, if you just couldn't bear being around them and thought someone else could do the job just as well. But winning to me is the most important thing. I can overlook interpersonal disagreements. I can't take losing."

Jalen looked at her, and she knew they were both thinking the same thing. "We appreciate your time today."

John rose and buttoned his suit jacket. "No problem. If there are any updates, please let me know. I'm hoping I can get this all put behind me soon and win this case."

"We understand." He only really was concerned about himself.

When they had gotten outside, she turned to Jalen. "We're on the same page, aren't we?"

"You want to check out Rhett McGee and see if any other lawyers have been fired so that Quinn could take over."

"It's a long shot but it's worth a try." They had to exhaust every theory.

"I'll take long shots right about now."

26

ate that afternoon, Jalen dropped her off back at the office. He was going to meet with the three men who were at Richard's happy hour and insisted that she go back and circle up with Wyatt. She thought he was trying to play matchmaker. It didn't matter to her. Nothing would happen between her and Wyatt and that was the end of the story. She was very interested to hear his thoughts on the case after spending the day immersed in the files.

She found Wyatt just like they left him in the conference room, but he had spread out documents all across the table and had taken over one of the blank white boards.

"You've been busy."

He looked up and smiled. "Yes, I have. I'm ready to talk if you are. Is Jalen around?"

"He had leads to run down, so you're stuck with me. I'll fill him in."

"Good. Okay, I believe, as I said before, that the stalker and the killer are the same. He has violent tendencies but is able to keep them under wraps but only to a point."

She sat down beside him fully engrossed in what he was saying. "What will the breaking point be?"

"When killing CEOs is no longer enough to quench his thirst for Quinn. I have no doubt that he will go after her directly. It's just a matter of time. The CEO kills have just been a proxy. He won't stop until he gets to what he ultimately wants, which is her."

"What's your profile?"

Wyatt ran his hand through his hair. "White male, mid-thirties to late forties. Smart, driven. Probably has an impressive career but that isn't enough for him. He isn't a guy stuck behind a computer all day or hiding out in his basement. People who know him would be surprised that he was a killer."

Hearing those words disturbed her. "Hearing it from your lips makes it all too real."

Wyatt leaned toward her. "It is. This guy is very calculated but highly dangerous. He is a cold-blooded killer and won't think twice about killing. This is about him. His wants and desires."

"But how do we stop him before he strikes again?"

"That's the tough part. With limited leads, it's going to be difficult. As he escalates though, he might make a mistake. I know you talked to John Rossi, but he needs to be on high alert. I think this pattern will hold. Quinn wins the lawsuit, then the killer goes after Rossi."

"And if she loses?"

"Rossi might get a reprieve, but it depends on how wound up our guy really is."

She locked eyes with him and again was struck by the intense blue color. "We'll follow up with Rossi."

"Good." Wyatt turned and looked at the clock. "I should be heading to the airport soon, but I'd love to hear updates and provide any continuing help if you need it."

She smiled. "We'd appreciate that."

"You and Jalen are doing everything right, so I didn't mean to insinuate otherwise."

"I didn't take it like that. You're the profiler, not us."

Wyatt started packing up his stuff. "How did you end up in violent crimes?"

"It's what I always wanted to do. The FBI had other ideas, so I spent my first couple of years in counterterrorism."

Wyatt frowned. "That had to be tough if it wasn't what you wanted to do."

"It was, but I'm in the perfect place now. How long have you been with the BAU?"

"About six years."

"Want me to give you a lift to the airport?" She wasn't sure why she had offered.

"You don't have to fight the traffic on my account."

"It's no problem. Helps me clear my head."

Wyatt smiled. "Great."

27

Quinn was dreading meeting with John. He had called her all worked up after his meeting with the FBI. Everyone was wanting something from her right now and it was getting old. She couldn't even focus on her work and the bigger picture because of all of these hassles and distractions.

The one positive was that she was back at home. The big negative was that John had insisted on coming over to her place tonight. He wouldn't take no for an answer. At least she still had the FBI security agent who would be outside her house. That gave her some small measure of comfort, but she had zero confidence that John would behave himself. Men like him rarely did.

When the doorbell rang, she took a steadying breath. She'd already let the FBI agent know that John was coming over so there wouldn't be any issues.

She opened the door and John rushed in, pushing her inside. "I need a drink."

Not even a hello. It wasn't going to be a small talk kind of evening. "What would you like?"

"Whiskey neat."

At least that request would be easy enough. "Have a seat and I'll get it."

She wanted him to choose his seat first. That would allow her to sit as far away from him as possible. He sat down on her sofa, and she poured the whiskey into the glass. She took another deep breath before walking over to him. "What's going on, John? It isn't like you to pay night visits." In fact, he'd only been over to her house once before. Unfortunately, she'd visited his on a few occasions.

He took a big gulp of whiskey before responding. "You need to tell me what's really going on here."

She sat down in her favorite armchair. "What do you mean?"

John ran his hand through his hair. "The FBI is being cagey. Super shifty. They aren't telling me everything, and I have a sinking feeling that they're leaving out parts about you that are going to end up impacting *me*."

That was possible. "Did they talk to you about the stalkers?"

"Stalkers? No. Who has stalkers?"

Before she could respond, he kept talking. "Don't tell me it's you." He leaned forward.

"Unfortunately, so."

He threw up his hands. "I *knew* this was all your fault."

She bit her bottom lip trying desperately not to lash out. "How is me being stalked my fault, John? Talk about blaming the victim." He was good at that. In the lawsuit and now.

"You're no victim, Quinn." He laughed. "The furthest thing from it."

"In this case I am, and I still fail to see how any of this is my fault."

After he finished his drink, he set down the glass. "If you weren't always putting yourself out there every opportunity on social media, you wouldn't have these freaks following you around. You asked for this, Quinn."

She'd had enough. "John, you don't get to talk to me like

that. You may mistreat everyone else in your life, but I'm not afraid of you, and so you need to stop it. Now."

"Are you threatening me?" He grinned. "This is rich, really, Quinn. You need me. You need this case. My business. You should be the one catering to me, not the other way around."

She wanted to quit. To tell him to get out of her house. But if she did that, there would be major firm fallout, and she didn't want to deal with that. No, she would have to stay the course. The trial started in a few days. That's what she should focus on. "Do you want to win this—yes or no? Because I'm beginning to think you want me to lose because you're a coward and are afraid about what might happen to you."

He jumped up out of his seat, and she thought he might come at her but instead he started pacing the room. "You might be right."

Okay, she hadn't expected that admission. She would have to walk him back. "You can't let some psycho damage your company out of fear. This case is winnable, but you're going to have to pull yourself together. The man you are right now screams guilty to a jury." And of course, she realized that he and the company did not have clean hands in this, but as their attorney, she had to zealously defend them even if she knew the cold hard truth.

He walked over to her bar and helped himself to more whiskey. "Before we talk about the trial, I am still confused about all this stalker business."

"The FBI now believes that one of the men stalking me could be the same man who killed my clients."

"But you said two stalkers?"

"There's another guy obsessed with me, but no one really thinks he is the murderer. He is the one who told the FBI about the other stalker because apparently two men have been following me."

"Quinn. That's why you have the FBI outside the door."

"Yup." She paused. "But enough about me. We have to get

back to you and how you're going to behave on the witness stand."

He sat back down. "I will be fine on the stand. I promise, they won't see any of this I've shown tonight. I'm very good at compartmentalizing."

She believed him on that. "I hope so because your testimony will be very important for the jury."

"I know you don't believe a word that comes out of my mouth."

"Ultimately, it doesn't matter what I think. It's all in the hands of the jury." She was skirting some lines with legal ethics regarding his testimony, but given all the circumstances, she could live with it.

"Are you worried this guy is actually going to come after you?"

"If he does, I'll be ready."

John's eyes narrowed. "That sounds ominous."

"It should."

John walked over to her and pulled her out of the chair. "Maybe we should work out some of our issues in bed. What do you think?"

She resisted the urge to knee him in the groin. "I don't mix business with pleasure."

John laughed. "You expect me to believe that? I know exactly how you service your other clients."

"I don't care what you believe. The answer is no. It's time for you to leave."

He pulled her close to him. "But I'm not ready to leave," he whispered in her ear as his hands tightened around her.

The walls started to close in. "I'm about to start screaming and that FBI agent is going to run in here. Do you really want that?"

"What would you say if I told you that I told the agent to take a coffee break."

Was he bluffing? Would the FBI agent leave his post? She

found that highly doubtful. "I'd say you're lying." She pushed him hard away from her.

He came toward her again, and she pulled the gun from the back of her waistband. "Don't come another step closer."

John stepped dead in his tracks. "Are you gonna shoot me?"

"Don't tempt me. Get out of here now, and if you ever touch me again, I will kill you."

The color drained from John's face. "You are psychotic. I should fire you right now."

"But you're not going to because I'm the best chance you have of winning this case. Get out of here, and I'll see you in court next week."

He shook his head in disbelief and walked toward her door. He turned around. "Women don't ever tell me no."

She still had the gun gripped tightly in her hands. "Yes, they do. You just don't want to hear them."

John slammed the door on his way out, and she set the gun on the coffee table and slid down deep into her couch. Yeah, she'd been a bit aggressive in her response, but John had left her no choice. She didn't trust how far he would've pushed it, and she wanted to set some clear boundaries. If he could smell weakness, he would pounce.

After a minute, she went and checked, and didn't see the FBI agent outside her door. Her stomach clenched, and she went back and grabbed her gun. Had John been telling the truth? Or had something else happened?

She texted the agent but didn't hear back quickly so she called Samira.

"Quinn, are you okay?"

"I'm not really sure." She quickly recounted what had happened.

"The agent should've never left his post. Something isn't right."

Her heartbeat thumped loudly. "Is it him?" Her thoughts went to the stalker. "Did he do this?"

"I'm not sure. But I've got officers en route to your place, and I'm on my way. Don't open the door for anyone who isn't clearly law enforcement. You said you had a gun. You should get it out."

"I already did." She didn't mention why she'd done it.

"Good. Sit tight."

Easy for her to say. Before she could keep talking, a loud crashing noise filled the air. She shrieked and instinctively dropped to the floor.

"Quinn, what was that? Are you there?"

Quinn looked at the brick that had been thrown through her living room window. Shards of glass were everywhere.

"Quinn. Talk to me!"

"Someone threw a brick through my living room window." She grabbed a whining Felix and held him close to her to protect him.

"Listen to me. Go upstairs. Lock yourself in one of the rooms with the gun. Do it now. Your life may depend on it. If someone enters that room and is not law enforcement, you need to shoot. Do you understand me?"

"Yes. I'll shoot him."

28

Samira sat with Quinn at her kitchen table. Jalen was leading a team of agents who were scouring Quinn's home and the surrounding neighborhood. Quinn had asked that Samira stay with her, and since she needed to be fully debriefed, it made sense.

"Let's start at the beginning," Samira said.

Quinn picked up her coffee cup with shaky hands but set it back down without taking a sip. "John came over tonight."

"For what?"

"You all freaked him out and he wanted to try to get more information out of me about what was really going on."

"And did you tell him?"

"Yeah, and that just made him more upset. Then we talked about the trial starting next week and how he needed to keep it together."

"What else?"

"Then he left."

"That's it?" Samira thought Quinn wasn't telling her everything.

Quinn nodded.

"Are the two of you involved?"

"Absolutely not," Quinn answered quickly.

"Does he want you to be?"

"He's pushed, yes. And I've been clear with him. That is not going to happen. Not under any circumstances."

A thought occurred to her. "You had the gun with you already because of John, didn't you?"

Quinn grimaced. "Yeah."

Samira's concern level ticked up a bit. "Did he do something to you?"

"Not really. He made a move and put his hands on me. That's when I pulled the gun." She sucked in a breath. "I know it may seem extreme, but I've dealt with him before, and he doesn't take hearing no well. I wanted to make sure that there was no chance of him actually doing anything to me."

Samira seethed thinking about John. He had no right to put that kind of fear into Quinn. But as detestable as John was, she didn't really think he was the killer they were looking for.

"John did tell me that he told the agent to take a coffee break. I thought he was bluffing but after John left, I looked out there and didn't see anyone. Everything was happening so fast. Then the brick came through the window."

"Take a deep breath." Had the agent left his post? If so, he could get fired. "We're figuring out what happened to the agent. He was found unconscious near the house."

"So he might have left," Quinn suggested.

"It's possible, but we need to debrief him and find out exactly what occurred."

"Why the brick? Why not just come after me? He was clearly right outside."

Samira had been thinking about the same thing on the way over. "He's engaging in psychological warfare. He is also warning you. I bet he was watching and saw John enter your home. That set him off. Just like you being seen with Richard."

Jalen walked into the kitchen. "The agent on duty is conscious now. According to him, the last thing he remembers is being right outside near the front porch. Then someone got the jump on him. Knocked him out cold with a blow to the head. The attacker must have moved him while he was out."

Quinn looked at Jalen. "So he didn't leave me like John said."

"What did John say?" Jalen asked.

Jalen hadn't heard their conversation, so he was a bit behind on all the facts. "John told Quinn that he'd given the agent a break."

Jalen shook his head. "No. This guy didn't leave his post willingly. I feel pretty confident about that. He's only a second-year agent. No way he would've risked his career."

"Our guy takes out the security detail and throws the brick through the window. We should check to make sure John got home okay."

Jalen pulled out his phone. "Let me make that call." He stepped away.

"You have every right not to be concerned about John given how he treated you, but we have to watch out for everyone even if they are jerks."

Quinn gave a weak smile. "I get it. The same way I have to keep representing him in court. It's my job."

Samira couldn't believe she was about to suggest this. "You could just walk away from this one, Quinn. Let someone else at your firm step in. In fact, I'm sure you could get a trial continuance. We'd even speak to the judge to explain the situation."

Quinn's blue eyes narrowed. "There is no way I'm backing down and letting this guy mess with my career and my life any further."

She had expected Quinn to balk at the idea, but the fire in her eyes let her know that Quinn wasn't going to budge. "I got that message loud and clear."

"I refuse to let this man take anything else from me."

"I understand that you're frustrated, but you may be playing into his hands by going forward with the trial next week. I want you to think about that. Just promise me you will."

"Oh, I'll think about it, but I am not changing my mind. He will have to kill me to stop me from taking that case to trial."

"Let's not talk like that." Samira had hit a nerve and Quinn was not handling it well.

"I'm telling you the truth."

"I know you are." There was no doubt in her mind.

Jalen walked back in. "John is safe at home. No issues on his end."

"Great." The sarcasm dripped from Quinn's response.

Jalen didn't take the bait. "The team is going to finish up its work inside the house. The perimeter search came up empty. We'll help board up the window and post someone at the house overnight, but I'm thinking you should go back to the hotel."

"I agree with that," Quinn said.

"We're also going to go door to door and see if any of the neighbor's doorbell cameras captured everything," Jalen said.

"Good idea," Samira responded. "Maybe we'll catch a break there."

Quinn frowned. "I wouldn't be so sure. This guy seems to know what he's doing. He's like a ghost."

"He's out there, and we'll catch him." Samira only hoped they could do it in time.

29

The next morning, Samira met Jalen back at Quinn's house. She wanted to do a walkaround in the daylight.

"How are you holding up?" Jalen asked.

"I must really look like crap this morning for you to ask that."

He placed his hand on her shoulder. "Just checking on you."

She smiled. "Thanks. I'm doing all right, but I'd be a lot better if we could nail this guy. Let's walk down the street and then back up. I'd like to get a feel for what the stalker saw and where he could be squatting around here."

They walked down the block and then turned around and looked toward Quinn's house. "Any luck with the doorbell cams?"

Jalen sighed. "There were less in the sub than I would've thought and the ones that did have them on didn't pick up anything."

"I wonder if he knew which areas to avoid. There's got to be some footage at some point of this guy if he's been here lurking around here a lot as I predict he has."

"We can subpoena the ring cam company," Jalen offered.

"Yeah. Let's do it. I'm really worried about the escalation and what set him off. Why make himself so visibly known now? Why go after Quinn instead of stay in the shadows?"

They walked by her house and then approached from the other angle.

Jalen stopped for a moment and looked around. "I don't have great answers to those questions, but he's clearly on the move and not afraid to act in a more direct manner."

Something still wasn't adding up to her, but she couldn't put her finger on why.

Jalen touched her arm. "I know that look on your face. Just tell me what you're thinking."

He knew her too well. "I'm concerned we're missing something. Something big. I can feel it."

"I don't know. We're just frustrated at how slippery this guy is. I'm not sure there's some grand mystery behind it. He's obsessed with Quinn and will do whatever it takes to get close to her."

"But we all know that story does not have a happy ending. Even if he isn't hurting her directly yet, he most certainly will. The question is how much time do we have?"

"As Wyatt suggested, this guy is smart. I'd say highly intelligent. He knows the trial is next week. He will want to watch and wait and see what happens. Then he'll make his next move."

She'd given Jalen the rundown on Wyatt's profile, but she hadn't told him about giving Wyatt a ride to the airport. She didn't need Jalen hassling her about it. He had good intentions, but she had to work through her love life problems, or lack thereof, on her own. "Where are we on the online investigation into Richard?"

"Coming up cold. I had high hopes, but right now there's nothing the analysts can find."

She sighed.

"What?"

"Maybe we're coming at this from the wrong angle."

"Then what would be the right one?"

"I'm still trying to figure that out. Whatever happened with Richard's friends?" she asked.

"They were really devastated with the news. They'd known him for years, a couple of the guys going all the way back to college. I don't think any of them are responsible, but just to be on the safe side, the analysts are doing a deep dive to make sure we're not missing any potential drug connection. The guys said Richard was upset and edgy but not suicidal."

"Did you ask them if Richard offered them drugs?"

"Yeah, I got a resounding no. Lots of booze and cigars. That was it."

"Any comment about his coke usage?"

"After a lot of pushing, one of the men admitted that Richard did use coke on occasion, but it wasn't an all the time thing."

"We need to find out how he got that coke, so have the analysts keep pushing on that." She looked down at her watch. "Let's go pay Rhett McGee a visit."

"I did some research on him last night. Works at a big competitor firm of Quinn's called Fritz & Edwards LLP. Their offices are also in a midtown high rise."

On the drive over she wanted to get her thoughts together. "Rhett was counsel for Horizon Pharma. He's fired by John and replaced by Quinn. Could losing out on a big case be motive enough to come after her?"

"What about the fixation piece of this? Could Rhett have wanted to know more about the lawyer he was ousted by. Given her reputation in the legal community he almost certainly knew her before, but once she replaced him, what if he started to try to learn more about her and in the process developed some sort of obsession."

"I like where you're heading with that, but I'm still a little iffy on the motive for killing the CEOs."

Jalen glanced over at her and then looked back at the road. "The same as we've been discussing in general, right? I don't think it's any different because he's an attorney. His obsession turned deadly."

"I would think for any of this to hold up for Rhett McGee, he would've had to have had some underlying issues. It will be important for us to see if we can notice any cracks beneath the surface." She paused. "It's more likely than not that Rhett has zero to do with this, but we can't disregard that information John gave us. We also need to talk to Quinn and see if she knows of her having replaced any other attorneys."

The office of Fritz & Edwards was strikingly similar to Quinn's firm. Modern art on the wall, expansive views of the city, and conference rooms galore.

When Rhett McGee walked into the room, she had a mixture of disappointment and relief because he definitely didn't fit the description Luke had given or look like the man in Luke's picture. Rhett was probably nearing sixty years old, with a full head of gray hair. He wore glasses and instead of a suit was sporting the business casual look with a long sleeve button down and khakis.

They exchanged brief introductions, and all took a seat.

"What can I do to assist the FBI?" Rhett asked.

He seemed calm but she could tell he was a bit on edge, probably worried about the trouble his clients could be in.

"Let me start off to put your mind at ease that this has nothing to do with your clients."

Rhett's shoulders dropped down. "Oh, then what is it about then?"

"We want to talk to you about Quinn Kelly."

Rhett's blue eyes widened. "Is Quinn under FBI investigation?"

He seemed a little bit too excited about that prospect. "No, but she's related to a case we're working on."

"What do you want to know?" Rhett asked.

Jalen leaned in. "We understand that you were working for

John Rossi at Horizon Pharma, and then he replaced you with Quinn. Is that right?"

"Yeah. Not my proudest moment. First time I have ever been fired by a client in my almost thirty-five years of practicing law."

"What happened?" Jalen asked.

She watched Rhett closely to study his body language.

"I try not to speak ill of any of my clients either during the representation or after, but since you're here, I assume it's important, so I'll tell you that John is bad news. I'm not saying he's involved in any illegal activity or divulging privileged communications. I'm just telling you that not only was he a horrific client to try to micromanage, he's not a good guy."

She'd already figured that out from everything that had happened with him and Quinn. But this was now a man saying the same thing. She needed to understand more. "Did John treat you badly?"

Rhett huffed. "That's an understatement. I'm used to taking heat from clients—being yelled at, the whole nine yards. But John was on another level. He was verbally abusive to me and members of my team. I could handle it because it's not my first rodeo, but I had to confront him numerous times about how he was dealing with my team, especially the women members."

John was a misogynistic, abusive pig. But what would be his motivation to kill? She still wasn't sure if that could make any sense. "How did you get fired?"

"One day, he pushed me too far, and I snapped. He wasn't used to someone standing up to him, and he couldn't handle it."

She had to ask. "How do you think Quinn is dealing with him?"

Rhett grimaced. "Quinn Kelly is one of the toughest trial lawyers in town. I have no doubt that she'd stand up to him like I did, but John would probably handle it even worse coming from a woman." Rhett took a breath. "Is John on your radar as some type of suspect?"

"We can't get into the details of our investigation," she responded. "But I would like to get back to Quinn. How well do you know her?"

"We run in the same circles and go after similar clients. Our firms are chief competitors with each other, so we aren't exactly friends if you know what I mean."

"But you respect her work as an attorney?" Jalen asked.

"I do, but I have to tell you, sometimes I just don't get how she convinces these juries. The nickname she has around here is the Pied Piper."

She found that interesting. "Really? Don't all lawyers tell their version of the story to try to zealously defend their clients' interests."

"That sounds like lawyer speak right there, Agent Haddad."

She smiled. "It's law school speak, and that's as far as I went down that road."

"You probably made the right decision. I tell people these days to think long and hard before choosing the career path I did. It will suck the life right out of you."

"Going back to Quinn." They needed to stay focused.

"Oh yes, I got sidetracked. Like I said, Quinn's a bit of an enigma. She gets the job done though, and that's what the clients care about the most."

Jalen looked at Rhett. "I guess I'm still not getting how Quinn is an enigma?"

"You would think a highly successful trial lawyer would be the life of the party, but she's not like that. From what I can tell she has a very small knit group of friends. She's single, no kids, but she has this uncanny connection with people when she gets up in front of them and talks to the jury."

Rhett's critique of Quinn hit far too close to home. He could've been talking about her.

"Sounds like you might be a little jealous," Jalen said.

She was glad he made the point instead of her.

Rhett smiled. "I'm hypercompetitive, so I definitely don't like losing clients, but I will tell you, I was much happier once I was done with John, so it all worked out in the end. I may not have Quinn's special sauce recipe, but I've held my own and done extremely well over my career. So really there's nothing to be jealous about." He stopped for a moment and looked at Jalen and then her. "You don't think I'm involved in whatever it is you're investigating, do you?"

She didn't. But this conversation had been enlightening. "We're just doing our due diligence and wanted to make sure we spoke with you."

He arched an eyebrow. "You realize you're the one engaging in lawyer speak now. That wasn't a denial."

"As we told you before, we can't divulge the details," Jalen said.

"I know the drill. Is there anything else you need before I get back to work?"

Samira stood. "That'll be it. We appreciate your time."

"You know where to find me."

Once they were back in their car, she was interested to get Jalen's take. "What did you think?"

"My biggest takeaway had nothing to do with Rhett and more to do with how he described Quinn."

"Yeah. I agree. I want to go back and watch the social media clips and interviews Quinn has given and see if we can put together anything she did that may have instigated our killer."

Jalen merged onto the interstate. "I forgot to tell you that I spoke to the psychiatrist evaluating Luke."

"And?"

"She believes he has some serious mental health issues but didn't divulge details because of privacy concerns. I discussed with her what we were looking at and in her professional opinion, it couldn't be him. Plus, he has the alibi for Richard's murder."

"Then we have at least two possible roads. One, we still have to consider that even with his issues, that he was right about the identification of the stalker. Alternatively, he was wrong, and we're nowhere on the stalker."

"And then you have three, which is the worst possibility of all," Jalen said.

"Which is?" She feared she knew his answer.

"That the stalker and the killer are two different men."

"That is the nightmare scenario, but right now, we have to focus on the stalker because we know he is actively stepping up his game and that provides us somewhere to focus."

"Also, the analysts have finished their review of Luke's phone. Nothing else on the stalker, but he was taking a lot of pics of Quinn. Nothing surprising though."

"It was worth a shot."

"Big plans for Friday night?" Jalen asked.

She laughed. "Watching Quinn videos. You?"

"Do you want me to join you?"

"Not if you have actual legit plans. I'll let you know if I find anything."

He smiled. "Thanks partner." He let out a sigh. "And Samira, I know I'm overstepping, but I have to say it."

"No, you don't. We've been down this road before."

"And I'm going to keep reminding you that at some point, you'll have to get out there again. There's no way you should be alone the rest of your life. I still think you need to stay in touch with Wyatt. Who knows where that could go."

She'd had the love of her life and he'd been killed five years ago on an overseas assignment for the FBI—or so that's what she was told. To this day she was convinced that Omar had been recruited by the CIA and that's why he'd gotten killed. But there were no real answers, only the emptiness in her heart. "I'm not ready, Jalen, and I'm not sure I ever will be. Can you just please let it go?"

He kept his left hand on the wheel but reached out with his right and grabbed her hand. "I didn't mean to upset you. I just care about you."

"I know." She couldn't think about the hole in her heart that Omar left. No other man would ever be able to fill it.

30

That night Quinn sat on the couch in her hotel suite with Felix curled up beside her. She had no desire to go back to her house. She'd barely slept last night having nightmares of glass crashing all around her and then her being smothered by John. She knew that he was a dangerous man, but the sad part was that he wasn't even the most dangerous man in her life right now.

She'd had enough of sitting back and being victimized. It was time for her to do what she did best. Fight. She needed to devise a plan. A way to trap the stalker and stop him for good. She would never have the freedom she needed to continue her work if he was always lingering around. No. The time had come to take action. It didn't look like the FBI was any closer to finding this guy than when he first popped onto the scene, and she couldn't afford to wait around on them.

She thought about the best way to go about it. And after much consideration, the most obvious answer stared her in face.

She would use herself as bait. Dangle herself in front of him. Something that was too good to turn down. And then it would be all over. She'd go back to life. Back to her work. Back to her home. Her safe space.

The suite doorbell rang, and she groaned wondering who it could be and not wanting to really see anyone. She still had an FBI agent on security detail outside the door, so she wasn't worried about it being a threat. More of an annoyance. A big one.

She went and looked through the peephole and cursed under her breath. It was the last person she wanted to see. Why was John hassling her again? She had foolishly believed that he wouldn't bother her after last night. He was proving to be a bigger problem than she had imagined.

Reluctantly, she opened the door and he barged in.

"What are you doing here?"

He moved closer to her. "That's no way to greet your client."

"Seriously. What are you doing here?" Her patience was waning.

"The FBI told me what happened and given what had transpired between us, I wanted to make sure you weren't attempting to throw me under the bus because I had nothing to do with it." John crossed his arms over his chest in defiance. He had some nerve.

She laughed. "I wish I had thought about blaming it on you, but honestly it all happened so fast, it didn't occur to me. They don't think it was you, so you have nothing to worry about. And thanks for inquiring about my safety."

"You don't need protection." He took a step towards her and then stopped. "You aren't going to pull a gun on me again, are you?"

"Depends on if you deserve it."

Now it was his turn to laugh. "Quinn, why can't you see that we could be good together? I don't know why you're being so stubborn."

She straightened her shoulders. "Stubborn? You just can't handle the fact that a woman turned you down and stood up for herself. You need to get it into your thick head that I'm not interested, and I'm never going to be interested. We have a job to do plain and simple. Your job is to testify, and mine is to win this case. And then we're gonna move on. And we won't see each other unless there's another case that I need to win for you and your company. Are we clear?"

John arched an eyebrow.

She could tell he was mildly amused, but she didn't really care. Bullies needed to be stood up to, and she was doing just that.

"You haven't offered me a drink."

"Are you going to be staying long enough for a drink? Is there anything else we even need to talk about?"

"I was hoping you'd have some more updates on the situation."

And then it occurred to her. He was using this as a ruse. Yeah, he still wanted to get into bed with her, but really what he wanted was some reassurance that *he* wasn't going to be targeted. That *he* was going to be safe. Because when she had called him a coward, she was a hundred percent right.

She wouldn't be providing him any comfort. "They're pretty tight lipped, and even if they weren't, I don't think they have anything. Actually, let me rephrase that. I think they have about zero. Yeah, there's the one guy who is undergoing psychological testing, but he is not the threat here. And we know that because he was actually hospitalized for the testing while all this other stuff was happening."

John took it upon himself and strolled up to the expansive suite minibar and fixed himself a glass of whiskey. Then he walked over and took a seat in the big navy chair. She decided she could sit down as well but didn't get anywhere near him.

"It's not like you to just sit back and let someone else fight your battle. Since the trial starts on Monday, you have to have a plan. So what is it?"

She hated answering to him. "My plan is to win our case. After the litigation is over, I can worry about the stalker guy, but I refuse to let him derail me. In the same way I won't let you."

John laughed. "You really do have an issue with men, don't you?"

"Since I deal with men like you, can you really blame me?"

John took a sip of whiskey. "I'm not really that bad. You don't get to where I got by playing nice. You get to where I got by breaking all the rules. You would know something about that. You're just as much of a rule breaker as I am, you just have a prettier face."

She'd had enough of him accusing her of things. They were nothing alike in her mind. "Did you get security?"

"Yeah, the company is providing it. I'm not messing around. If this dude wants to come after me, then let him. My guys will be ready."

"It's easier to be brave when you have someone doing the dirty work for you. I don't think you'd want to go one on one with this guy."

"Why do you say that?"

She was messing with him now and enjoying every minute of it. "This guy is a killer. I mean he's killed multiple people that we know of. And who knows beyond that. I'm sure he'd have no problem breaking your neck. Snap."

John slammed the glass down on the table. "You're just trying to screw with me. It's not working. Like I said, I don't have to deal with this guy one on one. He's not the one busting windows in my house and following me around. Something tells me that you're the one that needs to sleep with one eye open."

She smiled. "I always do."

31

Samira made herself a cup of tea with fresh mint and settled in on her couch with her laptop. She didn't have much of a garden, but she did grow mint because it reminded her so much of Sitti. The house always smelled like mint growing up. Her grandmother used mint in almost every dish, and it was a comfort to carry that small piece of Sitti with her. Having mint tea in the evenings as a way to unwind was one of the ways she still felt connected to Sitti.

But right now, loneliness washed over her in waves. That's probably why Rhett's comments about Quinn hit her so hard. Like there was something wrong with a woman who was single and didn't have kids. Men like him had no idea what women really went through.

She closed her eyes for a moment and allowed herself to do something she rarely did. Imagine her life right now if Omar had still been alive. Would they have been snuggled up on the couch together watching a movie? Would she be a mother?

She felt the tears well up in her eyes. She couldn't even remember the last time she cried, but for some reason she was feeling raw right now. She missed Sitti. She missed Omar. And while her father was still alive, he might as well be dead. He had always wanted her to become a lawyer, not join the FBI. She didn't expect him to understand her. He never had and never would.

She was alone. There was no other way to look at it. She was thankful for her friendship and partnership with Jalen. But she wasn't good at letting others in. And while she was quiet about her faith, she still had some, but not much. Many days she thought that God had abandoned her. And maybe he had. She tried to stay busy with work and refuse to wallow, but for some reason she felt really down tonight.

And even though a man like Wyatt was intriguing, she didn't have it in her to try to start a long-distance relationship. She didn't even know if she could function in any relationship. Every man since Omar she had compared to him—even Wyatt. But if she was being honest with herself, Wyatt seemed different from the other men. Mature, handsome, self-confident, but not overly cocky. It was clear to her based on their conversation on the way to the airport, that he would've been open to getting to know her better. He was single and seemed interested but not pushy. Who knows if their paths would cross again, but she tended to doubt it. She had accepted the fact that she would probably never marry, and just keep focused on her career.

Opening up her eyes and wiping away the tears, she had to get a grip. There was work to do and wallowing in self-pity wasn't helpful to her or to Quinn or the families of those who had been killed. She was better than that.

"Get it together," she said out loud.

Taking a big sip of tea, she looked at her computer and decided it was time to get to work. Starting with the coverage surrounding the first case in question involving Myers and Newton Plastics, she pressed play.

Gemma looked into the camera and introduced Quinn before the camera turned on her.

"Quinn, you just wrapped up your closing argument in the Newton Plastics trial. Tell me, how are you feeling."

Quinn looked directly in the camera, her bright blue eyes full of life. "I'm feeling confident, Gemma. The jury is now doing their hard work of deliberation, and we feel good that they will find in favor of Newton Plastics."

"There are some who say you were heartless in trying to poke holes in the plaintiffs' case given that children have died. How do you respond to that allegation?"

Quinn's eyes softened. "My heart breaks into a million pieces when I listen to those parents testify, but it's my job as an advocate to get to the truth. To make sure justice is served. By holding an innocent party liable, there is no justice. So you see, I'm not discounting what the plaintiffs have been through—just the opposite. I'm listening to their voices, and I empathize with their pain and loss. But the way to provide some meaning and justice to them is not by holding the wrong party accountable."

"And how can you be that certain that Newton Plastics is innocent here of any wrongdoing."

Quinn stood tall. "Because I follow the evidence wherever it takes me, and in this case, after reviewing all the evidence, there is only one logical conclusion. That Newton Plastics is not liable for these tragic deaths."

Samira stopped the video and typed up a few notes. She'd heard Quinn make similar arguments before, and she was sensing a theme would emerge. But if Quinn was wrong about the guilt of who she represented, then the entire premise of her defense would crumble.

What she was unsure of was how that would all fit into the stalker and his thinking. Another thought occurred to her. What if the stalker wasn't romantically drawn to Quinn? What if he became obsessed with her because he thought she was lying about getting justice, and that's why he had to take matters into his own hands by killing the CEOs? Then at some point, he got so frustrated, he came after Quinn directly. That certainly seemed like a possibility—less of a romantic angle and more of a vendetta against someone he saw as possibly corrupt.

Keeping those thoughts in mind, she turned to the Crown Bank footage.

"The jury just found in your client's favor, Quinn. What do you attribute that to?"

Quinn looked the part in this video as well wearing a gray power suit. "The plaintiffs did not meet their burden of proof. The jury was a smart group of highly engaged individuals who reviewed the evidence in front of them and found zero link between the lending practices of the bank and any violation of the law. The jury, to their credit, looked beyond the smoke and mirrors approach of plaintiffs' counsel who tried to paint the bank as an evil institution, but didn't have the receipts to back it up. I applaud the jury for focusing in so intently on such a difficult and admittedly often mundane and boring topic. But justice was served here today and that's the most important thing."

There it was again. Justice. And the focus on lack of evidence. She watched the other videos, and the message was entirely consistent. Then as she was scrolling through, she found an interview Quinn had done a couple of years ago for the Georgia Women Lawyers group. Curious, she started to play the video.

"We're here today with one of Atlanta's most successful trial attorneys, Quinn Kelly. We appreciate your time."

"I'm excited to be here." Quinn's enthusiasm actually seemed sincere.

"We fielded questions from the membership, and we got a lot of women wanting to know how you managed to rise to the top in this male dominated profession—and specifically as a high-powered trial lawyer."

Quinn gave a slight smile. "There is a lot to unpack there."

A laugh escaped the interviewer's lips. "We're really interested to get your thoughts."

"As a start, there is no substitute for hard work. That is the cornerstone of being a great attorney, but as women we often believe if we put our heads down, do the work, and are the best substantively at what we're doing, then that is going to be enough. I'm here today to tell you it isn't."

The interviewer leaned in. "Please tell us more about that."

"As most of the members know, law firms can be a cutthroat environment. An environment that is many times not welcoming to women and people of color. Things are improving, but with money comes power and for far too long, a privileged few have held onto that money and power. When people like me come and try to take some of that away, there's bound to be a fight. Bound to be fallout."

Samira kept watching intently.

"And how do you fight those battles and win, Quinn?"

Quinn smiled broadly this time. "Some will tell you that you have to be able to do whatever it takes. I will tell you that you have to be willing to do whatever it takes but you have to stay within your own moral principles. Integrity is vital in the legal profession. If you lose it, you can lose your reputation, and that means you lose everything. Men have the luxury that we don't have in that regard, but they're not judged as harshly. Women attorneys will be micromanaged, put under a microscope. Every decision we make will be second guessed, sometimes by our clients, sometimes by our colleagues. That's one of the reasons that it's so important that you have to know your own self and be true to it."

"For a young attorney, would you advise them to take the big law route, knowing everything you know now?"

Quinn looked down and then reengaged eye contact. "That's a difficult question. You see, I didn't take this road by choice. I had an enormous amount of student loan debt, and I was on my own. I had to take a lucrative firm job to be able to pay the bills, and once I got in and realized I was good at it, and I would be able to pay off my loans, then I made the decision to stay even longer than I needed to because I also realized another thing."

"What is that?"

"That I could make a real difference. That I could open doors for other women in the firm. That I could use my power and influence for good. All of that matters to me."

Samira finished up the interview and felt like she was beginning to understand Quinn even more, but what did her stalker see when he watched it?

Did he feel enraged at her success and her speaking truth about being a woman in a big law firm? Was killing her clients a way to get to her that he felt could ruin her reputation? She had made the reputational point.

She took another sip of tea as she pondered all these things and wondered how it all fit together and worried what the stalker's next move would be. She felt pretty certain that Quinn was being completely sincere during this last interview, but what was less clear for her was whether that was the case in the others. If Quinn really wanted justice so badly, could it really be that none of those clients she'd been defending had actually been liable. That seemed hard for her to believe knowing what she did about corporate America. Was it all part of her professional persona? So much so that she had convinced people that she was the one who made sure justice was served? And had someone agreed with her on the concept, but not about whether the CEOs should be held responsible?

She'd done the research on Quinn as a lawyer, but she wanted to dig further into Quinn's background and see if there was anything there that could lead her down the right path. One of the FBI analysts had sent her a zip file with everything they could locate, and now she had the time to finally review it.

Quinn was born and raised in Savannah. She already knew a little about Quinn's family. Scanning the screen quickly she came to a halt.

Quinn's father, John Kelly, had died by suicide but that wasn't the fact that shook her. John Kelly had been under investigation by the Savannah Police Department for multiple counts of child abuse and statutory rape.

When Quinn said her father had been abusive, she had

assumed violence, which was bad enough. But this? If Quinn's father was such a monster, she was certainly a victim of his abuse. While her own father had been absent, he had never done anything to physically hurt her. What Quinn's father had done was unspeakable.

She kept reading now, hungry for more information. Given the age of the victims, information was sparse, but she had seen enough to get the picture, and it was an ugly one. No wonder Quinn cared so much about her pro bono work. To say it was personal to her was an understatement.

After watching all the tape tonight, she had felt she had gained a better understanding of Quinn. But after reading this, she now understood just how difficult Quinn's life had been and it made her want to work even harder to find out the man who was coming after her. Quinn had already faced enough pain in her life. Samira had to stop this guy before it was too late.

32

On Monday afternoon, Quinn sat at counsel's table at the start of the Horizon Pharma trial. They'd spent the morning picking the jury and now that was done, opening arguments were about to ensue.

She didn't know how she was going to make it through the trial with John beside her. He had been even more of a pain than she expected during jury selection—to the point of insisting he wanted a particular woman on the jury because he believed he had already formed a connection with her.

She had let him drone on about what he wanted, but in the end, John was not the legal expert. That woman he was convinced would love him was one of the ones she was most concerned about, and she refused to bow to him over this. John was irate when she had struck his favorite juror, but this was her show—not his.

John leaned over to her. "If you lose this case, I will kill you."

She smiled and turned toward him, their faces almost touching. "Don't make threats you don't intend to keep."

He grabbed her wrist under the table.

"I'm going to win. Now let me work and play nice. Once the jury comes in, it's game face until after the verdict. Got it."

He let go of her and gave a reluctant grunt.

She feared keeping him in line during the trial was going to be a full-time job.

After the judge and jury entered the courtroom, it was time for opening statements. The plaintiffs were first. The day-to-day lawyer for the plaintiffs that she and Allie had been working with was not the one trying the case. They had brought in a woman trial specialist probably thinking that she would be more convincing especially given the subject matter. She'd never gone against Tasha Williams, so she wasn't quite sure what to expect. She'd had an associate do a deep dive into Tasha's history—top of her class at the University of Georgia for undergrad and law school. Tasha had been working on the plaintiffs' side since she graduated ten years ago—fighting the good fight, as they say.

There was no doubt that Tasha was probably going all in on this case. The narrative was in Tasha's favor, but no matter how motivated Tasha was, Quinn would always be more so because it was about more than just this case to her.

Judge Carter, a judge she had been in front of before, got things started. He was in his late fifties, no nonsense, and pretty middle of the road. His rosy cheeks against his pale skin indicated that he probably had high blood pressure. He took off his reading glasses and addressed the courtroom. "Ms. Williams, are you ready to begin?"

Tasha stood. "I am, Your Honor."

She sized Tasha up. Tall, even taller than her, with flawless copper skin and killer lashes. Her black skirt suit fit her curvy figure perfectly.

"Ladies and gentlemen of the jury, I'm Tasha Williams, we met earlier today during jury selection, and I represent the plaintiffs in this case. I want to start out by thanking you for your service, your time and attention." Tasha walked to the jury. She wasn't using any notes.

"The defendant in this case is Horizon Pharma, a multi-billion dollar drug company. But I'm not here today to bash drug companies and tell you how bad and greedy they are. No, I'm here today because the specific actions of Horizon Pharma caused the death or permanent bodily harm to my clients. This isn't an abstract debate, ladies and gentlemen. This is life and death, and the defendant is one hundred percent responsible. You see, Horizon Pharma manufactures a birth control device, an IUD, that my clients used. Many of my clients experienced internal bleeding, but unfortunately, it doesn't stop there. The damage caused led to infertility in my clients and even death." She paused, no doubt for dramatic effect to let her words sink in.

"These women put their trust in Horizon Pharma to provide a safe and effective birth control method, and instead, their bodies were forever harmed. And for my two clients who lost their lives, you'll hear much more about them during the trial, Tiffany and Monique, they have no voice to be able to testify about what happened to them. I will try to be their voice and make sure that justice is done here in this courtroom."

Tasha took a step back. "Now, you're going to hear a lot of talk today and throughout the trial about there not being enough evidence to show that the IUD produced by Horizon Pharma was the cause of the harm in this case, but I submit to you, that after you listen to everything, there will be overwhelming evidence to find the defendant liable."

Tasha continued for a bit longer going through some evidentiary issues and standards and some of the procedural hoops of the case. But she had come out swinging. There was no doubt Tasha had the stronger emotional argument but based on the evidence that was going to be put into trial, she had the upper hand. That was, of course, because John had destroyed damaging evidence. She had to play the hand in front of her and that was exactly what she was going to do.

Tasha finished up her opening statement and now it was her turn. By looking at the jury, she could tell she was starting from behind, but that was almost always the case. She glanced behind her and saw that Samira and Jalen were watching intently.

"Ms. Kelly, you can proceed," Judge Carter said.

Quinn took a deep breath and made eye contact with the jurors. She'd done this a million times, but the stakes were higher today, and she couldn't ignore that.

"Ladies and gentlemen of the jury. I would like to echo Ms. Williams' thanks for your service and attention today and throughout the trial. We'll try to be as efficient and effective as possible so as to not waste your time, but these issues we face are of critical importance. Life and death. You've heard from Ms. Williams about the allegations in this case. The contention that the IUD produced by Horizon Pharma caused internal bleeding, infertility, and yes, even death. If true, I agree with Ms. Williams that there has to be accountability, but the evidence will show that there is no link between the IUD usage and the specific harms alleged here." She paused. "I cannot even begin to imagine the pain and struggle that these brave women have gone through who are here and will testify in this case, but at the end of the day, their pain was not caused by my client, Horizon Pharma. No matter how much empathy you feel for these women, and believe me, I feel it too, you can't let your feelings dictate your verdict. This country is built on the rule of law. We have a justice system that sets forth a certain burden of proof for a reason. Once you have heard all the evidence, you will still have great empathy for these women and their families, but you will have no choice but to find in favor of my client because the evidence will not support any other finding."

She finished up and took her seat, not looking at John. She didn't want his feedback.

"Given a scheduling issue, we are going to adjourn for the rest of the day and call the first witness in the morning," Judge Carter said. He finished by reminding the jury about their responsibilities and then dismissed them.

John finally spoke after the jury was gone. "I was scared after their lawyer spoke, but you brought it back."

She turned toward him. "Did you honestly expect anything less from me?"

He laughed. "Honestly, yes, because I know you hate me. Hate what I stand for and would probably be fine taking a loss on this one just to get at me."

"That's not how I operate."

"I can see that now, but you have to keep it up."

"I plan to."

"I'm going to get out of here."

That was good with her. "See you in the morning. Tomorrow's going to be a tough day of their witnesses."

He rolled his eyes. "Cry me a river." He squeezed her shoulder too tightly for her liking before he walked away. The man was pure evil, and she had to do something about it, but her first priority was this case. She had a fiduciary duty to her client—Horizon Pharma. She didn't owe John anything.

Allie, who had been sitting right behind her, approached after John left.

"What did you think?" Quinn asked.

"It was solid. The jurors were engaged in both openings, but you definitely have your work cut out for you. At best, we're even right now, and they might be ahead just given their emotional appeal. But you did just what you needed to do. I want to be able to give an opening like that one day."

She grabbed onto Allie's arm. "And you will. We've got a couple of smaller cases this year where you will be first chair and will get that standup trial experience that you've been craving. I'll be by your side each step of the way."

"Thank you."

She looked up as she was packing her bag and saw Samira approaching. "The FBI is calling again."

"I'll take that as my cue to leave." Allie turned to walk away but almost ran into Samira.

"Agent Haddad, this is my right-hand woman, Allie Prince. I'm sure you've seen her here and around the firm."

Samira outstretched her hand. "Very nice to meet you, Allie."

Allie smiled. "Likewise. I'll let you two talk. I'll see you back at work, Quinn." Allie grabbed her bag and walked away.

"You were pretty impressive today," Samira said.

"Thanks. This is going to be a tough one."

"Yeah. Your opponent seemed ready."

She stood tall. "I never back down from a challenge."

Samira smiled. "How are you doing otherwise?"

"I'm okay. Anything more on Richard's death?"

"Still a work in progress." Samira moved closer to her. "Do you have a few minutes to talk somewhere in private?"

This couldn't be good. The last thing she needed right now was more bad news, but if there was anything else going on, she needed to know it. "Yes. Do you want to meet me back at my office? That may be best."

"Sure thing. Want some coffee? I'll pick it up and then meet you back at your office."

Coffee sounded amazing. "That would be great. Straight up black for me."

"You got it. See you in a few."

She wondered what Samira was up to. Guess she was about to find out.

33

As promised, Samira got the coffees and went to Quinn's office. She and Jalen had agreed that she was going to have this discussion one on one with Quinn in hopes of getting her to open up more.

She was escorted to Quinn's office and found her typing away on her computer.

"I come bearing gifts," Samira held out the coffee.

"Thank you." Quinn took the coffee and got up and shut the door. "So now are you going to tell me what's going on?"

"Yeah." Samira took a sip of coffee. "I don't want you to think this is creepy, but I spent Friday night reviewing a lot of your interviews that had been posted to social media."

Quinn arched an eyebrow. "Okay. Why?"

"I was hoping to see if I could find something that might have set the stalker off."

"And did you?"

"Nothing concrete, but as I was watching all of your tape, I had some questions."

"Shoot." Quinn leaned back in her chair.

"When you were talking about your commitment to the advancement of women in the legal profession, I could feel how much it meant to you. That made me wonder whether the stalker is a misogynist and decided to target you because you embody everything he hates."

"Well, that sucks when you put it that way."

Samira lifted up her hand. "It's just a theory, that's all. Anyway, I knew you believed what you were speaking about."

"I'm glad you think I'm sincere because it's the truth. It is how I feel and how I live my professional career."

Samira didn't want this to go down the wrong road. "I'm not questioning that at all, but I am still really struggling with what you do and how you talk about your cases."

Quinn placed her hands on the desk and leaned forward. "How so?"

"You don't sound like a lawyer who is defending big companies—just the opposite. You speak like a plaintiff's lawyer seeking justice and doing the right thing."

"And you think I'm full of it." Quinn raised an eyebrow.

"Honestly, I'm not sure what you actually believe, but I am wondering if the stalker took your words to heart but doesn't believe you're getting the job done. There are some that could argue that you're actually such a good attorney, you're able to win cases where the companies should've been held liable, and maybe the stalker doesn't appreciate that."

"Don't you think that's a bit of a stretch?"

She wanted to push her harder. "Is it, though? Look at your track record. You can't seriously sit here and tell me that every case you won, you think was actually carrying out justice, even if you said it was."

"I don't think I like your insinuation here, Samira. I'm doing my job, and I happen to be really good at it. Why should I be judged so harshly because of that? You wouldn't be asking a man the same question."

This wasn't going anywhere. "I'm not judging you, but I believe your gender is at play here and that there's a man out there—the stalker who may be not only judging you but acting on it."

"Meaning killing the CEOs."

"Exactly. You're out there expounding justice, and he has decided to take it into his own hands. In a way he believes you, but he doesn't believe you are carrying it out. Does that make sense?"

Quinn laughed. "You're asking me if the rationalization of a serial killer makes sense? Do you realize how crazy that sounds?"

"It may very well be, but I'm trying to get into this guy's head and the minds of serial killers are dangerous places."

"I guess you're right." Quinn's shoulders slumped.

"I'm not attacking you, Quinn. I'm trying to do everything I can to figure out who this guy could be before he strikes again, and you are key to us finding him. This is just an alternate theory I came up with. The other being that he is simply fixated on you, obsessive and killing the successful men in your life. Neither scenario is a good one."

"What do you want me to do?"

"You don't need to do anything except tell me the truth. If there's anything you've been keeping to yourself, no matter what it is, now is the time to put it all on the table."

Quinn's blue eyes locked onto her. "I've told you everything."

She had to retread over old ground. "No old boyfriends, or any other male figure in your life that you could be involved here?"

"You've already asked me that, and as I told you before, no."

"I hate to do this, but given the personal nature of these attacks, I'm going to need the names of your old boyfriends."

"Is that really necessary?" Quinn was becoming agitated, and she couldn't really blame her.

"I know this is super frustrating, but I need those names. We have to check everything."

"It's a very short list. There are only two men I've dated for any substantial amount of time. Felipe Maxwell and Cody Bisbee. Men have taken a back seat in my life and I'm fine with that."

She lifted up her hands. "Hey, no judgment from me. Thanks for providing that information. I will be completely honest with you. I feel like we're not seeing something vitally important here, and I'm doing everything I can to try to figure out what that is."

Quinn's face softened. "I understand. I feel like I'm caged up right now with the security and then of course, being in the middle of this trial. It's just a lot on my plate."

"And I don't want to make things any more difficult than they already are, but I guess I keep hoping that if I push hard enough that you're going to say something that will be able to help me figure this all out."

"I know you're doing all you can." Quinn smiled weakly. "But I hate to say that I don't think I have the secret formula here. Isn't it just possible we're dealing with a violent psychopath?"

Quinn's words put a sick feeling in her stomach because she feared that's exactly what they were dealing with.

34

Quinn had told her FBI security detail that she was going to be at the office until at least six o'clock, knowing good and well that she had other plans. It was imperative that she discovered who her stalker was, and this was the only way she could do it while still having the upper hand. This needed to be on her terms especially after her discussion with Samira earlier.

She was counting on the stalker following her every move. He was clearly escalating, and she had spent some time thinking up her own profile for him. Probably in his thirties or early forties, single, white and smart—but the trouble was that he thought he was smarter than everyone else, including her. She would show him. There had been too many men who wreaked havoc in her life since the day she was born. This particular man, she felt she could do something about, but there would be no point trying if her FBI security detail was stuck by her side. That's why she had to be discreet. The agent wouldn't be showing back up to take her to the hotel until six p.m. which meant she had a good three hours.

If she was wrong about the stalker following her twenty-four seven, then this would be a big waste of time, but something in her gut told her that this guy was on high alert and was getting close to making further moves against her which was why she couldn't afford to wait. Action was required now. Decisive action.

She thought about Samira's questions. They were starting to hit a little too close to home. Did everyone think she was a fraud when she talked about justice? They just didn't understand that she was doing what she had to do. Justice did matter to her, and she wished they could see that, but right now, she had to fight one battle at a time, and today her fight was with this stalker.

Not knowing exactly who she was dealing with, she wasn't coming unprepared. She pulled the gun out of her locked office drawer—her second weapon—and placed it in her purse. The firm prohibited firearms in the building, but that had never stopped her. She'd always kept it there in case of emergency, and this would seem to qualify. Kicking off her heels, she slipped into her flats. There was going to be a good bit of walking and she needed to be highly mobile, and her three-inch heels weren't going to cut it.

Once the fresh air hit her as she stepped out of the building, a little twinge of nerves set in, but she quickly pushed those away and gave herself a pep talk. She was strong enough to face down this lunatic. She wasn't sure if reasoning was going to do anything to help her, so that's why she was armed. Taking a moment, she walked down the sidewalk and just looked around. Was he there watching her now? The streets of Midtown Atlanta weren't completely full of people, but there were enough people out and about. Many of them taking an afternoon coffee break along with some moms with strollers and dog walkers.

If the stalker was watching her, she had to lure him somewhere more private as they clearly couldn't have an altercation in the middle of Fourteenth Street.

She walked slowly down the block before stopping in front of one of the delis and waiting for a minute. People were coming in and out, but she wasn't concerned about them. Her eyes were looking elsewhere. Trying to determine if *he* was out there.

What she was doing was a long shot, but she had to try. The existence of the stalker was causing her way too many problems, and the sooner she could deal with him the better. She started walking again.

It was probably another twenty minutes before she sensed him. There was someone following her. She didn't look back too many times because she didn't want him to know that she was onto him, but she felt this had to be him. She had to trust her instincts.

When she had stolen a glance, his description fit that of what Luke had told the FBI. Her stalker was an average height white male with dark hair. He was dressed in business casual attire. But she knew better than to judge someone based on their looks. People had done that to her for her entire life.

The plan was playing out as she wanted. Her next move was to slow down enough to make sure he could get to her when she entered the large parking garage.

She entered the garage and started going up the steps. Her goal was to go to one of the higher floors where there would be less foot traffic.

The stalker was still following her. She could now hear his footsteps a few flights below. Speeding up just a bit, she wanted to make sure she was situated before he got out of the staircase. All that extra cardio was paying off because her breath was still calm even after all the steps.

She exited on the seventh floor and pulled her gun out of her purse. Then she hid behind a white SUV and waited for him to walk out of the stairwell.

When the man did emerge from the stairwell, she got a good look at his face. This wasn't someone she recognized. What if she was wrong about this? Things could go really wrong in a split second, but she had to trust her instincts because they had gotten her this far in life. She stepped out from behind the SUV with her gun pointed directly at him. "Let me see your hands," she said.

"Whoa." He lifted his hands up. "What are you doing?"

She took a step closer. "Walk this way." She wanted to get him further away from the exit.

He followed her orders. "What are you doing? Who are you?"

"Don't play dumb. I know you're the man who's been stalking me, and I want to know why."

His expression changed from confusion to a sinister smile. "I never thought you were going to notice me."

She had been right. This was him. "Notice you how?"

"You never noticed me. Not in law school. Not after we graduated. Do you even remember my name?"

She seriously had no idea who this guy was, but she wasn't putting down her gun. "I'm sorry. I don't think I know you."

He laughed. "My name is Tom Malone. We were in the same class at Emory Law."

"There were hundreds of people in our class and that was many years ago. I'm sorry I don't have that good of a memory."

"I see you on social media all the time. I thought that maybe if you learned more about me, then I could make you see that we are right for each other. But you kept sleeping around with your clients instead of realizing what a great match we are."

"I did not." She couldn't let him say that about her.

"Don't lie to me." He showed no fear even with a gun pointed at him. "I was there. I saw you at their houses late at night. I know you weren't working on cases. I'm not stupid."

So he had been following her. "Tom, you're a good looking guy. You have to be smart if you were at Emory. You don't need to bother with me. Why the hassle?" She really wanted to know.

"Because we're alike."

She seriously doubted that. "I don't think we are, Tom."

"We both have secrets."

"We all have secrets." Her patience was running out.

"Not the kind like us."

Now he was making her extremely uncomfortable. "You need to leave me alone. Do you understand me? This has to end."

He took a step toward her. "No. I can't be without you, Quinn. I've tried and it's too hard to be apart from you for even a single second more."

"You're going to have to be."

Tom's eyes narrowed. "I've watched you for so long. I've studied your every move to make sure I could be the best man for you. I know who you really are. I see the real Quinn, not the one you put on display."

No one fully knew the real her. "Please, stop this. I'm going to ask you one more time."

He lunged forward, catching her off guard, and she stepped backward, gun still steady in her grip. That's when she saw that he had a gun in his waistband. This guy really was not only mentally unstable, but he was dangerous. Far from a harmless man who had taken things too far.

Tom dove toward her, and she quickly sidestepped him. When he went for his gun, she didn't hesitate, because she had learned that even one second of hesitation could get you killed. With his gun drawn and pointed at her, she pulled the trigger and shot twice before he had the chance. All that training had paid off because she hit him center mass.

Tom fell to the concrete floor.

She squatted down near him and called 911. She had acted in self-defense, and she wanted this done completely by the book.

It was only a few seconds before the life drained out of his light brown eyes. Tom Malone had picked the wrong woman to stalk.

35

Samira couldn't believe what she had just heard from Quinn. They sat across from each other in a conference room at the field office. "What were you thinking? You could've been the one lying dead in the parking garage. Do you have any idea how reckless what you did was? It was completely beyond the pale. Really, I'm so mad right now I can barely look at you." It sounded like she was scolding a petulant child, and that's exactly what was happening. When she'd gotten the call, she had no idea how bad things had really been.

Quinn hung her head. "I've already said I'm sorry."

"That's not good enough. Now the prime suspect is dead, and we aren't even able to question him about the murders."

"I was afraid." Quinn looked at her. "He was coming after me. He pulled his gun."

"I don't doubt that, but you should have never, I repeat, never, have been in that situation in the first place. You went rogue beyond any scenario that I could've ever contemplated. More than anyone I've ever worked with has done. I'm truly in shock right now at your behavior." Samira had a lot of questions about Quinn's story, and she intended to get answers.

"It just all happened so fast."

"Then why don't we back up. After I left your office, you decided that you wanted some fresh air and coffee, and you didn't bother to call your security detail? And I had just brought you coffee earlier. You needed more?"

Quinn groaned. "Yes. I'm tired, okay. I needed the caffeine boost. I didn't think it would be a big deal. It was broad daylight."

Samira was fuming. "That was mistake number one."

"I wanted to get out, breathe some fresh air, and clear my head, and I did have my gun with me. I have a permit to carry. It's legal."

She gripped her fists tightly under the table trying not to completely lose her composure. "I'm not worried about legality right now. You get outside for your walk and a coffee and what happened?"

"After I had walked a bit, I felt like someone was following me."

"Why didn't you call me or your security detail or 911?"

Quinn's shoulder slumped. "I don't know. I panicked. I just needed to get away from him. I thought there would be people in the parking garage so that's where I went."

She didn't think Quinn was telling her the whole story, but she kept standing firm in her account. "And then once in the garage, Tom Malone attacked you."

"Yes. He came for me. I saw he had a gun, and when he went for his weapon and pointed it at me, that's when I shot him before he could fire at me."

The questions flooded her mind. "Did you have any discussion with him?"

"Just briefly. I asked him why he was doing this, and it seemed like he was annoyed that I didn't remember him from law school, and he had been watching me and trying to figure out how to get into my life."

"Did you really not remember him?"

Quinn shook her head. "I didn't. I know that sounds awful,

but there were a lot of people in law school. He definitely wasn't in my circle of friends."

"We're checking to see if there's any surveillance footage at the garage."

"Okay. That's good."

Quinn didn't seem fazed by that prospect. Had it all happened exactly as she described? "We're tearing apart Tom Malone's life right now. We need to find out if he was the one killing the CEOs. It's a good bet that it's him, but I'd feel much better if we had evidence."

"Me too." Quinn sighed. "I know you're angry."

"Angry doesn't even begin to cover it." She couldn't remember the last time she'd been this mad. It was nothing short of miraculous that Quinn wasn't the one who was lying dead in the parking garage.

"But I felt so cooped up. I told you earlier how stressed I was," Quinn's voice elevated.

"So now this is my fault?" Samira couldn't believe where this conversation was going.

Quinn stood and started pacing. "No, but I'm trying to explain where I was coming from. I just needed a few minutes to myself. I had no idea that the stalker would try to track me down in broad daylight."

"We need to shift gears for a minute." She had to even though she was still furious. "You shot and killed a man today. I understand that it was self-defense, but I imagine you're going to have a lot of feelings to work through about that."

"Yeah," Quinn said quietly. "Honestly, I don't think I've processed everything yet."

Samira couldn't help but empathize with Quinn. She was still angry at her for taking such a stupid risk, but now they were going to have to deal with the very real fallout. "You might even feel numb for a while before it catches up with you. There is no right or wrong way to react. The simple truth is that how you feel is how you feel. Do you understand that?"

"Yeah." Quinn flopped down in the chair.

Samira wasn't sure Quinn understood the gravity of what she had done.

"So what happens now?"

"We're going to get you to your hotel where you will stay for tonight until you need to be in court tomorrow. I've got too much on my plate to be worrying about what you might do tonight."

"But if Tom is gone, doesn't that mean I'm safe?" Quinn's voice cracked.

Samira noticed that Quinn had said gone and not dead. Maybe this was going to be even harder for Quinn than Samira had imagined. "I hope so, but until we know that Tom Malone was the one who killed the CEOs, I'm not going to rest easy." She wanted proof.

Quinn reached out and touched her arm. "I really am sorry, Samira. I'm not trying to make your life any harder. I acted in the moment out of fear because I'm not a trained FBI agent. I did what I had to do to protect myself."

She needed to make sure Quinn fully understood the source of her anger. "I'm not upset with you for protecting yourself. I'm mad with you for putting yourself in that position to begin with." If Quinn hadn't acted before Malone, she probably would be dead, and Samira couldn't wrap her head around that.

Quinn averted her eyes. "I understand."

This was going nowhere. "There's nothing we can do about any of that now. I'll have an agent take you to the hotel, and I'm going over to meet Jalen at Tom Malone's house."

Quinn seemed to relent to the plan, and she left her with another agent so she could go to Malone's house.

By the time she got there, the place was swarming with agents and Atlanta PD had secured the scene and perimeter. She quickly found Jalen. "Talk to me. What do we have?"

He grabbed onto her elbow. "Most of the house appears to be

normal but come with me upstairs. I think it's the guest bedroom that Malone has turned into his own little shrine to Quinn."

Samira got a sick feeling in the pit of her stomach as she followed Jalen up the steps. She walked into the guest room and took a breath. It was covered with pictures of Quinn. News clippings about her cases. Lots of photos. Candid shots in many different situations and settings. "He's been following her for a while."

Jalen blew out a breath. "Yeah, that's what I'm thinking, and by the looks of some of the pictures, he's gotten much closer to her than I would've thought."

She stared at some of the pictures and thought about how violated Quinn would feel if she saw them. Pictures of her coming out of her office, going into the coffee shop, and notably, going into Richard's house. "We were probably right about him getting set off by her nighttime visits to Richard. Anything here tying him to the other CEOs?"

"Not yet but there are boxes of other pictures and clippings that he didn't hang up that we will need to go through." He lifted up one of the boxes to show her.

"What's your gut telling you? Is this our killer?" She wanted to hear his thoughts.

Jalen walked around the room for a minute. "This guy was clearly obsessed with Quinn. She was his focus. If he believed that Quinn was romantically involved with the CEOs, then that's one strong motive. It would tend to point to Maxine's death being an accident. What's throwing me a bit is the one CEO in the case she lost, Lew O'Malley, is still alive. As we've talked about before, is there some reason that CEO wasn't seen as a threat because he was on the losing side?"

"We need to ask Quinn about Lew and their relationship or lack thereof."

Jalen started typing away on his phone. "Samira, I don't think that will be necessary."

"Why?"

He showed her his phone. "Lew is the president of the Atlanta LGBTQ lawyers' group. If I found that out in a simple internet search, I'm sure Malone could've too and then that would make a lot of sense. Malone wouldn't have had to take Lew out because he wouldn't have wanted to be with Quinn. Simply put, Lew wasn't a threat to Malone."

For the first time, she started to feel like things were falling into place. "This all makes a lot of sense, but I'd really like to find something specific here linking him to the murders. Chances are, he's our guy, but even if there's a one percent chance he isn't, we've got to be prepared."

"I hear you, but I'm feeling pretty good the more that we've talked this through. His obsession turned deadly and there was no turning back."

She thought for a moment. "If it is Malone, then this could have nothing to do with winning and losing cases and all about his obsession with Quinn and how he viewed the men in her life."

Jalen nodded. "I say we get this all boxed up and taken to the field office where we can sift through it."

"Agreed. We also need to make sure we've torn this place up from top to bottom. I don't want to miss anything." She'd felt they had already missed too much. She could only hope that the killing had stopped with Malone's death.

36

Quinn had slept much better than normal. Having the stalker out of her life for good put her at ease. What had greatly disturbed her was Samira calling her last night to tell her about the shrines in Tom Malone's home. The thought of him following her for an extended period of time made her queasy. How had she missed that?

She prided herself on being aware, on having taken self-defense training, of making sure that no man could ever hurt her again. And Tom had come ever so close to changing all of that. She vowed to be more careful moving forward. She had to be.

Now she was back in the courtroom and had the unfortunate task of cross examining a highly sympathetic witness for the plaintiffs that had just broken down in tears on the stand. She could've sworn some of the jury members had teared up too. She had to engage in a delicate balancing act, or she was going to lose the jury and it would be all over. They might as well open up the company's coffers if that happened, and Quinn would never be hired by Horizon Pharma again.

Ms. Martin was a thirty year old suburban housewife with pale skin and light blue eyes. She wore her blonde hair in a short bob.

"Ms. Martin, you're convinced that the Horizon Pharma IUD caused your infertility, isn't that right?"

Ms. Martin nodded.

"I'm sorry, Ms. Martin, just a reminder that you'll need to verbalize your answer so the court reporter can take it down."

Ms. Martin looked directly at her. "Yes. I am convinced of that."

"Ms. Williams took us through your heartbreaking story in great detail so I'm not going to retread over that ground. I want to actually talk with you about the time period prior to you ever using the IUD in question."

"Okay." Ms. Martin bit her bottom lip.

She'd debated long and hard with Allie over how quickly to jump to this. Did she build it up with a lot of background, or did she just dive in for maximum impact? This topic was the subject of a pretrial motion. Tasha had tried to get the information excluded saying it was too prejudicial, but she won the argument on relevance, so she was able to present it. It wasn't until in that moment, that she made her final decision to go down this road. Just because you could introduce evidence, didn't mean you should. Especially on a topic like this. She was probably going to hate herself after this, but she couldn't lose sight of the bigger picture.

Once she dropped this bomb, there was no turning back. "Ms. Martin, isn't it true that you got pregnant five years ago?"

"Yes."

"And isn't it also true that you decided to have an abortion?"

A few gasps were audible in the courtroom.

Ms. Martin looked down. "It's more complicated than that."

"Actually, it's not, Ms. Martin. Did you have an abortion five years ago?"

"I did," she responded softly.

"And since that time, you have never been pregnant again, correct?"

"That's right."

"And you've tried to get pregnant again, correct?"

"Yes, once I got married two years ago. Then we decided the time wasn't right and I started using the Horizon Pharma IUD."

"Ms. Martin, you encountered difficulties during the procedure to terminate your pregnancy, did you not?"

"Yes."

"In fact, you suffered severe internal bleeding."

Ms. Martin looked at the jury. "I wouldn't characterize it like that."

She stepped closer to the witness. "Then how exactly would you characterize it because I have your medical records that indicate, there was, and I quote, severe internal bleeding."

Tasha shot up out of her seat. "Objection, your Honor. Facts not in evidence."

"I'll put it into evidence right now." Nothing was going to stop this train now. Her only hope was to press the gas and hope for the best.

"I'll allow it. Proceed, Ms. Kelly," the judge said.

She introduced the medical records and continued with her questioning by placing the blown up medical record on the large courtroom screen for the jury to view. "Ms. Martin, you'll see the language there that I quoted. Severe internal bleeding." She took a pause.

"Was that a question?" Ms. Martin asked.

She was starting to break her down. "Do you dispute the fact that your doctor documented in real time that you had severe internal bleeding."

Ms. Martin's face started to flush. "I don't think it was as bad as he said. Definitely not like the bleeding I had with the Horizon Pharma IUD."

"But you did have internal bleeding, and I'm not the medical expert here. We'll have those experts testify later, but I would think any internal bleeding would be a serious matter."

Tasha rose again. "Objection, move to strike, Your Honor, counsel is testifying."

The judge nodded. "Agreed. The jury will disregard Ms. Kelly's last statement."

That didn't matter to her one bit. She didn't care about evidentiary rulings. She cared about the thoughts that she put into the jurors' heads. So why not push the envelope because if she had miscalculated the damage was already done. Irreparable, beyond compare. She was betting on the fact that she'd played the better hand even if it was distasteful. "Isn't it true, Ms. Martin, that your infertility was caused, not by the Horizon Pharma IUD, but by an abortion that was riddled with complications?"

"Objection, calls for legal conclusion," Tasha said.

"Sustained."

"Let me rephrase." She turned to the jury, taking her time to make eye contact with all of them. "How do you know, Ms. Martin, that your abortion wasn't the cause of your infertility?"

Ms. Martin's face turned full on crimson. "I just know. I felt fine after the procedure. It wasn't until the IUD that I started getting really sick. I knew something was wrong."

She had made her point, as difficult as it was. "No further questions."

Tasha popped up quickly out of her seat and walked toward the witness. "Just one question for you, Ms. Martin. Can you tell the jury why you had an abortion?"

Turning, Ms. Martin looked directly at the jury. "Because I was raped by my uncle."

Oh no. She didn't know that fact, and if she had, she would've reconsidered her entire strategy.

Tasha moved toward the witness. "Thank you, Ms. Martin. That's all I have."

Well, Quinn had gone for it, and while she might have put doubt in the jurors' minds, Ms. Martin had just gained even more sympathy. And Quinn felt sick to her stomach at having put Ms. Martin through all of that especially given the revelation about the abuse. Something she knew all too well. But she couldn't let the jury see her real feelings. It was just one of the many ways she was forced to wear a façade. She would have to deal with her own emotional fallout later because it would surely come.

Once they had ended for the day, it was going to be brutal. John was right beside her ready to pounce, but first she had an incoming missile from Gemma.

But she waved both of them off and pulled a somber-faced Allie over.

"You've got to help me dig myself out of this hole. Whatever you can think of, okay?"

"I'm on it." Allie gave her shoulder a quick pat and then walked away.

Gemma didn't waste any time pushing past Allie. "Quinn, can I get a statement?"

"No comment."

"I need more than that and you know it. Today was big. Aren't you going to say anything?" Gemma held up the phone which was live streaming. This was bigger than just this one case. She had to keep her reputation intact. No matter how tough today had been, she couldn't and wouldn't display weakness.

"While my heart goes out to Ms. Martin, I believe the evidence presented today strongly points to the fact that her infertility was not caused by my client's IUD."

"Do you think it was wrong to bring up her abortion in a public hearing for all the world to see?" Gemma's eyes locked onto hers.

"It's not about right or wrong, Gemma. It's about justice. When Ms. Martin and her attorney chose to bring this case, they knew there was a big chance that all of her medical history would be fair game for examination given the nature of the claims presented. I simply go wherever the evidence takes me, and in this case, it clearly took me to there being another reason for the infertility. This was not personal against Ms. Martin in any way, but my client also deserves a full and fair hearing based on all the facts. There is a lot at stake here, and I will continue to do my job to make sure truth and justice are served. That's all I have for now."

Gemma put down her phone. "Thanks."

She walked closer to Gemma. "You owe me one."

Gemma nodded and walked away.

John grabbed onto her arm and his fingers pushed into her flesh. "We need to talk."

She figured as much. He looked like he was ready to explode. "Not here."

"I'll meet you at your hotel."

She didn't like that idea, but it was better than making a scene in public. And she still had the FBI agent on guard although she wondered if that would end soon. She also wanted to go back to her house but given the trial, she had decided to stay in the hotel to finish it out. The window repair was complete and with Tom gone, she felt like she could return.

She'd only been back in her hotel room a few minutes when John arrived in a blaze of anger, just as she had expected.

"What was that in there today?" He helped himself to a drink.

"What it was, John, was putting real doubt into the jurors' heads about the cause of Ms. Martin's infertility. You and I both know that the IUD does cause problems, but in this instance, there's a very real possibility that the infertility was caused by the abortion."

John turned to her, drink in hand. "But now the jury knows she's a rape victim. They feel even more sorry for her which I didn't think would even be possible until I watched you annihilate the woman."

"I had no idea about the rape. I weighed the risks based on all the information I had at the time, and I still think it's the right call. As emotional as it was in the courtroom today, when the jury gets into their deliberation room, that emotion will have worn off some, and they will remember the fact that Ms. Martin suffered severe complications from an abortion. That evidence will have a great amount of weight."

"I hope you're right."

She was about ready to strangle him. "I'm working with the facts that you gave me. I can't pull a rabbit out of a hat no matter how good of an attorney I am. You should lose this case. Hands down. And those women deserve every penny they are seeking and more from you."

John moved closer to her. "It's too late for you to get soft now."

"I'm not getting soft, I'm telling you the cold, hard facts. If I can win this case, it would be a miracle. We've discussed multiple times that the likelihood of losing is higher than winning."

John threw his now empty glass across the room, and it shattered.

A few seconds later the FBI agent had entered the room, gun drawn.

"Whoa," John put his hands up.

"It's okay," she said. "John's temper got the best of him, and he threw a glass. Not at me, thankfully."

The FBI agent raised a brow in suspicion. "Would you like me to stay in here?"

"No, thank you. We're good."

The agent did as she said and went back outside the door, but she felt more comfortable knowing he was there to keep John in check.

Not deterred much, John picked up another glass.

"Try not to break that one."

He frowned and faced her. "What are we going to do?"

"The only thing we can do. Fight as hard as we can. Their settlement number wasn't something the Board wanted to entertain, so we keep pushing."

"If today is any indication as to how this is going to end up, I hate to tell you, Quinn, but I think you lose."

"No. *We* lose."

He threw back his drink. "Speaking of that. I was informed that the stalker is dead. They didn't tell me how, but did you have something to do with that?"

"I shot him in self-defense."

His eyes widened. "Wow, Quinn. You really are crazy."

"What I am is still alive. I wouldn't be standing here with you otherwise. He pulled a gun on me."

"Then why do you still have security?"

"Because they're trying to figure out if the stalker was the one who killed my clients."

He frowned. "Isn't that a given?"

"Apparently not."

"Which means I'm still on the hook if we lose."

She laughed. "It's always about you, isn't it?"

"Shouldn't it be? The guy is killing CEOs. That's me, not you."

"I think they will find that the stalker and killer are one in the same, and we can move on with our lives."

He closed the space between them. "You're not still going to point that gun at me if I touch you, are you?"

"I wouldn't advise touching me. Go find some other woman who is actually interested in you."

Not listening to her, he pulled her close to him. She could feel his breath on her cheek. "Get away from me."

"You know you want me."

"I don't." The walls started to close in on her again as night-marish memories floated through her brain. She pushed him away with all of her strength, causing a little separation between them.

"You're so uptight."

"What I am is a woman who has told you no numerous times and will continue to do so. I'm not changing my mind about you."

He closed the space between them again and pressed his body against hers. "I'll convince you."

She'd had enough and she kneed him in the groin as hard as she could.

He moaned and doubled over.

How many other women had this monster preyed upon?

She walked over to the door and opened it, finding the FBI agent there. "Can you please escort Mr. Rossi out?"

37

On Wednesday morning, Samira sat with Jalen in a big conference room surrounded by boxes. They'd spent time yesterday working through the documents but had also taken time to go see the trial. Today Samira decided it was more important for them to push through reviewing everything taken from Malone's house. An FBI agent was stationed at the courthouse just in case anything happened during the trial.

"Let's regroup." She took a sip of coffee.

Jalen walked up to the big board. "I came back in last night because I was too wired up and I started putting together a chronology of photos."

Samira joined him to look at what he had done.

"I can't guarantee the timing is right on all of these. It's just my best guess and the fact that once certain people are killed, that obviously impacts the timeline."

She took a few moments and studied Jalen's work. "Do you think Quinn hasn't been completely up front with us about the nature of her relationships with these guys?"

"I had the same thought, but I imagine since they are all her clients, she didn't want to be judged for her actions, and I get that."

"Why else spend so much time over there at night? All of these pictures were taken during the evening hours." She pointed to photos. "First, Russell Myers, then Warren Cruz, then Richard Hale."

"To follow up on another point, I've checked everything that was recovered from Malone's house, and there are no signs of any types of drugs—prescription or otherwise."

"Any evidence of a storage unit? A key or anything like that?"

Jalen shook his head. "No. I had the same thought, but nothing so far. I have one of the analysts working through his bank and credit card records and I asked him specifically to flag if he saw any payments for a storage unit or payments to unknown entities."

"Good thinking." Jalen was always on top of things. "Our first priority has to be finding evidence to tie him to the murders because if none exists, then it's entirely possible that we still have a serial killer out there."

Jalen placed his hand on her arm. "You don't think Malone's our guy, do you?"

Samira had tossed and turned last night thinking about this very question. "Of course, right when this happened, it seemed to fit perfectly. The motive was there given his strong obsession with Quinn."

"But?" Jalen raised an eyebrow.

"I'm concerned by the cause of death. If his main driver was Quinn, why go through so much trouble to hide the murders. Wouldn't he want to almost show her what he had done for her?"

"True, but could it be a timing issue? Maybe he wasn't ready yet to reveal himself."

"Possibly. But without anything tying him to the actual murders, I'm very uneasy."

"I hear you."

"Take the Warren Cruz murder for example. Play that out for me. How could that have happened?"

Jalen paced around the room for a minute before turning back to her. "Malone gains entry to Cruz's home. Maybe he talked himself in or was able to break in so that it wasn't detected by those working the scene. The police arrive and work it like a straight up overdose."

"How does he get Cruz to take the pills?"

"Maybe he holds him at gunpoint. Gives him the choice—the pills or the gun, and Warren takes the pills."

"And where did the pills come from?"

Jalen went and picked up one of his notebooks. "I double checked that fact again first thing this morning. They were Warren's prescription sleeping pills."

"And how did Malone know that Warren had those meds."

"Malone goes in with the intent to kill Warren, but he wants to be discreet. Maybe he checks the medicine cabinet or Warren had the pills out in plain sight."

"But if Malone went there with the intent to kill, he had to have had a plan, right?"

"Could've been planning to shoot him until the pill option presented itself."

"That's possible." She let out a big sigh.

"I can tell you're still not fully buying it. Let's play out Richard's murder."

"The difference there is the cutting agent in the cocaine." A thought occurred to her. "Any evidence at all that the two of them knew each other?"

Jalen leaned against the table. "You're thinking that Malone comes over and offers coke to his friend? How does he get past the guard?"

"The guards Richard hired seemed fine enough, but if you really know what you're doing, I bet someone could've gotten around them."

"I would agree with that. We need to look at both men and see if there is any connection no matter how small. I'm going to have the analysts cross reference their phone records." He made the call while she stood staring at the board of photos in front of her.

What are we missing? She took a step closer and studied each photo. It made her wonder why, if her suspicions were correct, that Quinn would've had relationships with these guys. Quinn was an attractive, wealthy woman. Surely, she could've had her choice of men.

It was also possible that Quinn had been telling the truth, but that Malone had seen what he wanted to see because of his unhealthy fixation.

Jalen moved toward her. "They can run that cross reference, so we should know something soon if they ever called or texted each other."

"Good. If there is a connection there, that would help push this thing toward Malone."

"We have that appointment with Felipe Maxwell in a few. We should head over to his office." Jalen grabbed his keys off the table.

"On the way over, you can tell me what happened with Cody." They had to close the loop on the past men in Quinn's life.

Once they were in the car, Jalen glanced over at her from the driver's side. "Cody is living in California working in a startup tech company. He's been there the last five years. There's no way he could've killed the CEOs because he was in Europe for a work trip during the time they were murdered."

"At least we're able to eliminate him. Did you get anything from him about his relationship with Quinn?"

"Cody wasn't that chatty on the topic. Said they dated for almost a year, but most of it was long distance. Quinn was a workaholic but so was he, so that wasn't a problem. He said their relationship was very transactional—his words not mine.

They didn't get to know each other very well, and he felt Quinn was guarded with her feelings. Never really let him in."

"How did it end?"

"Just fizzled out. Nothing dramatic. The distance and their work schedules got in the way, and neither one of them was invested enough to make a big push." Jalen cleared his throat. "Quinn's almost forty and only two serious relationships. She's dating like a man."

"There isn't anything wrong with that."

"Didn't say there was."

Now was the time to tell Jalen what she had found out about Quinn's past. "I believe she has good reason to keep men at a distance. I discovered that her father was under investigation for child abuse and statutory rape. She'd told me he was abusive, but this is on a completely different level."

"What happened with the investigation?"

"He killed himself before they could put him on trial."

Jalen blew out a breath. "That's heavy stuff."

"Yeah. Tell me what you've dug up on Felipe?"

"He was her most recent boyfriend but that was still almost two years ago. Big banker. No real red flags that I could find."

"Good. I'll feel better once we close this off."

They arrived at the high rise in midtown and went in to be greeted by a receptionist at the main entrance. Then they got visitor badges and went up to the thirtieth floor where they were escorted into a conference room.

After waiting for a few minutes, the door opened and a tall, handsome man with curly dark hair and big brown eyes walked in. "Agents, I'm Felipe Maxwell." He offered his hand to each of them.

"I'm Supervisory Special Agent Haddad and this is Special Agent Smith."

"Please sit." Felipe unbuttoned his navy suit jacket before he sat. "I understand from my assistant that this meeting isn't about banking business, so I don't have my counsel present, but I just wanted to confirm that."

Once again, the FBI's presence made someone nervous. "No, this is a personal matter. It has nothing to do with the bank."

"How can I help you then?" Felipe asked.

Jalen leaned in. "We want to talk to you about your relationship with Quinn Kelly."

Felipe's dark eyes narrowed. "I must admit I didn't see that coming. What would you like to know? Is Quinn okay?"

"Quinn is fine, but we are investigating a case connected to her. She hasn't done anything wrong."

Felipe rubbed his chin. "Things ended with us about two years ago, I'd say."

"Who ended it?" Jalen asked.

"I did." Felipe blew out a breath. "It's a bit complicated."

"Relationships usually are," she said. "Why did you break it off?"

"Quinn's really a remarkable woman. Brilliant, probably the smartest person I've ever met, in fact. And of course, she's beautiful, radiant, and charming. But to be completely honest, I felt like I never really knew the real Quinn Kelly. She kept me at arm's length. I was nearing the point in my life where I wanted to settle down, and I couldn't see Quinn taking that next step."

"What do you mean?" Jalen asked.

"For instance, I kept trying to get her to meet my family because family is so important to me, and she always found an excuse. Cancelled at the last minute multiple times. And don't even get me started about her family. She would never talk about them. To this day, I'm not sure whether Quinn even has any family."

She shifted in her chair. "Did you stay in touch?"

"Not really. Initially after the breakup we spoke a couple of times. I wondered if I had been too hasty. I felt bad, but it was almost as if she was relieved it was over. I don't want to talk out of turn, but Quinn has some pretty big emotional issues.

Baggage that weighs her down even when she puts on this completely cool and put together exterior."

"Why do you say that?" she asked.

"Sometimes Quinn would pull back and retreat from me. Things were really stressful for her at work. I know she was seeing a therapist."

That got her attention. "Do you know whether male or female?"

"A woman."

That was probably a dead end then.

"Agents, what's going on here?"

It was time to tell him what they were really doing and check his alibis. They took a few minutes comparing dates and calendars and Felipe was out of town at a banking conference in New York for one of the murders and had solid alibis for the other dates, so he was ruled out as the killer.

"Is there anything else you can think of that might help us?" she asked.

Felipe ran his hand through his thick hair. "I don't think so, but based on what I know, this guy who is out there killing is probably not that close to Quinn even if he wants to be because she doesn't let anyone get that close."

"Thanks for your time." She stood.

"If you need anything else from me, don't hesitate to ask."

They exited the building and walked back to their car.

"That was interesting," Jalen said. "I know you aren't loving it, but everything keeps pointing to Malone. It makes the most sense."

"It does at a high level, but I'm just concerned about the details and..."

"And what?"

"That we're still looking for a serial killer."

38

After another long day in court, the last thing Quinn wanted to do was to deal with John again, but he said he had to talk to her. He'd actually missed the afternoon witnesses and another company representative had sat in his place. There had been a big meeting he couldn't miss—or at least that's what he told her.

"Are you sure you want me to let Mr. Rossi back in tonight?" Mateo, her FBI security detail asked her. She liked the guy. He'd been on duty on most of the night shifts, so he had figured out the situation.

"I don't really want him here, but he says he has to talk about the case, so I can't say no. I know you'll be right outside."

He stepped closer to her. "You don't have to put up with that kind of abuse. I can hear him yelling and throwing things."

"And I appreciate your concern. I feel safe knowing you're right outside."

Mateo gave her a small smile. "I don't know enough about how it works with lawyers, but if you can fire a client, I'd suggest you think long and hard about it. I've already far overstepped my place, so I won't say anything else. I'll let him in when he arrives and will be outside if you need me."

She gave his shoulder a friendly pat. "Thank you, Mateo."

There weren't many decent men out there, and her gut was telling her that Mateo was one of the few.

Heading inside her hotel room, she petted Felix who had grown to like his suite. But because John had become so volatile, she didn't trust him around Felix. She grabbed Felix up and put him in her bedroom with a fresh bowl of wet food to try to appease him. "There's a mean man coming here again, and I don't want him to hurt you." She closed the door and felt better that Felix was out of the line of fire.

She took a few minutes trying to get her head on straight. Running a brush through her hair, she looked at herself in the mirror. She didn't look her best. The dark circles under her eyes were more than likely stress induced. When was this nightmare going to be over?

Thankfully, she was good at compartmentalization, because when she allowed herself to think about the things Samira had told her about Tom Malone, it made her skin crawl. At least with John, she knew the threat existed. He was upfront and in her face. The things she most worried about were those things lurking in the night. Like Tom. Like what had happened to her as a child. A chill shot down her back and for a moment she thought she might get sick. The last thing she wanted was for John to see her falter. She'd put up with his antics far too long for that.

She sat on the couch and only waited a few minutes before John came in.

"We need to talk." He made a beeline to the bar.

"I figured that's why you're here. What's going on?"

"I had a board meeting this afternoon."

Her stomach clenched. "You didn't tell me that it was a board meeting."

"I didn't want to chance throwing you off your game in court, but it was a very eventful meeting. The board members watched your statement to Gemma yesterday, and while they commended you for your efforts, they are now worried about a PR fallout even worse than what we already have."

"What are you saying? Am I getting fired? Because I guarantee there's not a single lawyer in this city or elsewhere who could've handled that any better than I have."

He held up his hand. "Slow down. You're not getting fired. The board still loves you. The men all want you and the women want to be you."

Yeah right. "I don't understand."

John plopped down on the couch with his drink in hand. "The board wants to settle."

"Settle? After all of this?" She couldn't believe it. "I brought them settlement as an option at the outset before this got so ugly and they told me, as you will remember, in no uncertain terms that they would never settle this case. Ever!"

He pulled her down on the sofa beside him. She eased back an inch. "Even though you told them how bad it could be, it's different when it actually happens. They're willing to put big money on this to get it done."

"You realize their number will have gone up since the last settlement demand? Tasha's a very bright attorney. She has the leverage now and will exert that to get every dime."

"I get it, but the board has faith that you can negotiate a settlement. You make people believe lies all the time. Just make her believe that we're in a better position than what we are."

His words cut deep because they were so true. "What's the number?"

"I have authority for two hundred million for this class of plaintiffs."

"That might do it. But she will push for two fifty at least. I can make the call right now. Do I have authority to go to the judge to get a day off of trial to try to make this happen?"

"Basically, you can do whatever you need to do within that dollar amount and then come back to me if you need more money and I'll take it to the board."

"I can call her now."

"Good. I'd like to listen."

"Sure." She grabbed her cell and pushed Tasha's contact, putting it on speaker.

"This is Tasha."

"It's Quinn Kelly."

"Hi Quinn. What's going on?"

"My client is ready to restart settlement discussions, and I wanted to see if you would be amenable to that?"

Tasha laughed. "Wow. It's even worse than I thought."

"To the contrary. I believe the risks have been highlighted for both of us. Yes, you've got the emotion card, but I poked serious doubt into the cause of your client's condition, and you're smart enough to know I'm right."

There was silence for a moment. "Okay. What's your offer?"

"One eighty five."

"Too low."

"Then counter me."

"I need to think about that and confer with my clients."

"I suggest we go to the judge asking for a brief continuance and you and I meet tomorrow to try to figure this out."

"Let's meet at eight thirty in the morning and talk to the judge's clerk."

"See you then."

She ended the call and looked over at John.

He clapped. "Bravo. As usual."

She had mixed feelings about this settlement, but one thing she was crystal clear on was getting John out of her life for good.

39

Samira sat by herself at home going over everything that she and Jalen had discussed today. They were getting heat from their boss to close this case. When she had expressed her fear to him that Malone might not be the killer, he didn't take it well. But he trusted her enough to let them continue their work.

Her phone rang and her stomach dropped when she saw it was Quinn. Hopefully nothing was wrong.

"Quinn, what's going on?"

"Hey. Just wanted to let you know there's a good chance the case is going to settle. I'm meeting with opposing counsel tomorrow."

She was relieved it wasn't something bad but needed to understand where this came from. "Isn't this all out of the blue?"

"It's driven by my client and their fear of losing and continuing with some bad PR."

Samira quickly tried to think about how if she was right and the killer was still out there, how a settlement would impact him.

"Are you there?" Quinn asked.

"Yes. Sorry, I'm processing."

"You're still concerned that Tom wasn't the killer."

"Yes, and I don't know how this settlement news fits into everything."

"Believe me, I'd like to finish trying the case, but ultimately, it's not my call. The client gets to make that decision. There's always a chance that negotiations will fall apart tomorrow, but my client is highly motivated to get out of this one, so I follow their direction."

"Understood. I'm assuming you haven't had any other issues I need to know about?"

"None at all. If this does settle tomorrow, I'll be moving back home ASAP, and then we need to discuss whether I even need this security detail."

It was a strain on resources and with the stalker now dead, it would probably be hard to justify it, but if the killer was still out there, then Quinn could be at risk. "Let me think about how best to handle that. If Malone wasn't the killer, then we have to figure out how he will react to a settlement. John could still possibly be a target."

"I'll let you be the one to talk to him about that. I have to deal with him enough already."

"Don't worry. We'll handle John." She wanted to say something else. "I know you're probably bummed about this case not going to the jury, but maybe in the end, it's a good thing. You've had to deal with so much over the past few weeks."

"Yeah. I hate settlement in general. People bring me in when settlement isn't usually possible, but given all the circumstances here, I'll take an end to this, especially having to deal with John."

"Has he done something else that we need to talk about?"

"Nothing beyond his regular routine. I just continue rebuffing him."

"Do you want me to talk to him?"

"No way. That will just make it worse. Let's just see if I can settle this thing tomorrow and hopefully get him out of my life, at least for the time being. I'll keep you posted on how it goes tomorrow."

"Thanks. And if you need anything, just call."

"Will do."

Samira set down her phone and then saw a text from Jalen pop up. The analysts found no connection whatsoever between Richard and Malone. She sat up on the couch and took a few more deep breaths.

She had to assume right now that Malone wasn't the killer. If she put all that aside regarding the stalker and the obsession with Quinn, then they were back at square one with their initial theories. The question was whether any of those made sense. Could the killer be one of the impacted family members who has taken on vendetta? But then why spare Lew? Was it because the jury found his company responsible?

Could Quinn in fact have a stalker and there be a killer who was obsessed with her? The likelihood of that just didn't seem that high to her, but she couldn't rule it out.

And then there was that sinking feeling that she was in the dark about something big, but what could it be? She rubbed her temples to try to fend off the impending headache.

John Rossi was a womanizing, abusive man, but he couldn't be the killer because he had alibied out. Who else was there in Quinn's life? Was she keeping her relationship with someone secret? Maybe a relationship that she wasn't proud of?

She threw her head back and groaned, realizing she was grasping at straws. Why wouldn't she take Quinn at face value that there wasn't a man in her life? Because it didn't fit within the narrative she was desperately trying to create.

Maybe she was wrong. Maybe Malone had killed the CEOs and now that he was dead, the threat was gone. She'd sleep a lot better if she was certain of that. Until then, she was still on the hunt.

40

The next evening, a flurry of emotions were running through Quinn as she walked back into her house with Felix in his carrier. "We're home, buddy." She opened the carrier and Felix darted out. No doubt, happy to be back in his own kingdom.

She'd spent a good chunk of the day with Tasha, and unfortunately, John since he was the one holding the settlement authority. But it had ended up settling, and she had said goodbye to it all. Hoping for a quiet night, she took a deep breath.

The FBI security detail had been released—largely due to her insistence and to her promise to Samira that she wouldn't do anything reckless. With Tom gone, no one was going to try to hurt her unless John came back in the picture. She still had to figure out what to do about him. The case was over, and hopefully that would mean he would leave her alone, but she had this feeling that he wouldn't be able to let her go because he wasn't the type of man to lose out on a conquest.

John would probably be looking over his shoulder at least for the next few days because the FBI had told him point blank that they couldn't guarantee that he was in the clear given all the unknowns about the investigation.

When her cell rang, she dreaded looking to see who it was. When she saw, she was shocked. "Felipe?"

"Quinn, how are you?"

"I'm okay. I have to admit, I'm surprised to hear from you. Is everything all right?"

"That's what I should be asking you."

"What do you mean?"

"The FBI showed up at my office yesterday."

Uh oh. "What did they want?"

"They were asking a lot of questions about our relationship. About you. And they were making sure I wasn't some killer they were looking for. Quinn, are you in trouble?"

Felipe didn't know all her secrets—no one did. But he knew more than most. "I'm not sure what they all told you."

"Not much."

"I had a stalker. He's dead now."

"What?"

"He tried to shoot me, and I killed him in self-defense."

Felipe let out a low whistle. "How does that fit in with this killer they're looking for?"

"Basically they are trying to figure out if they are one in the same. If not, then there's still a killer on the loose."

"Quinn, this sounds extremely dangerous."

"The killer hasn't targeted me. He seems focused on my clients."

"Still. Is there anything I can do to help?"

She thought for a minute and in her time of weakness, considered inviting him over to blow off some steam. But ultimately, that wouldn't be good for her. "I don't think so."

"Well too bad. I'm outside in your driveway."

"What?"

"Will you let me in?"

"Of course. Give me a second." She hung up and ran upstairs

to survey how she looked. Not her best, but there was nothing she could do about that. She reapplied some lipstick and mascara and then ran back downstairs to open up the door.

When she saw Felipe, it all came flooding back to her. Why she had pushed him away. Because she had been afraid of actually falling in love with him and that's something she couldn't allow to happen.

"Quinn." He walked through the door and grabbed onto her hands. "I feel so much better just seeing you. Those agents had me really worried."

She gave his hands a squeeze before taking a step back. "Let's sit." They walked into the living room.

She sat down beside him on the couch, but not too close.

His eyes met hers. "Tell me what's really going on here. I know there's more to this than what the FBI was telling me."

"I wish I knew. We just settled a case today, and it's been a hellacious few weeks."

"What's the deal with this stalker you had?"

"It was actually a guy I went to law school with. I don't remember him at all, but I guess he developed some obsession with me. My face is on social media all the time. If you want to find content with me, it's there."

"Yeah, he had to seek you out. That's creepy. Have you talked to someone about what you had to do to save yourself?"

"I've got an appointment to see Dr. Lane."

"The FBI actually asked me about whether you had a male or female therapist."

That was odd. Then it hit her. "They were trying to figure out if my therapist could be a suspect. But they believe a man is behind all of this. No way Dr. Lane is involved."

"Are you seeing anyone?" he asked softly.

She hadn't been expecting that question. "No. Honestly, I haven't been in a relationship since we broke up. Easier that way."

He took her hand. "Quinn, you don't have to live your life

like that. I know you've been through a lot. You only told me a small amount about your childhood, and it was enough for me to understand that you suffered trauma. You're in a different place now and you shouldn't just push everyone away. There are good guys out there. I promise."

"Like you."

"And yet, you also pushed me away. It's why I ended things, remember?"

Like it was yesterday. "Yes. You're no doubt better off without me. I'm sure you've found a less damaged woman."

He raised an eyebrow. "I've dated, but I definitely haven't found anyone that even begins to compare with you. I have to admit, I hate the circumstances, but I'm glad I had an excuse to reach back out to you."

She lifted up her hand. "Don't get the wrong idea, Felipe. I'm the same messed up woman you were with before. Nothing has changed." If anything, she was even more damaged now.

"Don't go running away. I'm not asking for anything but a little bit of your time and company tonight." He brought her hand to his mouth and placed a gentle kiss on it.

She'd dared to dream that things could be different with Felipe, but her demons always found a way of overtaking her. "I can handle that."

"Does the FBI think you are in danger?"

"Not really. I had a security detail but once the stalker was out of the picture, I told them I'd had enough. I had to stay in a hotel for a bit because he threw a brick through my window."

Felipe picked up his glass. "I'm glad he can never hurt you again."

"Me too. That self-defense and firearms training probably saved my life." A chill shot down her back thinking about what would've happened if she hadn't been armed. Would Tom have killed her? She felt certain the answer was yes.

"I remember how dedicated you were to your training."

"And you thought I was being a bit paranoid."

"You ended up being right, and I'm so glad you didn't listen to me."

Felipe had said he would protect her, but she knew better. She needed to be able to defend herself no matter what. "Enough about all of this stuff. What's new with you?"

"I was promoted again."

"Congratulations. I have no doubt that you might even become CEO one day at the rate you're going."

"It's even longer hours than it used to be, but I'm married to my job."

"I'm all too familiar with that concept."

"I recognize this isn't the best time given all you've gone through, but would you consider letting me take you to dinner again sometime. I really do think we have something special, and we're both hyper focused on work, and we never judged each other because of it. I want to make sure we're not missing out because I was an idiot and broke up with you."

"As I said before, I haven't changed. The commitments you ultimately want from me, I don't think I'm able to give."

"Would you at least consider dinner? I'm not asking for a life-time commitment right now."

"But isn't that what you ultimately want?" She knew he did. They had talked about it.

"Yes, but I haven't exactly been successful in that pursuit with anyone. What if I was too hasty pushing you away because you were doing the same thing to me. All I'm asking is that you think about it."

Her doorbell rang.

"Were you expecting anyone?" Felipe asked.

"No. But I have a bad feeling it's my client."

His eyes narrowed. "At this hour?"

"John's a disaster. I'm going to send him away."

She walked to the door and noticed that Felipe wasn't far behind.

Opening the door, John stood on the other side. His eyes

widened when he saw Felipe. "Ah. I see you're otherwise engaged."

"Yes. What is it, John?"

He stepped by her into her home. "I just wanted to regroup."

She turned to face him. "There's nothing to regroup about. The case is over, the settlement documents were executed about an hour ago.

John's face started to redden. "But I do have questions about the settlement."

"Nothing that is pressing."

"There are payment terms to discuss."

"All of that can wait until tomorrow."

John's nostrils flared. "I don't think it can."

Felipe cleared his throat. "Man, she said you could talk tomorrow. You need to leave. Now."

John ignored Felipe and looked at her. "Is he the reason you kept turning me down? Because you were screwing him?"

"Wait a minute." Felipe stepped in between her and John. "Don't speak to her like that."

The two men stood facing off and neither giving an inch. The last thing she wanted or needed was a physical altercation between the two of them. "Enough. John, please leave. If there's any legitimate legal matter we need to discuss, it can wait until tomorrow."

John stood his ground a moment before turning around. He muttered foul things about her as he slammed the door on his way out.

Felipe turned to her. "You seriously need new clients."

"Tell me about it. Now that the case has settled, I shouldn't have to deal with him as much. I'm actually hoping they don't hire me again."

He pulled her into his arms, taking her off guard. She thought about pushing him away, but especially after dealing with John again, it felt too nice and comforting. She was making a mistake, but John had pushed her to the brink.

Taking a moment, she just enjoyed having his strong arms wrapped around her. As good as Felipe felt in her arms, she knew it was just fleeting. She was too damaged to have a healthy relationship with him or anyone else. "You should probably go."

He pulled back. "Are you sure?"

"Yeah. It's getting late, and I can't give you what you need."

Felipe squeezed her hands. "Call me if you need anything, Quinn."

She watched as he walked out of her life again.

41

Quinn woke up and had tried to put Felipe out of her mind. She had needed him last night for a lot of different reasons, but nothing had really changed. It hadn't worked out between them before, and sadly, it wasn't going to work now.

She had decided to work from home today, and now in the middle of a Friday afternoon, her decision seemed wise. Given the stress of the past few weeks, she didn't need to be in the office today.

She still had to figure out what to do about John. She hadn't expected him to show up last night. But she had to be careful. Given what had happened to Tom, she had no choice. She really couldn't afford to have a situation like that to happen again. She understood that and would have to keep her emotions in check about John even if he was a complete weasel of a man.

How was she going to get John off her back?

What did he really want from her? Why was he so persistent? Could it really be a macho male ego thing? That would be really pathetic if it was the case. Maybe she was missing something. Whatever it was, she had to bring it to a stop. And quickly. She needed to move on, work her cases, and reach her goals.

The settlement had thrown a wrench in everything. She hadn't really dealt with a situation exactly like this before and was still trying to work through what the right move was.

The FBI would probably be on the lookout to try to protect John, in case they are wrong about Tom's involvement in the CEO killings.

Maybe if John thought the FBI was going to be monitoring him, he would give her a little space. She would at least put that idea in his mind. She clearly didn't see any agents last night when he'd rudely come over uninvited. She needed to check with Samira to see what they were doing with him. Felix jumped on her lap. She moved her computer to give him a moment of attention. She thought back to last night with Felipe. She wished that she could entertain the thought of having him in her life on a more permanent basis, but she was no fool, and knew that would never work.

He simply wanted things she couldn't give him. She'd made the decision a long time ago that she would probably be alone the rest of her life. And she'd come to accept that. She rubbed Felix's ears as she thought about her dilemma.

Her productivity level hadn't been that high today, mainly dealing with her emails that had stacked up because of the trial. That was fine, she deserved a little bit of a breather.

She closed her eyes for a moment to try to decompress. The next thing she knew, she was awakened by a noise. She couldn't believe she'd fallen asleep. It was late and now dark outside.

Hearing Felix hiss loudly, she jumped up from the couch and that's when she saw him. John had broken into her house.

"John, what are you doing here? Have you lost your mind?"

"You wouldn't answer my calls or your door, but I knew you were in here." He moved closer to her, the smell of whiskey undeniable on his breath.

"So you break into my house? That's not acceptable behavior, John, even for you. You've gone too far this time." She put on a brave face, but she didn't have her gun. It was upstairs, and even with her training, his strength would prove too much in hand to hand if it came to that.

He quickly closed the space between them and grabbed onto her wrists hard. "I got fired today because of you."

Her stomach clenched. John was out for blood. "You can't blame that on me."

"Can't I? The Board didn't like the settlement and the only reason we had to do it was because of your idiotic idea to bring up that woman's abortion."

She broke free from him and took a step back. "You would've made the exact same call. It was the only play we had. We were losing."

His face reddened. "You didn't do your job. And because of that, I'm out."

"I'm sorry, but there's nothing I can do about that."

"Another point on which we disagree." He grabbed her tightly by the arms. "Why won't you just admit that you want me."

"Because that would be a lie. I detest you."

"You know I have the upper hand here." His nostrils flared.

"What is your plan then? To take me by force? Then what happens when I report you to the police and you get arrested?"

John laughed. "You would never do that. You'd be too humiliated, and no one would believe you with your track record of sleeping with clients."

She gritted her teeth. How could she handle this? Could she try to de-escalate and hope for a chance to gain back some control? "First of all, I don't sleep with clients, not that it's any of your business. Why don't we just take a step back and act like rational adults."

"That's rich coming from you. Don't you think I know how messed up you are?"

"You don't really know anything about me."

He raised an eyebrow. "Don't I?" He refused to let her go.

She had to come up with a plan, and fast. "Okay, what do you want from me?"

He pulled her up against him. "I think that's obvious. You screwed me over. Now it's my turn."

She'd lived through rape and assault before when she was young. More times than she wanted to remember. Standing there now, locked in his arms, she knew no amount of self-defense training was going to be able to stop him. He outweighed her by a good seventy-five pounds and was much stronger. Without her gun, there was only so much she could do. "I'm telling you no."

He picked her up, and she started kicking and thrashing.

"The more you fight me, the more I'm going to enjoy this."

She feared he was right, and she had to enter into survival mode. The most important thing now was staying alive. There was far too much left to accomplish in her life, and she couldn't let him kill her. He was in such a drunken rage, she feared he might do it. She could delay the inevitable, but there was no way she could stop him.

He threw her down hard onto the floor, and she tasted blood in her mouth. A vivid reminder that she was still alive. Survival. It was all that mattered. Her body may be ravaged as it had been before, but he could not steal her soul. She refused to let him.

John held her down. His body heavy against hers. The smell of his pungent cologne brought on a wave of nausea. When she had been raped as a girl, she'd closed her eyes. But right now, for a moment, she stared directly into John's dark eyes, feeling like she was peering into the gates of hell. His rage and complete hatred of her were on full display.

As the assault continued, she struggled against him, and ended up in a very dark place trying to block it all out just like she did when she was a young girl. No longer wanting to gaze into the eyes of the devil. Fresh tears rolled down her cheeks.

She recreated the melodic tune from the music box ballerina and tried to focus only on that. Not on the monster forcing himself on her. Each note was a continuing reminder that she was still alive. That she had faced this horror many times before and had gotten back up to fight another day.

One thought drove her through the horror of it all. To survive. Because then she could get revenge.

42

The next evening, Quinn stared at herself in the mirror and tried to shut out the horror from last night that was so fresh in her mind. She wanted to believe it had been a haunting nightmare, but it had been all too real. She'd thought about going to the police, but she had another plan. One that would protect her from having to relive the pain ever again.

Now she had to execute on it. And in her mind, there was no time to waste so she'd spent the day in meticulous preparation. This was her opportunity to make things right. She'd been on the fence before given how things had gone with her case, but now there was no doubt in her mind what she needed to do.

When she arrived at John's house, she took a deep breath and rang the doorbell. Thankfully, there was no security presence. They'd been called off after he'd gotten fired. A fact she'd learned last night from his own lips.

When John opened the door, his eyes widened. "What're you doing here?"

"Aren't you going to invite me in?"

He looked for a moment like he might slam the door in her face, but he stepped aside, and she walked in.

She could do this. She had to do this. "No big plans on a Saturday night?"

He raised an eyebrow. "Are you asking me out?"

She smiled. "No." She was careful to keep space between them.

He reached for her, but she took a large step back.

"I have to admit, I didn't think I'd be seeing you again so soon."

"What you did last night was wrong." That simple fact had to be stated.

John groaned. "C'mon. Don't act like it was that big of a deal. You liked it rough."

She couldn't even listen to his sickening words any longer.

He looked down. "And why are you wearing gloves? It's eighty degrees outside."

She pulled the stun gun out of her jacket pocket and before he could react, she had him writhing on the floor. One more zap and he was unconscious. Now her work would really begin, and she wouldn't have long before he regained consciousness.

There was so much she wanted to do to him. Pain she wanted to inflict, but now wasn't the time to lose control. She had way too much on the line and as much as she wanted him to feel as violated as she had felt, it just wasn't going to be possible. She'd come to terms with her decision today as difficult as it was.

Working quickly, she pulled his body onto the couch, sitting him upright, and binding his hands behind him carefully, so as to not leave any marks. He felt even heavier than he looked, but adrenaline rushed through her body, and she was more than able to get the job done.

She'd brought her gun, just in case, because there's no way she was going to let him touch her again. But shooting him wasn't the plan. Pulling the bottle out of her purse and the syringe, she filled it with liquid. Not wasting any time, she opened his mouth and shot the liquid down his throat. He started to cough as his eyes fluttered open. But he'd swallowed the liquid just as she had planned.

That's when she saw the amazing look in his eyes. It was the one she'd been waiting for. The look of fear.

He started to squirm, and it hit him that his hands were tied up. "Quinn, what was that? Did you roofie me?"

She couldn't help but laugh at the thought. Of course that's where his mind would go.

"Why are you laughing? This isn't funny. Let me go."

"How does it feel to be powerless, John?" How many women had he made feel that exact same way—including her. There was no doubt in her mind that John had raped countless other women in his life. Sadly, she had not been his first.

John's nostrils flared. "I can't believe you think that what you're doing to me now is anything like what happened between us last night."

"There was no *us*. There was you, forcing yourself on me."

"You know you wanted it. You always have since the first day we met."

"I didn't and I was very clear about that."

"What are you going to do to me now?" His voice cracked.

She took a steadying breath, knowing there was no turning back. "Kill you."

Now John laughed. "That's a good one, Quinn. You threatened me with a gun before, but I knew you wouldn't ever use it then and you're certainly not going to use it now."

"I didn't say I was going to shoot you. You're going to die of an Oxy overdose. That's the concoction I just shot down your throat in liquid form. Enough to kill a man twice your size because I wasn't taking any chances."

His eyes widened and he started to flop back and forth on the couch like a fish out of water.

"You're only going to make it worse doing that."

He shook his head in denial. "I don't believe you. You're just trying to get back at me. You don't have it in you to kill anyone."

"I killed Tom Malone."

John rolled his eyes. "That was in self-defense."

"And isn't this too?"

"No. It's murder!" His face reddened. "You're a lawyer. You know that."

She could no longer hold back a smile. "You're right. I do."

Tears started to well up in his eyes. What a pathetic excuse for a man. He was a coward.

"You're serious, aren't you? You're psychotic. Let me go. Call 911. You still have time. Do the right thing."

"Like all the right things you've done in your life? No. You deserve this. Justice is going to be served here tonight."

"Justice? I'm innocent," he hissed.

"You're not or I wouldn't be doing this. I don't kill innocent people."

He looked down and back up. Then his dark eyes grew large. "It's you," he whispered.

"What are you talking about?"

The color faded from his cheeks. "You're the one who has been killing those CEOs. You win their cases, but then you kill them. You are messed up beyond belief."

He was the one who was messed up. Not her. "Some would say that I'm just balancing the scales of justice."

"I can't believe this. You will be caught."

"I doubt that. I'm not an amateur."

"How many people have you killed?" his voice cracked.

"Enough."

"Please. Don't do this. Call for an ambulance."

She flashed back to last night. The horror of his body on top of hers. How he violated her. The pain he inflicted again and again. "Remember when I begged you to stop, and you didn't? Why should I stop now?"

He struggled but couldn't break free.

"I know I'm not your first. How many other innocent women have you raped?"

His dark eyes narrowed. "More than I can count."

"I only wish I could've made your death more painful, but at the end of the day, you'll still be dead, and that's just going to have to do." It took everything she had not to hurt him but that was way too far outside the killer's MO. Her MO. And deviations could get her caught.

John made one more effort to get off the couch, but getting woozy, he fell back down onto it. He was no longer a threat, so she removed the bindings from his wrists.

She leaned down close to him and whispered in his ear. "I'm going to be here until you take your final, pathetic breath, because I want my face to be the last thing you see. If only you would've just left me alone. You brought this upon yourself."

"I never imagined that you could've been the killer."

"That's a fact I'm banking on."

43

Late Monday morning, Samira and Jalen walked into John Rossi's home in Buckhead.

She walked over to Atlanta detective Perez. "What do we know?" She pulled on her gloves.

He ran his hand through his thick dark hair. "The housekeeper found him this morning when she arrived. She thought he was asleep having passed out on the couch, but when she tried to rouse him, she realized he was dead. She freaked out and immediately called 911. When I got word of this, I feared the worst. The CEO killer has struck again."

Samira nodded. "Looks that way."

Perez's brown eyes narrowed. "I was hoping that this case would end with Malone."

"Us too," Jalen responded.

They walked over to the body.

Jalen nudged her arm. "You were right about Malone."

She got no joy in that fact. "I wish I wouldn't have been because then John Rossi would still be alive. I don't know why he would have called off his security." John was a proud, egotistical man, and it may have cost him his life.

"We still have to rule out suicide or an accidental OD, but we both know where this will most likely lead."

"His case ended in settlement, not a victory."

Jalen moved back from the body so the ME and her team could work. "Maybe the killer is shifting. Or he considered a settlement close enough to a victory to act."

"I dread making another phone call to Quinn. Although I imagine that she won't take this death nearly as hard as she took Richard's." Although a murder was still a murder, and it wouldn't be good for her that another one of her clients had been killed, she knew that Quinn didn't like John at all.

"Let's look around," Jalen said.

They did a walk-through of John's expansive home. He lived alone, and there were some aspects of the place that did scream bachelor pad even though other areas seemed more sophisticated.

"No sign of forced entry," Jalen said.

"That seems to be a theme."

They combed through his place and ended back up in the living room. Samira squatted down and pulled a strand of red hair off the carpet and placed it into an evidence bag. "Guess we know who this belongs to. We'll have to ask Quinn when the last time she was over here."

"I'll add that to our list of follow up. You know the bigwigs aren't going to be happy that we aren't able to close this case. Hopefully Quinn doesn't have another trial anytime soon."

"I hear you, but even if she doesn't, I still worry. He's killed a lot lately. He's hot. I don't know that he will have the necessary discipline to go into sleeper mode until Quinn has another case go to trial."

Jalen touched her arm. "We should stop by Quinn's office, and discuss bringing back her security detail. If you're right that the killer is in the hot zone, at some point, he may fully snap and go after Quinn."

"Agreed. And we can't let that happen. There have already

been way too many lives taken by this guy. I don't know what his end game is, and I really don't want to find out. We have to find a way to stop him."

"Maybe Quinn will be the key to that."

"If we make her untouchable, then who would be his target? That's what we have to determine, because this guy's going to be looking for a fresh kill far too soon."

44

Quinn watched as somber faced Samira and Jalen walked into her office. "What's happened now?"

"I'm sorry to inform you that John Rossi is dead." Jalen's brown eyes locked onto her.

She sucked in a deliberate breath. "How?"

"A drug overdose, but we believe it's the work of the killer," Samira responded.

"So now you don't think Tom murdered my clients?" Of course, she'd known that the entire time.

Samira tucked a strand of dark hair behind her ear. "No, we don't, but that also means that we are now very concerned about your safety."

"Why do you think that?"

"Because this guy might be running out of targets, and you could be his ultimate one," Samira said.

Now that John could no longer hurt her, she wasn't afraid, but she was prepared for this new security push. She had to put on a good show here. "What's going to happen to me?"

Jalen cleared his throat. "We're going to put your security detail back on and increase it to a two-person team."

"Do you think that's overkill?"

Samira shook her head. "Unfortunately, not. I believe you could be in real danger, and given what has transpired, we can't take any chances. If John hadn't called off his private security, there's a good chance he'd still be alive."

That told her that they didn't know yet that John had been fired and his security pulled by the company. "I'll do whatever you think is best. I thought this nightmare might be over, but I guess I was wrong."

"I know you're frustrated," Samira said. "We are too, but if we're right, the killer could be coming to his final target."

They believed that target was her.

Jalen leaned in. "What's your trial schedule like?"

"My next trial is over two months away."

Samira frowned.

"Why is that a bad thing?"

Samira crossed her arms. "Because I'm worried that the killer won't be able to slow down now. He's going to need a new target, and if there isn't one related to your lawsuits, I'm not sure what his next move will be. Hence, the need to protect you."

She didn't think they were playing her. They really didn't have a clue, and she had to keep it that way. "Like I said, I'll accept the help. I would prefer to stay home though."

"That won't be an issue." Jalen jotted down something in his notepad. "We'll have the security stationed at your house."

"Will they be with me wherever I go?" Best to set the ground rules.

"That's the way I would prefer it. Especially right now." Samira's expression was grim. "I don't think we can overstate the threat level to you personally."

They really were concerned. She hadn't seen the two of them this on edge and had to make sure their efforts stayed focused on their current track and not on her. "Well, I don't do that much besides come to the office and run random errands."

"Your security detail will be able to accommodate whatever you need," Jalen said.

Samira lifted up her hand. "Within reason. Now isn't the time to take unnecessary risks, but we realize you have to keep living your life."

"Understood."

Jalen's cell rang and he excused himself from the room.

Samira's dark eyes softened. "I know you're conflicted about John."

"You're right. He was not a good person, but I don't think it's sunk in that I'll never see him again." But it would.

"When was the last time you were at his house?"

They must have found evidence of her being there. Thankfully she had planned for this and had taken it into account. "Saturday afternoon. I had to drop off some paperwork for him. He was in a really foul mood." She'd driven to his place Saturday and done some recon for door and surveillance cams, plus if anyone checked her GPS they would see when she had been there. She had to cover her tracks.

"I'm assuming that's the last time you saw him."

"He also came over to my place Friday night to hassle me."

Samira raised an eyebrow. "Is there anything we should know about that?"

She shook her head. "No. Just John being John. He didn't stay too long. He wasn't quite sure what to think about the settlement. Ultimately, it had been the Board of Director's call and not his."

"Did he mention anything about why he decided not to use security anymore?"

She knew exactly what had happened. "No, but if I had to guess, I'd say that he thought he was untouchable. Men like him don't ever really think they're in danger."

"He was wrong, and it cost him his life."

Quinn hung her head, fighting to keep up the emotional wall. It would have been so freeing to tell Samira what that monster had done to her, and how she'd gotten revenge, but she still had so much important work to do that she couldn't afford to take that risk. But the temptation to open up was almost overwhelming. She gritted her teeth.

"Look, his death isn't on you, Quinn."

"I appreciate you saying that. And at the risk of sounding selfish, at some point, no one is going to want to be my client. They'll be afraid of what will happen to them and rightfully so, I guess." That much was true, which was another reason why after she killed John, she'd been thinking about adapting her game plan.

"That isn't selfish. You've worked too hard in your career to be sidetracked by this guy. I know I've asked you a million times, but is there anything or anyone else you can think of that could be involved in this."

Quinn wanted to choose her words carefully. It would've been ideal if she could've had a fall guy. Tom Malone had taken any heat off of her for a while, but now that it was clear that he wasn't the real killer, she had to think about whether there was anyone else that she could point them to. A little wild goose chase would do her some good. The problem was that she was still trying to figure out if there was anyone she could give up, if nothing else, to buy more time and get them off track. "Not right now, but I'm going to give it some more thought. I'll review my old case files and look back at my notes. I know it's a long shot, but I want to help any way I can."

"I'd appreciate that. For what it's worth, we did speak to Felipe and Cody, and they both had solid alibis."

She feigned a sigh of relief. "They are good men. Sometimes things just don't work out, you know? I'm soon going on forty, and I am not seeing a place in my life for a man. I realize you know all this stuff about me, and I don't know anything about your life. Are you married? I don't see a ring, but given your work, I could understand if you didn't wear one." The answer was no, but she wanted to hear it. To try to get further into Samira's head.

Samira's shoulders slumped. "No. I'm focusing on my career right now."

There were waves of sadness coming off Samira. This was about more than her career. "I find it hard to trust men given all that I've been through in my life."

Samira made eye contact. "Quinn, I find it hard to trust anyone."

"Who hurt you to make you feel that way?" She was trying to break down any walls.

Samira sighed. "Far too many people." She paused. "We'll be in touch about your security. They'll be here to escort you home today. No taking chances."

"Thank you."

Samira stood. "And I have to say it because of what happened with Tom Malone. Don't go rogue on us. Let us do the investigating, Quinn. If you think of anything, no matter how insignificant, it's not something you should be running down. It's for us to do that. Am I clear?"

"Crystal. I promise."

"Good. I'll check in with you later."

Samira left her office and she let out a breath. She kicked herself for not planning for a better fall guy option in all of this. The stalker had really thrown her off, and then she hadn't counted on having to deal with John.

She closed her eyes for a moment and tried to block out what he had done to her. She hated herself for not taking him seriously enough. Yes, she had underestimated him and had paid the consequences. That was a lesson she would always carry with her. Just one more emotional scar that she didn't need.

His death had shown her something important though. The feeling of killing him had been different from the other CEOs. In her mind, the others definitely deserved to die. She had given each and every one of them the chance to fess up, and make things right, but none of them had been strong enough to accept it. When she had killed them, it was something that needed to be done.

Russell Myers was her first CEO victim and killing him had almost been too easy. He was more than eager to take the cocaine from her that unbeknownst to him was laced with fentanyl. The same cocaine she used to kill Richard. It had been risky to secure the cocaine in the first place, as she had driven out of state and then kept it in one of her safe deposit boxes. But it had been well worth it, killing two birds with the same stone. And now there was no evidence of it ever existing. She wasn't sure when he would actually use the coke, but within a week of her giving it to him, he was dead. Which also ended up taking any possible heat off of her.

As far as Cruz went, it was easy to use his own sleeping pills against him. And then she took the Oxy from Richard's place to use on John. Richard's bathroom had been a treasure trove of drugs, but she had remained disciplined and only taken the Oxy.

She had no regrets about the four CEOs. Working at a big firm had been a necessity for her, but she quickly learned that the concepts of justice she'd learned in law school and had been so passionate about were nothing but a mirage. If a company had a good enough lawyer, and the adequate resources, they could win the majority of cases where they should've been held liable. This sickened her. Even more so when she realized her part in propping up the system. That's what had jumpstarted her into action. To make sure that justice really was served.

It wasn't that hard to kill the CEOs because they weren't the first men she had killed. But now, she felt that her purpose needed to circle back to where she started. She wasn't born a killer. Her father and those men he let ravage her had made her into one.

She cursed and picked up her office phone to call Allie. What she wouldn't do is let John impact her in death the same way he had done in life. She asked Allie to come down and after a moment she arrived.

"What do you need?" Allie asked.

"I have to share some news with you. Have a seat."

"Is everything okay?"

"John Rossi is dead."

Allie's blue eyes widened. "What? How?"

"The FBI is investigating it as a murder."

"Wow. This guy is coming after all your clients. Who is next? You? Have they told you that?"

"There is concern on the FBI's part, yes."

"But I thought the stalker was the killer."

"It appears that might not be the case unless John killed himself."

Allie huffed. "That's highly unlikely. What is the FBI doing to protect you?"

"They're providing me security, and until this gets resolved, I want you to keep your head down and focus on the Murray case. That will be your chance to first chair and even though the trial is three months away, I want you to start your trial prep. Let me worry about this mess."

Allie bit her bottom lip. "I'm worried about you."

She grabbed Allie's hand. "I will be fine."

"I hope that's a promise you can keep."

45

The next morning, Samira and Jalen walked into Horizon Pharma for their meeting with Eric Chang, the chair of the board of directors. Samira wanted to talk to him about what had happened to John.

They were escorted up to a large corner office on the top floor of the building and greeted by Eric. The short, slender man with dark hair and sporting a trendy, designer suit greeted them warmly.

"Agents, I have to say I'm still in shock about what happened to John. I can't help but feel I'm partially responsible."

"Why would you say that, Mr. Chang?" Jalen asked.

Eric hung his head. "The Board made the decision to fire John after we were forced to settle this lawsuit over our IUDs. I guess it might have just sent John over the edge. I never would've imagined him for one who could've taken his own life."

Now she got his point. "I agree with you. We don't believe this was death by suicide."

Eric's eyes widened. "What?"

"We believe he was targeted and killed by the same serial killer who has murdered other powerful CEOs."

"Wow." Eric blew out a breath. "I just assumed when I heard

how he was found, that it was suicide. I knew he had security for a time, but after the firing we pulled his security."

"It's not your fault," she said. Although having security there could have possibly saved his life, it hadn't saved Richard's.

Eric took a step and stared out the window. "I didn't sleep last night with the weight of this on me. But murder? I guess I should've allowed the security to continue."

"I'm sorry that this has happened, but none of this is your fault. Do you know how many people knew about John being fired?"

"Just the Board. We were going to keep it quiet for a bit to try to give him time to find another position. I guess John could've told others, but I can't see that being something he would advertise. John was a very proud man."

She agreed with that. John would've been too embarrassed. He would've also been angry.

"Mr. Chang, if there's anything you could think of that you believe might be helpful to our investigation, we'd really like to know it." They were desperate for any leads.

"I'm really at a loss."

"How well did you know John?" Jalen asked.

"We worked very closely together but there wasn't a lot of sharing about our personal lives. I can say that about most of my working relationships—they are just that. Focused on work, but from the personal standpoint, I do know he wasn't married and was very popular with women."

"Is that because he told you that?" she asked.

"He didn't have to. When we would go out to social events, women were always hitting on him. He had no intention of ever settling down from what I could tell. My wife didn't like me spending much time with him because she claims he was a bad influence."

Smart woman. "I take it John didn't say anything to you about any threats or feeling like he was being followed or anything like that."

Eric shook his head. "Not a word. And frankly, he didn't act the least bit concerned. All John was focused on was his professional future."

This was a dead end. "We appreciate your time. If you do think of anything, please let us know."

"Of course." He escorted them to the elevator bay, and they said their goodbyes.

Once they were back in the car, Jalen looked over at her. "I guess all we learned from that meeting was that John was fired, but I have a hard time seeing how that's connected to the killing."

"Yeah. I had the same thought. Guess John was too embarrassed to tell Quinn because she didn't mention anything about that."

"Well, we knew he had an overinflated ego."

"Guy gets fired and killed within a matter of days."

"Tough break."

Jalen started the car. "I get the sense your sympathy level isn't that high."

"He wasn't a good man, but we still have to find out who killed him and the others." Her text message chimed, and she looked down at her phone. "It's the tox screen results. It was Oxy that killed him. Straight up Oxy and a lot of it."

"I guess that also means we have to keep the suicide possibility on the table."

"Yeah, but I'm still not buying it."

She had to tell him something else he didn't want to hear. "I got chewed out by Myron and Strickland early this morning."

"And you're just now telling me about it?"

"Wouldn't change anything." She took a breath. "They are *this* close to pulling us off the case. If we don't get answers soon, they'll have no choice but to shake things up."

Jalen groaned. "Sounds like a threat to me, and you know I don't deal well with those."

"We don't really have much of a choice. He's right. We

haven't produced any results. We need to go back to square one."

"Don't make any assumptions. Basically, a fresh case."

Something had been on her mind. "I have an idea."

"Shoot."

"We've been operating around the assumption that our killer is male and is fixated on Quinn. We started down that road given the strong connection to the stalker, who we eventually found out was Malone. But as we initially discussed, the MO is consistent with how a woman would kill. What if there's a woman out there who is obsessed with Quinn, and she's the one doing the killing?"

Jalen let out a whistle. "We have to look at our profile and reconsider the possibility of a female and see where that takes us."

"What if Quinn's picked up a female admirer who took things too far?"

"Let's run with it. At this point, we don't have anything to lose."

<h1 style="text-align:center">46</h1>

That evening Quinn sat on her couch with Felix curled up in her lap. She'd called and made an appointment to see Dr. Lane. It had been months since their last session but after what John had put her through, she needed to clear her head, and while she couldn't be completely honest, Dr. Lane knew her history of abuse and it would be good to speak with her to make sure she could move on from all of this.

She sipped on her chamomile tea and thought about her next move. Now was a critical time, and she couldn't afford to make any mistakes. She had two FBI agents standing guard outside of her house. If they only knew that the true threat was inside, but she wouldn't ever harm them. That wasn't how she operated.

What she needed to do was to make sure her plan was airtight. John had been a deviation. Something she'd never done before, but sometimes adjustments had to be made and he was one of them. When she decided to take on this mission, she had drawn up the rules in her mind in the same way she'd draw up a contract. First and foremost, for her to take action, the men had to be guilty. Beyond that, she had made the decision that she wouldn't kill those in any of the cases she lost because she wanted them to have to pay the price for their actions in the way that the judge and jury had determined. Her role, as she saw it, was to bring about justice when injustice had occurred.

Granted, John's kill had nothing to do with the settlement. It was an act of revenge pure and simple, and she wasn't going to lie to herself about that. She could rationalize the move and fit it into her operating framework, but there was no point. Killing him had been one of the most fulfilling things she'd done in her life. He had deserved to suffer more, but she couldn't have it all.

More than I can count. John's words still rang in her head. She wondered just how many other women John had raped and assaulted. At least he could never hurt anyone else again.

Now the question was whether that move on her part had caused any suspicion to be directed at her. She hoped not. But she wondered at some point if they would start to put things together. That meant she needed to lay low and not act again until the heat was off of her. At least she had a breather from trials which would make things a bit easier.

But she really did want to shift her work. Was what she was doing really that impactful anymore? Wouldn't her skills be better put to use killing men like John? Those men who abused women but never got caught? The prospect thrilled her, but she would have to bide her time. Patience was the name of the game.

She'd taken a call from Felipe who had wanted to see her again, but she had turned him down. Yeah, she'd needed him the other night, but there could be nothing real between them. After what had happened with John, the last thing she wanted right now was to be with a man. Hopefully, Felipe would just move on as he had done before.

The doorbell rang, catching her off guard. Maybe it was her security detail wanting to talk to her. She set Felix down on the floor and walked over to the front door. Looking through the peephole, she saw Samira.

Taking a deep breath, she opened the door. "Hi, is everything okay?"

Samira nodded. "Yeah. Can I come in?"

"Sure." She stepped aside. "Can I get you anything?"

"No. I'm good."

"Then let's have a seat and talk." She wasn't sure what Samira wanted, but she was on high alert.

Samira sat down in one of the large living room chairs and Quinn sat on the couch across from her. "Do you have any updates?" That seemed like a benign enough question.

"Jalen and I spent the better part of the day using a clean slate approach."

"What does that mean?"

"We started over at the beginning and tried to not bring any assumptions with us. It's one of the ways to try to see things we hadn't seen before."

She didn't like the sound of that. "And was it successful?"

Samira looked down. "It was a useful exercise, but we're still struggling with possible suspects."

"I know I'm not a criminal lawyer, so maybe I'm way off here but what about DNA evidence?"

"You're not off, but this killer is meticulous. And the DNA evidence we do have doesn't match any known DNA in our database."

"So it's possible the killer has never been in the criminal system before?"

"Absolutely. My money is on the fact that they've been operating under the radar for years. I think he or she has killed more than we know."

She let out a gasp but this time it wasn't feigned. "You just said he or *she*. I thought the killer was a man."

Samira straightened her shoulders. "Our strongest theory was that it was a man due to the linkage to a male stalker, but now that we know Malone isn't our guy, those assumptions have changed. Also, the manner of death, how the killer is murdering the victims, is more consistent with a female than a male. We knew that from the get go, but we were following a different path based on where the best evidence at the time led us. Now we have to shift course."

"Wow." This wasn't good. She thought she would have more time to develop next steps.

"Yeah. So one thing I wanted to talk to you about are the women in your life. I know it's hard to believe that anyone could do this, but I need you to really think hard about whether you've made enemies that could end up wanting to hurt you, or just the opposite—that you could have some woman obsessed with you."

She felt a bit of relief that this was the direction the conversation was going. "I've made enough enemies in the legal community—both men and women. As you know though, I've done a lot of work on women's issues and mentoring women. I'm not sure that I've done anything to any woman that would rise to the level of them acting this way against me."

"Like I said, though, it's possible she's in the other category. That she's enamored with you. Ultimately, a powerful obsession that has caused her to act."

She clenched her hands in her lap. "I'm not that close to many women."

"You might not be. In fact, this is someone who probably sees and admires you from a distance, but most likely someone you've interacted with before. What about the associate Allie Prince?"

Quinn couldn't help but laugh. "Allie is a vegan pacifist. If she won't even support the killing of animals, I know she isn't a murderer. Besides that, she isn't obsessed with me. She's obsessed over her career—as she should be. You can talk to her if you want, but it will be a big waste of your time."

"We'll still want to speak with her. How about others?"

The last thing she wanted to do was throw someone under the bus, but she might not have much of a choice. "I can give you the names of the women I serve on several committees with."

"Okay. That would be good. What about the domestic violence work you've done?"

Her head shot up. "No way. There's no one involved in that who would hurt me."

Samira got up and sat down beside her. "I know it's really tough to believe that, but we have a killer out there who is one step ahead of us. We have to think outside the box."

"And I'm telling you that the women I've helped have much bigger problems in their lives."

"But think about the motive. It could be there. A woman who was abused, and you came to the rescue. She would have animus against men, especially powerful men who she felt got away with bad things."

Samira had no idea how close she was getting to the truth, and it was making her palms sweat. She had to stay cool. She really didn't think Samira suspected her at all, and she had to keep it that way. But she also couldn't allow innocent women to be harassed by the FBI. That was against everything she believed in. "I'm at a loss here."

"Please think about it and provide names as soon as you can. We can't waste any time. I know it's hard to think about someone you stood up for and fought for doing this to you, but it is possible."

"I know that in my head. Sometimes emotions take over." She had to walk the line between being worried but not going over the top as that wouldn't be consistent with her prior behavior.

"I get that." Samira paused. "On a completely different topic, did John tell you he had been fired?"

Her eyes widened. "No. He didn't mention it."

"We met with Mr. Chang at Horizon Pharma, and he told us."

"Wow." She ran her hand through her hair. "No wonder he was in such a foul mood."

"He probably didn't want to admit failure to you. That didn't fit into his macho image."

"I know this is probably a long shot but given that information, is there any possibility that John took his own life and that his death isn't connected to the killer?"

"It is a theory on the table, but even if John was upset about being fired, do you really think he would've done that? It doesn't really fit to me."

She was walking the tightrope again. "I guess you're right, but he was upset. Maybe he wanted an escape, and it went too far. Did you find out what drug it was?"

"Oxy. He didn't have a prescription for it."

"That doesn't mean much. Men like John have ways of getting their hands on things."

"I agree with you. We're working all avenues on this one. How are you holding up?"

She took a deep breath. "Yeah. If I'm being honest with you, the death is starting to weigh on me. It's everywhere I turn." That was a lie. She felt exhilarated by it all but hopefully she was convincing to Samira.

"It's completely natural for you to feel that way. If you told me you were a hundred percent fine right now, I'd know that you were lying."

"What do you think is going to happen next?" The more information she could get out of her the better.

Samira sighed. "The killer is on a short fuse. Once he or she realizes that you're not going to be an easy target, they're going to shift their anger some other place. I just hope we can find them before that happens."

She had to keep up the charade. "Me too. I am appreciative of the security. Otherwise, I wouldn't be able to sleep at all, but this isn't any way to live in the long term."

"We know that. Hopefully, we'll be able to get you back to your regular life as soon as possible, but we can't take risks right now. This killer is cunning, smart, and out for blood."

She didn't really know what to say.

Samira touched her arm. "Quinn, we will get you through this, and I know you didn't like what I said a few minutes ago, but I really will need those names. Give it some thought, and I will touch base in the morning, okay?"

She didn't have any choice in this matter. "All right."

"Remember you're not alone in this." Samira stood up and she followed her to the door.

"Hope you can get some rest tonight," Samira said.

"Me too."

Samira left and Quinn let out a huge breath. Malone had bought her time but now things were heating up. Now she had to come up with a list of names which she absolutely hated doing. It seemed to go against everything she was working for to support women. The good thing was that there would be no way that any of them would ever seriously be considered because no evidence existed to tie them to any of the crimes. On the flip side, at some point, Samira might get too close to the truth, and she needed to be able to throw them off the scent.

It was going to be a long night because she was going to have to adjust her battle plan.

47

The next afternoon, Samira and Jalen huddled up in their war room at the field office.

Jalen opened his notebook. "I met with Allie Prince this morning. She isn't our woman. Solid alibis and doesn't fit any of the boxes."

"Quinn was adamant that it wasn't her." Samira looked down at her notes. "Quinn sent me the list of names. There was one I recognized."

"Who?" Jalen asked.

"Gemma Holland."

"Really?" Jalen laughed. "I find that a bit hard to envision."

That was her first reaction as well. "Me too. But I guess Quinn took the task seriously even though she clearly didn't want to do it. At least we know she was being comprehensive."

Jalen tapped his pen on the table. "You know, maybe I was too quick to judge. We should look at everyone with fresh eyes, including Gemma."

"You're right, as usual." She thought for a moment. "Gemma had the access to Quinn. She did all the videos. Is it possible that she became infatuated with her?"

"Possible, yes. Probable? I'm having a hard time imagining it. What would be her motive for killing?"

She bit the inside of her cheek. "Maybe to get Quinn's attention. To demonstrate her commitment? What if Gemma believed that Quinn didn't think her clients were truly innocent and took matters into her own hands. But we shouldn't go too far down the rabbit hole without talking to Gemma again. If she alibis out, we don't want to waste our time."

"I'll set up a meeting ASAP." Jalen pulled out his phone.

She typed up some notes while Jalen spoke to Gemma.

"She's available now. I asked if she could come to us and she's good with that. She seemed excited about coming to the FBI. I don't think a serial killer would act that way."

She agreed but they had to see this through. "We might just make Gemma's day until she realizes where the questioning is going."

They made some additional notes and did some research on the other names of the list while they waited for Gemma to arrive.

Once Gemma got there, they escorted her into a conference room.

"Does this mean there's a break in the case, and you're giving me the exclusive you promised?" Her eyes lit up.

"Not exactly," Jalen said. "Please have a seat and we'll talk."

Gemma sat down, bright eyed and tuned in to what they had to say.

Samira was ready to get down to it. "Gemma, do you have your calendar with you on your phone?"

"Of course." Gemma picked up her phone.

Jalen started the questioning and went through each date where there was a murder. Unfortunately, Gemma didn't have real alibis for any of them, at least from what she could tell based on her calendar.

"Do I need a lawyer?" Gemma finally asked.

"That's up to you," Samira said. She didn't think this was a serial killer sitting across from them, but they had to do their due diligence. She'd read too many case studies where law enforcement had the perpetrator in custody and didn't think they were viable suspects, to find out they were guilty.

Gemma tapped her fingers on the desk. "I don't have anything to hide here. I had nothing to do with any of this. You both can't seriously think that I'm a killer. It's ridiculous. I'm a member of the press!"

"Did you know any of the victims?" Jalen ignored her little rant.

"Not really. I saw them in the courtroom and tried to get statements from all of them because that is my job, but Quinn usually did all the talking." She took a deep breath. "The investigation can't be going well, if you're resorting to pointing the finger at the journalist. You really have no idea who is responsible for this and now I'm paying the price for your wild goose chase."

"We have to be thorough." It sounded weak even as she said it, but it didn't change the fact that they had to go through the motions.

"But what basis do you even have to think that I could be behind it?"

Jalen leaned in. "We're the ones asking the questions here, Ms. Holland."

Gemma laughed. "Maybe I should get a lawyer. I don't like where this is heading."

"That is your right," The last thing the Bureau needed was a lawsuit over this related to them threatening not only Gemma's first amendment rights but also her right to an attorney.

"What else do you want to know?"

Samira knew that Gemma was conflicted. In a way, she didn't want to shut the interview down because she felt she could use it for a story—potentially a huge story—but she also wanted to protect herself. Which would win out? "Have you ever been inside the homes of any of the victims?"

"No," Gemma said quickly. "Absolutely not. I have no clue where they even live."

One more push. "Would you voluntarily submit to a DNA test?"

Gemma lifted up her hand. "No way. I'm not that stupid."

"But you said you had nothing to hide," Jalen shot back.

"It's the principle of the matter, and with that, unless you tell me that you are going to charge me with something, I'm out of here."

She was a bit surprised by Gemma's assertiveness. She had to give it to her, the young woman was smart and understood her rights and their limitations under the law. "We aren't charging you, but cooperation would go a long way here."

Gemma sighed loudly. "I am cooperating, but when you're wrongfully accused of *murder*, it doesn't exactly make you want to sit around and take it."

Samira decided to keep prodding for information. "Do you know any women who you think may have wanted to hurt Quinn? Or had an unhealthy level of interest in her?"

"I get it now." Gemma leaned forward. "Something made you think the killer is a woman and you're starting at square one with any women in Quinn's life. That's why I'm here. But why the shift in thinking now?"

"You know we aren't going to answer that," Jalen said.

"I don't know of any women I could think of that could do this—including myself, obviously."

She glanced at Jalen. Gemma has turned uncooperative. This wasn't going anywhere. Gemma was now just trying to get information from them and not giving anything in return. "That's all for now. We'll be in touch."

"All right." Gemma stood.

"Someone will escort you out."

Gemma walked out of the room clearly not liking what had just gone down.

"What do you think?" she asked Jalen.

"I don't think she's good for this. Nothing about it fits to me."

She let out a breath. "It sure would've been nice if she had an alibi so we could eliminate her."

"Not a thing is breaking our way, and to hear you talk, if we don't produce results soon, we won't even have the case anymore."

"I don't want that to happen, but even more importantly, I don't want another murder. Let's start working our way through the rest of the list Quinn gave us."

48

Quinn had received a call from a high-strung Gemma who had begged for a meeting. Quinn had a feeling she knew why Gemma was acting that way, so she invited her over that evening for a drink. She wasn't going to tell Gemma that she had put her on the list that she provided to the FBI, but it wouldn't have mattered anyway. Once the FBI started to think the killer was a woman, Gemma was going to be interviewed no matter what Quinn said, so it wasn't as if she was really placing a target on her back.

Gemma blitzed through her living room bursting with energy. "The FBI has lost their minds."

"Why do you say that?"

"They questioned me today as a freaking suspect." Gemma's eyes widened. "Can you believe that?"

Quinn wanted to tread carefully. "I'm not that surprised given the fact that they just told me they now think a woman is behind the killings."

"But I didn't do it," Gemma's voice cracked.

"Sit down and take a few deep breaths. I'll get you a glass of wine, and we can talk this through. Everything is going to be fine. You have nothing to worry about." And Gemma didn't. There was no way she'd be pinned for this by the FBI.

"Thank you. And obviously this is an off the record conversation. I appreciate your help and trying to talk me down. I wouldn't ever share anything we said in confidence. You have my word."

Quinn wasn't worried about that. She actually needed Gemma and her plan was to get as much information as possible. She poured them each a glass of Chardonnay and walked back over to Gemma. "Now take your time and tell me what happened."

Gemma took a sip of wine before answering. "I was so naïve. I thought the FBI was calling me into the field office to give me an exclusive. Like they had broken the case and it was going to be huge for me." Gemma laughed. "I was an idiot."

"You're not an idiot." Quinn patted her hand. "It was completely logical for you to think that, and there's no way in the world you could've imagined that they would've wanted to question you as a possible suspect."

"Anyway, I get there, and it quickly becomes apparent to me that there is no exclusive, it's more like an interrogation."

That sounded a bit much. "Were they aggressive with you?"

"No, but they were firm, and very insistent. They wanted to know if I had alibis for the murders, which of course with my bad luck, I didn't. I'm going to dig deeper back into my social media though to try to figure out where I was on each of the dates. Hopefully, I wasn't at home alone during all of them."

"Did they seem to have any clues about who the real killer was?"

"You'd know better than me." Gemma laid her head back on the couch for a moment. "I should've gotten a lawyer right away, but the desire to get the scoop for a story pushed me not to. I was hoping for some good intel but there wasn't much to go on."

Quinn appreciated Gemma's ambition. "I understand why you did that especially since you have nothing to hide."

"They wanted me to give a DNA sample and I said no way. I know that's a big no no."

Gemma made a smart move on that one. "You're right. Once they have your DNA, it's in the system forever."

"If they come at me again, I will get a lawyer. I have to ultimately protect myself. I get the feeling they are desperate for answers and are starting to grasp at straws, so who knows what they might do. It's not a good look for the FBI to still have a killer on the loose."

Quinn sighed. "I know. You saw my security detail outside."

"They think you're in the line of fire now, don't they?"

"Yes, and I appreciate the security. I'm not sure who is behind this."

"You're not convinced it's a woman?" Gemma raised an eyebrow.

"I'm not, but honestly, my life has been turned upside down from all of this, so I don't know how clearly I'm thinking about everything."

Gemma's shoulders slumped. "I'm so sorry. I come over and dump all of this on you and you're having a much tougher time than me. You're actually in danger because of this maniac."

"Don't give it a second thought. Being questioned for a serial killing would make anyone on edge. They realize that there's no way it could be you, but under this new female theory, they're probably in the process of elimination. You're one of the women who has had a lot of access to me. It's natural they would want to rule you out so they could move on."

"I hope they exclude me quickly from the pool of suspects. I find it hard to believe that they think I could really be a cold-blooded killer." Gemma lifted up her glass. "I mean, look at me. It's ridiculous."

"This killer doesn't have to be strong and menacing. That's the problem. The way the victims were killed doesn't take brute force."

Gemma bit her bottom lip. "I guess you're right. That's

another reason they're looking at women. Have you thought about everyone you know? Is there anyone you could see being responsible for this?"

"No. The thought of it being someone in my life is scary though." She didn't take joy in this little charade with Gemma. She actually liked Gemma well enough, but right now she had to do everything in power to protect herself.

"I'm glad you have that security detail." She set her glass on the coffee table. "I guess now wouldn't be a good time to try to pump you for information on what happened with your stalker."

"If it's off the record, then yes, but if you want to publish it, then no." She refused to get any more publicity that wasn't from her lawsuits.

Gemma twirled a lock of hair around her finger. "I guess at this point, I'll just take knowing what happened. I've been in the dark."

Quinn took a few minutes and told Gemma a sanitized version of what happened, particularly leaving out the fact that she lured Tom to the garage.

Gemma's mouth dropped open. "Quinn, that is horrible. I'm so glad you're okay. He could've killed you."

"I know." She looked down. "And then to find out that Tom wasn't the killer."

"Isn't there still a chance that John Rossi killed himself? That Tom really was the killer?"

"I'm holding out hope, but the FBI is skeptical." If only it were that easy to have it tied up neatly in a little bow.

Finishing her glass of wine, Gemma placed it on the coffee table. "I'm sorry again for barging in here. It was rude of me."

"I told you it was fine. Would you like anything else?" She might need Gemma in the future and wanted to keep her close.

"No. I should be going."

She stood up when Gemma did. "Everything is going to be fine."

Gemma turned toward her. "You need to be careful. Enough people have already died because of this psychopath."

She so wanted Gemma to understand her motivation. To know that she wasn't a cold-blooded killer like what Gemma believed, but a thoughtful woman who took the actions that she had to for the greater good. But she couldn't tell anyone her secret. Not now. Not ever.

49

That night Samira sat at home having watched the footage from the garage multiple times. It had taken forever to get it. First, she'd been given the runaround and told that no video existed. But after prodding further and going all the way up the chain of the garage management company, the video did indeed exist and now she had the footage. And much to her surprise, there was audio as well. She was still trying to process through what she had witnessed.

She started to play it again from the beginning and watched the screen intently.

Quinn was ready for Malone. She was up the steps first and lying in wait. Her gun drawn. A few good seconds ticked by before a wild-eyed Malone came bursting up the stairwell door.

A couple of things troubled her about the video. Starting with how Quinn acted. She knew that Quinn had gone through extensive self-defense training probably because of what had happened in her past, but she was cool as a cucumber even when Malone went for his gun. And then, the even stranger thing was the conversation that happened between the two of them. Quinn clearly didn't seem to know who he was, but he knew her. That much was evident. Malone probably had psychological issues – serious ones. And his obsession had come to the point that he was willing to take her life. If he had done that, there was a piece of her that wondered whether he would've then killed himself. But that isn't how it played out.

She pushed stop and rewound it to play again. Malone kept saying how much he and Quinn were alike which Quinn summarily dismissed. But it was one of the final things he said that really bothered her. *I know who you really are.* What in the world did Malone mean by that? Did Quinn have some sort of illicit life? Quinn had secrets, didn't everyone, but was there something in particular about Quinn's secrets that had intrigued Malone. Was this the cause of his obsession, or at the very least, had it accelerated his feelings for her?

She might be grasping at straws, but the whole thing disturbed her. After watching a couple more times, another thought struck her. Quinn was fed up with the entire situation and had made that clear. Had she purposely gone out walking that day trying to get Malone to follow her?

No matter how skilled she was, it didn't seem like a rational move. And while she didn't know everything about Quinn, she was quite certain that Quinn was highly rational.

So why act irrationally now? Why would she have put herself in such danger? Tons of questions flooded her mind as she tried to fit the puzzle pieces together. She watched how Quinn checked Malone for a pulse with almost medical precision. She wasn't screaming or shaking. Completely even keeled. Not like what she expected to see especially given how frazzled Quinn had seemed when they talked after. Everyone reacts to trauma differently, she reminded herself, so it could've been a delayed reaction.

But another thought came into her mind. Something so outlandish that she pushed it away. She couldn't go there. Not yet. She needed to get Jalen's take on the video, and thankfully, he was going to be at her place any minute. She had called him once she'd gotten access to it that evening.

She made some mint tea, and by then, Jalen had arrived. She didn't want to prejudice him in any way. She wanted his opinion without influencing him, so she played the tape one time through without saying a word. Jalen stared at the screen.

Once it was over, he turned to her. "Not exactly what I was expecting."

"What do you mean?"

"I expected that Quinn would've been more frightened. More freaked out about what had just happened. She almost had a law enforcement coolness about her. I'm not judging her because of that, and maybe her intensive self-defense training really paid off. Her survival instinct was strong. She was totally in control of the situation—not Malone."

She agreed completely with his assessment. "What do you think about the things that Malone said to her?"

Jalen cocked his head to the side. "Will you play it one more time?"

"Sure." She played the video again and they both watched closely, not saying a word.

Jalen turned to her after it finished. "Malone clearly thought he knew something about Quinn. Maybe something about her personal life?"

She hadn't really thought about it like that. Jalen had a good point. "Yeah, that's possible. It's just very confusing. The certainty in his words is striking. And what doesn't sound certain is her response. I have another question for you."

"Shoot."

"Do you think there's any chance Quinn used herself as bait to set him up? She left the office, had her gun with her, and decided to stroll about all afternoon supposedly getting coffee. She told me she had to get some air, but I'm not so sure that adds up. I'd just gotten her coffee not long before that. Something is off."

"I'm thinking." Jalen stared back at the screen before turning to her. "What kind of woman would do that? If you know you have a deadly stalker after you, why would you put yourself directly in harm's way, even if you are trained in self-defense and are carrying."

Her thoughts exactly. "Unless the situation had become so untenable, she felt she had no choice. She was backed into a corner. Maybe we are underestimating the very real impact of her history of abuse. Just look at her relationships and what we've learned there. What if she felt we weren't cutting it, and she couldn't live like that anymore being hunted down by a stalker. It was either her or him. She might not look scared, but on the inside she was."

Jalen put his head in his hands for a moment before speaking again. "That doesn't look like a woman who is afraid. It looks more like a woman who was on a mission."

And that's exactly what she feared. "How else might we have underestimated Quinn Kelly?"

Jalen raised an eyebrow. "Samira? What are you saying?"

"I'm not saying anything yet."

Jalen stood up and started pacing in her living room. She learned that was when he did his best thinking. She let him pace for a couple minutes without interrupting his thought process. Her mind was already on overload.

He walked back over to her and sat down beside her on the couch. "It doesn't make sense. Yes, Quinn is probably pretty messed up, and rightfully so after what we've learned about her abusive father, but the motive is not there."

She had to make sure they were on the same page. "Just so we're being crystal clear here. We're talking about Quinn being a suspect, right?"

"Aren't we?"

Her stomach clenched. It seemed unthinkable at first, but as she was letting it sink in, she wondered if they could be onto something.

"Let's not get ahead of ourselves. We need to think this through. Methodically, like what we would do in any other situation. Take the emotion out of it and what we think we know about her."

Now it was time for Samira to stand because she couldn't sit still any longer. "She had the opportunity. She is super close to all of her clients. She could've gotten to them. And think about it. The cause of death, the MO, while not the exact same each time, is consistent with a female killer." Now that the words had come out of her mouth, it felt all too real, and she wasn't sure how she felt about it. Almost like she was betraying an innocent woman who she was supposed to be protecting. But what if she had been wrong about Quinn? "And she was at a legal conference on the day that Russell Myers died, but what if she had given him the coke the last time she saw him? She told us that had been about a week before he died. And it just so happens, that's when he decided to use it. Same thing with Richard Hale. She was at his home Monday night."

"I'm with you on the opportunity. It totally makes sense and would explain how she got access." Jalen walked over to join her. "But where I'm struggling here is motive. These were clients. Her clients. She worked as hard as she could to win these cases, and I have no doubt about that. Her passion for her work in the courtroom was evident. I don't think it was fake. So then she what? She kills them after she wins? Why would she do that, Samira?"

"You know I watched all those videos of her. There was a common theme. Something I questioned her about. Why is she defending big companies when she cares so much about justice, and her response was that she had to work at a big firm because she had no family and had massive student debt, so a big corporate defense firm was her only path. When she found out she was gifted at trial work, it became almost impossible for her to step away from that success and security. Now all of that makes perfect sense if she wasn't so gung ho on the justice angle."

Jalen snapped his fingers. "But maybe this is the Quinn Kelly style of justice. Yeah, you may win your case, because you have the best lawyer in town, but if you're truly guilty, if you should be held responsible, she comes after you because she knows the truth about whether her clients are really innocent or not."

Samira ran her hand through her already tousled hair trying to clear her head. "We're talking in extremes here."

Jalen laughed but there was no humor behind it. "Of course it's extreme. If we're right about this, we're talking about a serial killer. A woman who has killed multiple times and who knows how many others are out there that we don't know about. She's hiding behind a highly complex and effective façade, and I bet no one would've ever picked up on it. The stalker entering into the picture might just be the thing that exposes her in the end."

She was worried that they were both moving too quickly down this road. "Let's not go off the deep end just yet. This is just a theory. A theory we need to play out. We must do our homework. There is no reason to convict on the spot. We have a lot of unknowns here and could be wrong. Completely wrong. This woman has been victimized multiple times in life, and we don't want to do that to her again. We have to be absolutely certain."

"I couldn't agree with you more. Let's keep this between me and you right now. No one else. Not even Myron and Strickland."

She bit her lip. "What about Wyatt?"

He raised an eyebrow. "Are you looking for an excuse to call him or do you really want his opinion?"

"What do you think?" Romance was the last thing on her mind at the moment.

"Fine. But ask him to keep it to himself."

She looked up at him. "We've opened Pandora's box."

"And there's no closing it."

50

The next morning Samira and Jalen had both arrived early to the office to get to work.

"How did you sleep?" Jalen asked.

"I didn't. I kept trying to replay everything over and over in my head." She took a big sip of coffee.

"And did you have any revelations?" Jalen opened up his bag and took out his laptop.

"I called Wyatt after you left last night."

"And?"

"At first he was taken aback but as I laid it all out for him, he started to believe we were onto something. We talked a bit about female serial killers and how they are different from their male counterparts. Wyatt felt the childhood sexual abuse was a key factor here in shaping Quinn's sense of justice." Staring up at the big board they had in the conference room, there was no easy way to do this. "Let's start at the beginning. Or at least what we know as the beginning now."

Jalen walked up to the board. "The death of Russell Myers."

"The scene was worked as a death of natural causes so nothing much to go on from an evidentiary front. So Quinn goes over to Myers's house, and she gives him the coke that causes the heart attack. But he doesn't actually take it until the next week." She opened up one of the many file folders in front of her.

Jalen walked over and looked at the documents again. "Coke can cause heart attacks, but if Quinn truly wanted to kill him, she would've been taking a risk because there is no guarantee that the coke would've induced a heart attack. The coke could've had cutting agents that the ME didn't detect."

"Right because they weren't looking for it." She took a breath. "We'll let Myers sit for a minute and talk about French. We're both in agreement that we should take her out of the equation here for a lot of reasons."

"Agreed. Which leads us to Cruz. Overdose of his prescription sleeping pills."

She had a couple of theories on this one. "One possibility is the same one we were assuming when we played this out with Malone. Quinn could've threatened to kill him by some more violent means unless he took the pills."

"Or?" Jalen raised an eyebrow.

"Or, she could've crushed up the pills and put it in his drink. Cruz would've never known."

"Seems like a very passive way to kill, but if Quinn really is on a justice mission wouldn't she want the guilty perpetrators to know that they were going to die to pay for their crimes?"

She bit her bottom lip as she thought. "Yes. She could've had the conversation with them before they died. Basically conduct her own trial as judge and jury."

Jalen let out a low whistle. "That sounds scarily possible when you think about it."

It was too early to claim victory. "We shouldn't pat ourselves on the back yet. For one, we don't know if we're right, and the even bigger problem from a legal standpoint is we have no proof. Let's move on to the next murder."

Jalen went back up to the board. "This scene we actually worked ourselves. Richard Hale."

"We have the common element of coke from the Myers murder, but this time we have the fentanyl. And he was taking pills and drinking too."

"Quinn could've given Richard the laced coke that Monday night. Then after his happy hour with his friends he decided he didn't want the party to end, so he did the coke."

Jalen nodded. "Sounds plausible."

Which led them to the last murder. "And then we have Rossi. Killed by an Oxy overdose."

"Quinn had to have been able to get her hands on coke and prescription drugs, but I'm guessing she covered her tracks very well. Can you imagine Quinn hitting the streets and buying drugs?"

Things had changed quickly. "Before I saw that garage tape, I would've said no way that the proper Quinn Kelly could do that, but the way she handled herself with Malone, I totally think she could've and probably would've because I bet she would've thought paying someone else would be too risky. It could tie her to the drugs. No. I think she did this on her own. Her need for control is too strong."

Jalen turned to face her. "That means that there's a dealer out there who might remember her. She's pretty striking."

"Memorable, yes, but a drug dealer's word versus a highly esteemed attorney? We might be in trouble on that one."

"Here's another thought. If we're working on this Quinn Kelly justice theory, then she must have believed settlement was too easy for Rossi."

It was time to provide more details to Jalen because what before was not relevant, was now. "It might've been more personal than that."

Jalen raised an eyebrow. "How so?"

"Rossi kept trying to push himself on Quinn. She rebuffed him numerous times, but he definitely put his hands on her."

"Disgusting. But as bad as his actions were, it still doesn't give her license to kill him unless it was self-defense, and I fail to see how an Oxy overdose could be."

"I agree." As bad as John was, vigilante violence was never the answer.

"How are we going to play this? Do we really have anything at this point to tie her to the murders beyond opportunity?"

"Not much, but let's check the door cams in Rossi's neighborhood. Quinn told me she last saw John that afternoon, but maybe we'll catch a break and find something else."

Jalen huffed. "We haven't caught a break this entire time."

"Then we're about due. I want us to have an initial conversation with her. See if we can catch her in any lies or anything we could use. Now that we have a new working theory, it will change everything about how we approach her."

"Do you think it would be better if you did it one on one?'

"Why do you say that?"

"Quinn will let down her guard more around you. I'm beginning to think that her issues with men permeate everything she does."

She was still struggling to piece it all together. "Can you imagine there actually being a serial killer who also volunteers as an attorney for domestic violence victims? It goes against so much of what we're taught about the pathology of serial killers."

Jalen moved toward her and leaned on the edge of the table. "Remember your own experiences. Sometimes people don't fit within the neat boxes that the world wants to put them in."

"You're right. Just like the idea that people aren't all good or evil. Quinn has done a lot of good, but I'm just having a hard time getting my head around how she could think murder was the answer to the justice problem."

"In her mind, there may be no other way. The legal system failed the victims, and she had a role in that, so she had to make things right."

"You know what really scares me?"

"What?"

"The very real possibility that we know Quinn's a killer but not being able to do anything about it."

51

The next afternoon, Quinn sat in her office across from grim faced Samira. She decided to jump in. "Do you have any updates?"

Samira averted her gaze. "Unfortunately, none of the names you provided us have turned into any solid leads."

"I told you that I thought you were going down the wrong road." The FBI was spinning their wheels. She had expected more from them, but she also had to cut them some slack given Tom Malone had thrown everything into a tailspin. Now that he was squarely out of the picture, she was interested to see how long it would take them to get closer to the truth.

"Quinn, let me assure you that we're going down every road at this point and your security detail will remain until we have answers."

"Are you rethinking whether you were right initially about the killer being a man?" She hoped that the grand detour of women had discouraged them from continuing to focus on that direction.

"No. In fact we're putting all our resources behind the female killer theory. I've been brushing up on female serial killers."

Now this was getting interesting. "I must admit that's not

something I really know anything about." The lie rolled off her tongue in a compelling fashion. She was sure of it.

Samira leaned forward. "Most people assume serial killers are men because of the notorious male killers out there."

"I guess that makes sense. What are you looking for now?" She wanted to hear what Samira had to say about female killers.

"Female serial killers usually employ a much less violent mode of killing. Just like the situation we have here."

"Yes, that's why you started to examine this theory to begin with, right?" She remained calm. Almost eerily so given the pressure she should be feeling.

Samira nodded. "Absolutely. One theme about female serial killers is the angel of death."

"What is that?"

"Killing because they believe they are helping someone ease their pain. It's misguided, of course, but it is a theme."

"That doesn't make sense here though." She wasn't sure where Samira was going with this.

"You're right. This killer is unique. She doesn't quite fit the mold, but I do believe she is a purpose driven killer." Samira paused. "She isn't killing just for the thrill of killing. She believes she is righting a wrong."

The game of cat and mouse was truly about to start. In a strange way it thrilled her, pumping adrenaline through her veins, even at the risk of getting caught. She'd gone over it multiple times in her head realizing that at some point the FBI would finally clue into what was going on. The key was that they didn't view her as a viable suspect. "So you're looking for someone who doesn't like big company CEOs."

"That's a fair way of putting it. A woman who believes that the legal system isn't getting it right, and she takes it upon herself to make sure justice is served. What I don't know is what triggered her to start killing in the first place."

If only Samira knew the true horrors that Quinn had faced. Most women wouldn't even be alive now, but Quinn thrived on being a survivor no matter the circumstances. "A lot of people are against big corporations and don't go out and kill people."

"Exactly. I was hoping to pick your brain about that." Samira didn't break eye contact.

"I'm not sure what help I can be." Quinn couldn't appear to be too overeager and knowledgeable about any of this even though it all struck right to the core of who she was.

"You're close to this even though I know it's the last place you want to be, but I feel like your perspective could be really valuable here." Samira took a breath. "You're a passionate advocate of justice. What would make a woman take matters into her own hands?"

It was refreshing to finally be able to talk about this with Samira. She had assumed this conversation would've taken place much earlier but given the twists and turns of the investigation, that hadn't happened. Until now. "Maybe the killer feels like there is no other choice for her. No options out there. The system has failed her time and again."

"That's a strong point because one thing prevalent among serial killer profiles is violence and abuse during childhood. That might be a possibility here as well."

Silence filled the room. As she looked directly into Samira's big, brown eyes, for the first time she believed that Samira was actually suspicious of her. She wasn't sure how this turn of events had happened and what had ultimately given rise to the suspicion, but Quinn believed she still was firmly in control even though Samira probably thought she had the upper hand. She remembered their discussion about her abusive father. Samira was trying to make a point to see how she reacted. "Childhood trauma shapes people's lives forever. I see it in my clients I work with in the domestic violence clinic. Everyone handles that trauma differently, but the impact is still huge."

"I agree with that. Abuse leaves more than physical scars, but you understand that all too well, don't you?"

Was this empathy? Even with Samira's concerns? "Yes, unfortunately. Not everyone is able to pull themselves out of the darkness and live a productive life. It wasn't easy and that's one of the reasons I still visit a psychologist to this day. Pain like that never truly goes away."

Samira reached out and patted her hand. "I know and I'm sorry to have brought up such bad memories for you, but I do truly believe your insight could help us find the killer."

"I'll help in any way I can." She hadn't been sure how she would feel if this day ever came, but it was oddly exhilarating.

"One avenue we're pursuing is how the killer got her hands on cocaine."

"Powerful corporate executives doing lines of coke. It happens more than you would think."

"Did any of them ever want you to party with them?"

Quinn laughed. "Yes, all the time, but as I told you before, my vices stop with alcohol. No drugs for me." She had to stay as in control as possible.

"Do you have any idea where they would've gotten the coke?"

"These guys have people." She'd learned that early on as a naïve, young lawyer at the firm. "If you have money, you can pretty much get your hands on whatever you want, whenever you want."

"Another example of the rich and powerful not being held accountable."

"That's the way of the world." Now Quinn had power and money that she could've never dreamed of, but it was important to her to use her influence for good.

"We're getting all the door cam data from John's neighbors. Maybe we'll catch a break."

"That would be good." Quinn had prepared for that. There would be clear evidence supporting her story about going over there earlier in the day on Saturday, but she'd taken multiple precautions when she'd gone back that evening—including taking MARTA and then a cab ride paid with cash that dropped her off on the street behind John's house. She was careful to evade the homes that had the door cams or other outside surveillance. She'd done her homework. It might not be fool-proof, but it had been a risk she had been willing to take.

Samira stood. "I know all of this has taken a toll on you, but hopefully it will be over soon. We'll catch this woman and put her behind bars."

"You still think that she's a threat to me."

"I do. We can't ever be too careful. The killer could be right under our nose."

52

That night Samira sat in Jalen's living room having pizza for a working dinner.

"I want to hear all about how it went with Quinn," Jalen said.

Frustration bubbled up inside. "I wish you would've been there. I know you thought I would get more on my own, but I need you there the next time."

"Why do you say that?" Jalen took a bite of a huge slice of the cheesy pepperoni pizza.

Samira had racked her brain the rest of the day after the meeting. "I'm second guessing myself."

"About whether Quinn could be the killer?"

"Yeah, but I'm not sure if that's because I feel sorry for her and just don't want to believe the truth. This woman has been victimized. She suffered severe trauma during childhood."

Jalen picked up his soda. "All the more reason to believe she could have done these things."

"I guess so. It just doesn't seem fair."

He reached out and touched her arm. "Nothing about life is fair, Samira. We both know that."

Samira stared at the pizza crust on the plate in front of her. "Based on what we know, Quinn was abused, but I fear that something beyond our comprehension happened to her to make her do these things."

"I get that you feel for her, but it doesn't change the fact that she may very well be guilty of killing multiple men in cold blood. Pre-meditated murder."

"Is it really that clear cut?" She was experiencing a lot of angst over all of this. Yes, she wanted justice for the victims, but she felt a need to understand more what made Quinn tick.

"Quinn's backstory and motivation may not be completely clear, but the pre-meditated murder part is." Jalen set down his plate. "Samira, it's not like you to let your emotions play into your investigations. In fact, I've never seen it before in the five plus years we've been working together. Why is Quinn different?"

She'd asked herself the same thing. "I see a lot of myself in her."

Jalen raised an eyebrow. "I'm not sure I agree with you on that. You would never murder in cold blood. I'd bet my life on it. Yes, you've gone through many trials and adversities in your life, but that's made you stronger, and you don't need a violent outlet to handle your emotions. The things you feel like you have in common with Quinn are surface level."

It felt deeper than that.

He grabbed onto her hand. "Hey, talk to me. Is there something about your past that I don't know about that would impact your ability to be objective? You know you can tell me anything."

"No. I've never endured anything like what Quinn went through. I would tell you, but I'm just still getting my head wrapped around this." She had completely different types of secrets, but now wasn't the time to air them out.

"It's a lot to process. We've been around Quinn for over a

month now, and there's nothing that would've indicated to us that she could've been good for this."

She hung her head. "But now here we are thinking exactly that."

"Tell me more about the conversation."

"Quinn was cool and collected. She held her own. I watched for any signs of distress, nerves, or worry, and I didn't see them."

"Remember she is a seasoned trial attorney. She thrives on stress. Being able to put on a good show is what she excels at so what you describe doesn't surprise me."

"Yeah, I guess it was too much to hope that she would slip up."

"She's much too smart for that. Do you think you tipped your hand at all?"

"I don't think so, but Quinn has proven to be more than a worthy adversary so I can't say for sure. For instance, she didn't flinch at the mention of us looking at surveillance footage."

Jalen's dark eyes narrowed. "It could be that she's that confident she will get away with this."

"Well, she'd have good reason because right now we don't even have enough to hold her, much less charge her."

"We'll have that cam footage this weekend. I'm holding out hope that we'll catch a break. And on the bright side, Quinn can't do anyone else harm right now because of her security detail."

That gave her some small measure of comfort, but it wasn't a permanent solution. "That can't last forever which is another reason we need to bring this to a head quickly. Quinn planned all of this out masterfully. She had easy access to the CEOs, reasons to be with them so that any physical evidence found at the scene would have completely innocent explanations. What are we missing that she could've faltered on?"

"What about cold cases? What if she wasn't as meticulous before?"

"I appreciate the thinking, but it would be truly a needle in a haystack."

"I know you aren't going to like this, but depending on what we turn up, at some point we're going to need to confront her and see how she acts."

Samira feared she knew exactly how she would act. Like a serial killer.

53

On Monday morning, Samira was sailing on an adrenaline rush as she'd gotten word from Jalen that the neighborhood surveillance footage was in.

They huddled up around the conference room table ready to watch.

"Settle in. This might take a while," Jalen said.

"I'll let you be in charge of fast forwarding the tape." Samira took a big drink from her coffee mug and got ready to watch.

They sat in silence for about an hour as footage played but nothing useful was there. Then a figure emerged.

"Stop," Samira said.

"I'm on it." Jalen rewound for a minute and replayed.

The tape quality wasn't great, it was dark, but there was a figure walking in front of a house. You couldn't see the face, but the build matched that of Quinn. She was wearing a hoodie and moving quickly.

"Which house is this from?" She asked Jalen.

He started flipping through his notes. "This is from the street directly behind the Rossi house about three doors down."

Fixated on the screen, she realized she was holding her

breath. The blurry figure was moving toward the camera, and then, there it was. It could be Quinn's face.

Jalen smacked his hand on the table. "Isn't that her?"

She had to give them both a reality check. "I think you and I believe that is her, but the quality of the picture makes it a questionable match at best. It also doesn't put her inside Rossi's house."

Jalen grabbed onto her arm. "Samira, this is time stamped. This puts her on the street behind his house during the window of the murder. What reason would she have to be there other than to see Rossi. She lied about the last time she saw him. I do think that's something."

"Is it proof beyond a reasonable doubt?"

"Maybe not in isolation, but we can build a case around it using a lot of circumstantial evidence."

Thoughts flooded through her mind.

"You're being quiet."

"I'm thinking." Which was true. "I don't think that even confronted with this, we'll get a confession."

Jalen nodded. "True. But it's worth a go at it. We have nothing to lose."

"But Quinn sure does. If it gets out that she is a suspected serial killer, her legal career is over."

"We can build a case around this, Samira. It's not like we're accusing someone wrongfully here."

"I hope you're right."

"Nothing about this case is easy, but we're going to see this through. I've got your back."

"I know you always do."

54

The next afternoon, Quinn knew she was in trouble. That morning she'd been summoned to the FBI field office under the ruse of some new information, but she wasn't falling for that. This meant they were about to make their first real big move. She wasn't sure what they had on her, but she was convinced it was related to John because that's the only time she had ever been so reckless. Having thought long and hard about it, even if she got caught, killing him had been worth it. But there was no way she was giving up. She would fight this. Including getting the best criminal defense attorney in the city. Mike Gregory was on call and would be ready.

In the unlikely event that she was wrong about this meeting, she wouldn't end up needing him, but she was pretty certain she would.

She was walking into the lion's den, but she was oddly both calm and thrilled at the task of trying to outsmart the FBI—specifically Samira. Samira saw a lot of herself in Quinn and she agreed. She had been trying to develop that relationship from the beginning. Now she'd see if any of that would pay off. She'd worked far too hard and gone through way too much to let Samira take her down now.

When she arrived at the FBI, she was escorted to a conference room and told to wait. She wondered if they were on the other side of the glass watching her now. Seeing if there would be any telltale signs of guilt. There would be none. That was one thing Quinn was completely certain of. She would not crack under pressure. Ever.

After a few minutes, Samira and Jalen walked in and took a seat.

"This is the first time you've invited me on your turf for case updates. Usually you visit me at my office." She wanted to set the tone at the outset that she was in control here. Not them.

"Thanks for coming down and accommodating our request," Jalen said.

She flashed a confident smile. "Of course. What's going on?"

Samira shifted in her seat. "Quinn, you told us the last time you saw John Rossi was Saturday afternoon?"

"Yes."

"And that you had to take him some paperwork? What type of paperwork?"

"Documentation related to the settlement agreement."

"But why would you have done that since he no longer had any authority after being fired as CEO?"

If this was all they had, then Quinn was entirely unimpressed. "I didn't know he had been fired. He didn't say anything to me about that, and the company certainly didn't let me know."

Samira leaned forward. "Why were you in John's neighborhood Saturday night?"

So this was the big get. As careful as she had been, there had to have been some type of surveillance that put her there. While she really hated to do this, she had no choice. She'd been living, eating, and breathing the law for her entire adult life, and now was no time to play games and engage in risky behavior even if the cat and mouse game would've been much more fulfilling. If being in the vicinity of his house was all the evidence they had, then she wasn't that worried, but she also wasn't stupid. "I would like to speak to my lawyer."

Samira's dark eyes widened. "Just like that? Quinn, are you sure you want to lawyer up?"

She crossed her arms. "I don't like the tone of this conversation. I want my legal counsel present. It is my right as you surely know."

"You can call a lawyer, and we'll wait for one to show up." Jalen stood and exited the room with Samira.

Quinn picked up her cell and advised Mike to take his time because she wanted Samira and Jalen to sweat a bit. Mike had come to her place earlier in the day, and she'd told him about some of the possible exposure, but she didn't tell the truth. He didn't need to know that to defend her. She wanted him to be in the best position possible.

Mike was a fifty something year old, good looking, high powered defense lawyer. She'd met him at various legal events and his reputation was outstanding. He'd jumped at the chance to help her. He was no fool and knew this type of exposure would be great for his career—while it could destroy hers. She hoped it wouldn't get to that point which is another reason she wanted him involved at the outset. Damage control.

Once everyone had been introduced, Mike spoke. "Is my client being charged with a crime today?"

"That might depend on her level of cooperation," Jalen responded.

"I'm listening," Mike said.

Samira looked at Mike. "Before you arrived, we were asking your client why she was in John Rossi's neighborhood the night he was murdered. Let me play you the video footage so you're up to speed."

The video ran and then Mike spoke. "I don't think you can even demonstrate that is my client on the video. I'm advising her not to answer any questions surrounding that tape."

Samira frowned. "Mike, I'm not sure you and your client

fully appreciate the gravity of the situation here. We're talking about serial murder. The deaths of Russell Myers, Warren Cruz, Richard Hale, and John Rossi."

Mike's hazel eyes narrowed. "I fail to see how any of those murders are connected to my client. Do you have any evidence at all besides this highly questionable video?"

Jalen cleared his throat. "Your client had easy access to all the CEOs who were killed. She was at all of the crime scenes around the time of the murders."

"I fail to see how that shows that Ms. Kelly is guilty of murder. Serial murder at that. My client had every reason to have a close working relationship with the CEOs for the companies she represented. You haven't breathed a word about motive because there simply is no motive."

Mike was good and she had no problem letting him take the lead. As much as she wanted to speak, this was no longer her show. When she'd made the mistake of getting caught on tape, she'd lost the ability to run things the way she wanted. Now she had to defer to Mike. Her actions had consequences.

Samira straightened her shoulders. "We have a strand of red hair from John's home that will surely match your client."

Mike let out a dramatic sigh. "First, my client was admittedly inside Mr. Rossi's home for business purposes and secondly, you don't have a warrant to get my client's DNA."

"Actually, we do have a warrant." Jalen pulled a piece of paper out of his jacket pocket. "We'll send someone in to do the collection when we're finished with our questions."

Mike looked at the warrant. "Probable cause here is extremely weak. It will be basis for a reversible error if it ever comes to that point."

Samira gave him a weak smile. "That's a risk we're more than willing to take."

"Knock yourself out, but there's still a completely innocent reason for my client's DNA to be at the Rossi house. That alone doesn't prove anything."

"Luckily, we have more than that."

"You're grasping at straws here, agents," Mike said. "My client is a highly respected woman in the community. You're trying to smear her good name, and I will fight you every step of the way."

Samira shook her head. "No. We're just trying to get to the truth. I don't know that the DA would have any appetite to work out a deal with your client given the heinous nature of the crimes, but I do think her cooperation would go a long way instead of stonewalling us."

Mike laughed. "You two are so far ahead of yourselves on this one, and you're going to regret it. I'll ask again. Are you actually charging my client with anything?"

"Not at this moment," Samira said calmly.

"Good," Mike responded. "Also, there's the matter of the FBI security detail. Given you are now accusing my client of serial murder, I want that detail removed immediately. It's basically unlawful surveillance."

"We will remove the detail." Samira paused. "We're done for now, but we will have the DNA sample collected and will be in touch."

Quinn wasn't concerned about the DNA given how she'd set things up, but she did wonder if the FBI had any other surprises up their sleeves.

55

Two days later and the DNA results had proven what Samira already knew. The hair was Quinn's, but that wasn't going to get them very far.

"We have her DNA now if nothing else," Jalen said.

"Yeah, but that doesn't help us for this case we're trying to construct in the here and now."

"You had a nice bluff about additional evidence when we interrogated her."

"I don't think Quinn bought it. Talk about an ice queen. If you were being questioned for serial murder and your whole world threatened, wouldn't you have broken a sweat?"

"That tells us what we're dealing with here." Jalen leaned against the conference room table.

"The problem is we don't have anything else." She looked at her watch. "The District Attorney should be here any minute. I want him involved sooner rather than later."

Jalen touched her arm. "You're worried he isn't going to go for this."

"Yeah. It's like Mike said. Quinn is a highly respected woman in the legal community. Lawyers don't like going after their own, especially if the hard evidence isn't there."

"Don't be such a downer. We're making progress here."

"Such an optimist." They were so different in that way.

"We caught the bad guy, or this instance the bad girl. Now we just have to make it stick."

And that was exactly her concern. In her gut, she felt they didn't have enough—nearly enough for a conviction, and maybe not even enough to make an arrest. But they would see what the DA had to say.

A little while later Alex Lopez walked into the FBI conference room. The forty something DA was tall and well-built with dark curly hair and smoldering brown eyes.

After they made introductions and sat down, Alex looked at her. "What's going on here, Agent Haddad?"

"Please call me Samira. We have a sensitive case that we need to talk to you about."

"I'm all ears." Alex pulled his legal pad out of his briefcase.

Samira and Jalen took about half an hour and told Alex everything they knew including showing him the video. He took copious notes but didn't ask any questions, letting them finish before he started talking.

Alex put his pen down and looked at both of them. "I'm very rarely at a loss for words, but agents, right now I am close to that."

His response was not what she was hoping for, but she couldn't be that surprised. "I know it's a long shot, but we do have a lot of circumstantial evidence."

Alex cleared his throat. "What you have is a ton of conjecture. A woman who was stalked and almost killed. A pillar in the legal community. And you want to convince a jury that she's not only a murderer, but a full-fledged serial killer? Killing those people she had worked tirelessly to defend in highly televised litigation? To make the jury believe that she's on some warped vigilante justice tour? And to do it with next to no hard evidence? I'm sorry, but it's just not going to fly."

"I don't think it's as bad as you make it out to be," Jalen said.

Alex frowned. "With all due respect, it's probably even worse."

"What about her lying to us and the video footage?" She wanted to get his unfiltered take.

"Based on what you told me, I don't actually see the lie. You didn't ask her the last time she was in Rossi's neighborhood. You asked her the last time she saw him. The fact that you may, and I repeat may, be able to prove that is Quinn on the tape, doesn't prove that she was at his house, only in his neighborhood. And unless I'm mistaken, she hasn't provided you an answer on why or if she was there. That's when she lawyered up."

Samira gritted her teeth. "You're right."

Alex's dark eyes softened. "Look. I get that the two of you are hot on this right now. You've been busting it trying to get this serial killer and now you have a theory that you believe makes sense, but unfortunately, you just don't have the evidence yet to act."

"What are we supposed to do then?" Jalen stood and started pacing. "Just let her go and keep on killing?"

Alex sighed. "You have to let her go but keep tabs on her. At some point, if you are right, and that's a big if, she will slip up and you'll have to be able to construct an actual legal case against her."

There was something weighing on her. "And if she doesn't slip up but more people die?"

"It's your job to make sure that doesn't happen." Alex leaned in toward her. "And you also have to do more legwork to make sure that you've got the right woman. The last thing you want to be doing is spinning your wheels on Quinn if she isn't the real killer."

Jalen sat back down "Why are you so skeptical about the possibility of her guilt?"

"It's my job to be skeptical. To vet cases. You are too close to this to be objective, both of you. If you take a step back and listen to what you presented to me and evaluate it rationally, I have no doubt that you'd come to the exact same conclusion that I did."

As much as she hated to admit it, Alex had a point. They were too close and needed more. "We probably showed our hand to Quinn too soon. That was my call and my mistake."

Jalen shook his head. "I agreed with you. There's no way we can go back now. It's like Alex said, we have to find a way forward."

Alex pushed back from the table. "If you do get something else, let me know, but you're not there yet."

"We appreciate your time." She stood to see him out.

"Of course. I'm always here if you need something."

Once he left the room, she and Jalen stood, staring at each other.

"Now what?" he asked.

"We plan for the future. Alex's right. We're only going to get one real shot at this. Someone like Quinn isn't killing for the fun of it. She's killing for a purpose, and while she may be able to cool off for a little while, it won't last."

Jalen grabbed onto her arm. "The need to keep going will overtake her, and we'll have to be ready for it."

"I just hope we can stop her before we have blood on our hands."

56

That evening Quinn poured herself a generous glass of Cabernet and took a few deep breaths. Things had been radio silent since the FBI interrogation. She had feared that there would be more evidence against her, but even given what Samira had said, she didn't think they were holding back evidence. They had been bluffing. If they had more, they would've certainly used it by now, and she would have been arrested, but instead she sat safely snuggled up on her couch with Felix by her side.

All of that told her that while it was a close call, she was in a much better position than she had imagined going into the meeting. And Mike had agreed with her. They'd had a long talk today and were on the same page. The DNA evidence was meaningless, and Mike explained that they were probably pushing for it more for a future use than a present one. She would have to be careful in the future when she decided to start working again.

Taking a sip of wine and patting Felix on the head, she thought about how all of this would impact her work. Her future. Not her work at the firm, because without being formally charged, no one ever had to know about any of this and she could go on. But her real life's work would be impacted. After

John she could no longer go on killing CEOs she represented and now under the FBI microscope, it was completely off the table.

But she wasn't deterred about her larger mission. One that John had fueled.

When the doorbell rang, her stomach clenched. Surely it wasn't the FBI about to bust down her door looking for something that they'd never find. Taking a big drink from her glass, she walked to the door and looked through the peephole. It wasn't an FBI team. It was just Samira. She should've known.

Quinn took a steadying breath and then opened the door.

"Can I come in?" Samira asked.

"That depends. Are you here on official FBI business? Do I need my attorney present?" She knew that was not going to go over well.

A frown pulled down on Samira's lips. "I don't think you need your attorney, but that is your right. I'd prefer this to be an informal discussion."

She didn't need Mike for this. She could handle Samira right now. "Can I get you anything? I'm having a glass of wine. Would you like to join me?"

"Sure, but just water for me."

"Ah, so are you still on the clock." Quinn hadn't expected Samira to say yes. Samira wasn't going to give up easily on this case, and she was curious to hear what she had to say. She poured a glass of water for Samira and topped her wine off.

"What brings you here?" Quinn offered Samira the glass of water, and they sat down on the couch.

Samira took a sip before speaking. "You need to stop doing what you're doing."

"And that would be?"

"This would be a much easier discussion if we just stopped this silly charade."

Samira was a worthy adversary, but Quinn would ultimately win this game. "There is no charade. You accused me of being a serial killer. I'd say first I'd like an apology."

Samira huffed. "That is something you won't get from me." She paused. "I don't condone what you have done, but I think I know why you did it."

Of course she wasn't going to speak to that, but she was interested in what Samira had to say.

"I also realize that you know that killing CEOs isn't going to cut it now, so I imagine you've already been thinking about how to shift course. That's why I'm here tonight. I want you to get the help you need to face down your demons and stop the bloodshed."

"You aren't making any sense." She actually was making perfect sense, but she couldn't say that.

"You know exactly what I mean." Samira's eyes narrowed. "Just stop the killing, Quinn. You may have been able to get away with what has happened in the past, but I know who you really are now, and you won't be able to do that in the future."

"Does anyone ever truly know a person?"

"Don't speak in riddles, Quinn. I'm here to help you."

Quinn laughed. "Trying to arrest me is your idea of help?"

Samira set down her glass on the coffee table. "You proclaim to care about justice, and seeking justice is what I'm trying to accomplish. This time I didn't have all the evidence I needed to act, but you won't be so lucky next time, Quinn. You will be caught, tried, and found guilty. Then you'll spend the rest of your life in prison. That can't be what you want."

Samira's impassioned plea confirmed one important fact. Samira cared about her. Empathized with her. She could use that to her advantage moving forward. Yes, Samira was trying to do what she thought was the right thing, but she didn't understand fully what drove Quinn. How could she? Samira hadn't experienced the pain that Quinn had, although she felt there was much more to Samira that she didn't know. "I do want justice, and that's what I fight for every single day in the courtroom."

"I'm not talking about what you do inside the courtroom. It's what you're doing outside that is the problem." Samira touched her arm and then pulled away. "I know you've been through trauma in your life. Quinn, I read all about your father. About the heinous charges against him."

Her stomach clenched. "You had no right to dig into my life like that."

"But I had to. I am truly sorry for what your father did to you."

Quinn looked directly at her. "It's not what you think."

"What do you mean?"

Samira had unwittingly poked at a wound that was all too fresh. "Yes, my father was physically abusive. Extremely so. But not sexually. I guess he had to draw the line somewhere." She fought off a wave of nausea. "He left that part to his friends, and unfortunately for me, he had way too many so-called friends."

"No one should have been forced to endure what you did but killing won't make the pain go away." Samira's voice broke. "No matter how hard you try."

That's where Samira was mistaken. It did help with the pain. It helped to be doing something active to fight for what was right. To hold those accountable who have done wrong. "I'm sorry. I don't know what else you want me to say."

"Say you'll stop this. Now. You have the perfect opportunity to change course. I can even refer you to some excellent medical professionals. I believe there is hope for you but only if you seek help."

She needed to change topics. "Why are you spending your evening at my place instead of having a life? Maybe you should focus more on you and less on me."

Samira laughed. "From the woman that is completely tethered to her job."

Quinn smiled as she raised the wine glass. "As I told you before, we have more in common than you think."

Samira turned to her. "I thought that too for a while, but I've learned our differences are more stark than I realized. I could never kill people like you do regardless of what they've done."

"You can try to claim the moral high ground if you want, but if you took a good, hard look at yourself, you'd admit I'm right about the two of us."

A frown spread across Samira's face.

Quinn was getting to her. She decided to press her advantage. "We all have secrets, Samira. I've learned enough about you to understand yours are dark and deep. Just like mine."

"I never said I didn't have secrets, but I haven't acted out killing people to deal with my baggage." Samira took a deep breath. "I believe that Tom Malone knew your secret. That's what he was talking about the day you killed him. I think that since he'd been following you, for who knows how long, he'd figured out what you were up to."

Quinn fought to keep her expression neutral. "I don't have any idea what Tom was talking about. He was clearly troubled."

"No doubt, but I also think he was speaking the truth. I went back through all the evidence from his house hoping there would be something there I could use, but I think Tom, in his own way, was trying to protect you and purposely didn't leave any direct evidence that would connect you to the murders."

Quinn had to admit she was impressed. Samira was doing all the right things. "You're really grasping at straws here."

Samira's dark eyes narrowed. "I know I probably can't prove it just yet, but if you continue going down this path, one day I will. You can't keep playing judge and jury."

She took another sip of wine, enjoying how the conversation was going. Samira wasn't finding what she was looking for, but Quinn surely was. "I'm a lawyer. An advocate. I never claimed I was ever judge or jury."

"Actions speak a lot louder than words. You realize that better than most."

"I don't know why you've gotten so glum on me."

"We're done here for now." She stood. "But I meant what I said Quinn. Get some professional help. Don't resort to violence.

It won't fill the emptiness. Causing others pain will never solve your own."

Quinn ignored her. "It was nice for you to come over. I do always enjoy our visits. I hope we can continue them even though the investigation is over."

"Don't push me, Quinn. I have a badge and a gun. I swore an oath to protect. To protect people from killers like you. Regardless of your past and your motivations, I won't hesitate to act if I need to."

"I'd expect nothing less from you." She walked Samira to the door.

Samira turned around and looked at her again, as if she wanted to say something else, but then walked out.

Samira had been right about one thing. She had to be careful. The FBI would be breathing down her neck for who knows how long, but she also knew that at some point, they'd have to be working on other cases and she would become an afterthought. How patient could Quinn be? Very.

Yes, she'd take her time and do the legwork. Since she was shifting the focus of her work, she needed to make absolutely sure that the men she targeted were fully deserving of her brand of justice. To do that, it would require time, effort, and solid research.

Let the FBI spin their wheels, and then once their guard was down, she would strike. No one, not even Samira, would be able to stop her.

NEXT IN THE DEADLY JUSTICE SERIES

Secrets Chase Her
Deadly Justice Book 2

A brutal murder. A deadly secret. A lawyer who won't back down.

When high-powered attorney Quinn Kelly finds her protégé brutally murdered, she's plunged into a nightmare—one that points directly to a ruthless serial killer. FBI Agent Samira Haddad takes over the case, but her complicated past with Quinn threatens to cloud the investigation.

Blackmailed by a powerful tech mogul who holds incriminating evidence against her, Quinn is forced to take on his defense to keep him silent. But she refuses to sit on the sidelines while Samira hunts the killer who took her friend's life. Quinn's search for answers uncovers a chilling truth: someone close to her is in the crosshairs—and she may be the reason why.

The killer is watching and lying in wait. With trust in short supply, both women must decide how far they're willing to go for justice—and survival.

———

Preorder **Secrets Chase Her** today.

EXCERPT FROM OUT OF HIDING

Sadie felt the bullet whiz by her head as she crouched down in the wet dirt. Darkness surrounded her, but she wasn't alone. Her gut screamed loudly that something was terribly wrong. And she always trusted her gut. She had company, and if that bullet was any indication, they meant business. The sound of the crackling leaves told her someone was moving quickly in her direction.

Dressed in all black, she lay flat on the ground in the dark woods. No one was going to see her. That bullet wasn't meant for her but was intended for someone else. Who? She didn't want to stick around long enough to find out. She prayed that Megan wasn't out here in the woods tonight—alone, scared, and with bullets flying. It was no place for a sixteen-year-old girl.

She checked her gun and kept her position low against the damp, muddy ground. Her night vision goggles were a blessing. It was then she saw what she dreaded the most. The letters FBI on a dark-colored flak jacket as an agent trounced his way through the woods. Why the FBI was involved in whatever was happening in these woods she didn't know, but she didn't like it. They were invading her turf.

Sadie had her first solid lead on the Vladimir network in El

Paso, and she didn't want to give up the opportunity. She'd been on stakeouts for weeks, desperately trying to determine if Igor—the man who had taken everything from her—was in El Paso. Her intel had been that something related to the Vladimir crew was going down in the woods tonight. She had hoped that whatever it was wasn't going to involve Megan—the missing girl she was looking for. Sadie knew that Vladimir's crew was responsible for her disappearance. That's why she'd sought out the job just days ago.

Technically, she was still in the Witness Security Program commonly known as Witness Protection, although they didn't consider her to be in immediate danger anymore. She'd followed all their rules over the years. Her new life, her new name, everything. Done by the book. Not a single deviation from the protocol given to her by the U.S. Marshals. There was no way she'd let them know what she planned to do now that she had confirmation Igor sought to set up shop in her own backyard. It was only a matter of time before Witness Protection realized Igor's activities had expanded down to El Paso, and then they'd want her to move. She needed to act fast if she had any chance of taking out Igor's network.

She slowly stood up using a large tree as a shield. Thankfully, she was small of stature. By the time she'd registered the crunch of a stick right behind her it was too late. A large hand grabbed her shoulder with another muffling her scream.

"FBI, don't move," the deep voice said directly into her ear.

Didn't matter who he was, when a man put his hands on her, he was going to pay. She'd trained for moments like these. She slammed her foot down on his, and he groaned. But he didn't loosen his grip. Was this guy made of iron?

Trying another approach, she went limp in his arms, shocking him into loosening his grip, giving her a moment to slide away. She'd only taken two steps when he tackled her, knocking her to the ground. She could barely breathe. She squirmed against him, but she was no match for his size and strength. He had to have been at least a foot taller and a hundred pounds heavier. For a moment, fear seized her. She said a prayer asking God to keep her safe and then fought back.

"Stop struggling," he said quietly, his voice steady. "I promise I'm not going to hurt you."

She didn't believe him. She knew better than to trust the Feds. Trust them, and she could end up dead like her parents. He adjusted his grip just enough for her to knee him in the stomach. Big mistake on her part. Now he seemed raving mad.

"I'm trying to save your life here. You have no idea what you've gotten yourself into. You should not be here in these woods right now."

The thing was, she actually wasn't a stranger to life-and-death situations. So this one didn't faze her too much. "I already dodged one bullet and was doing just fine on my own."

"You'll have time later to explain how you ended up in the middle of an active FBI investigation packing heat and wearing night vision goggles. For now, let me get you out of here safe and sound."

She shuddered. Those promises had been made to her before. And they'd been broken—every single one of them.

"I'm not going anywhere with you," she hissed. She struggled against his secure grip.

"Yes, you are, ma'am. Listen to me." He paused, his breathing ragged. "Things are only going to get worse. You might not be as fortunate the next time a bullet gets fired. And I don't want to have your death on my conscience. I have enough guilt to last a lifetime. So when I say three, we move for that next tree. You hear me?"

Realizing her current options were limited, she relented. He was right. Her best move for now was to retreat. She'd taken a taxi tonight and made her way to the woods on foot. It wasn't as if she had her own ride out of danger. She'd have time to get away from him once they got to safety. "Okay."

"One, two, three, go go go!" he said in a low voice. They

sprinted from their current position to the next tree and squatted down. That's when she heard another round of gunfire. Automatic weapons this time. Her heartbeat quickened, but now was not the time to panic. She'd been in worse situations without the valuable experience that she now carried with her after years of being a private investigator.

"What next?" she whispered, trying to catch her breath.

"Make a run for that far tree. My Jeep is beyond it. I'm hoping that will work."

"And if not?"

"I'll think of plan B."

He sounded so sure of himself. Typical for FBI types. She wasn't going to count on him to get her out of here safely. She'd survey her options once they made it to the next tree before she jumped in the Jeep of a total stranger—even if he was in the FBI. Hadn't she already learned that tough lesson?

"Now," he barked.

She ran ahead of him using her small size and speed to her advantage, making it to the tree first. Though he wasn't far behind. She saw the dark Jeep parked behind a cluster of trees providing them with additional cover.

"Let's go for it," he said.

Making a split-second decision that she prayed she wouldn't regret, she slid into the passenger side and ducked down low. Before she could even steady herself, the FBI guy had turned the ignition and floored it. The bumpy ride had her on high alert as he navigated the vehicle over the rough terrain.

She stayed down not knowing if they were safe from the gunfire and started plotting her escape. No way was she being taken in by the FBI to "explain herself."

They drove a few minutes in silence as the Jeep weaved through the wooded area and onto the country road that would eventually lead back into town. Then he spoke after checking his mirrors. "We're in the clear."

She eased up into her seat and looked around at her

surroundings, including the man driving. She wasn't wrong in her initial assessment. This guy was tall and bulky. She already knew from the encounter in the woods that he was strong. His brown hair was cut short. She couldn't see his eyes since they were focused on what lay ahead. She told herself to remember that he was one of them.

He glanced over at her. "You want to tell me now what you were doing out in the woods?"

"My job," she snapped. Who knows what he thought she was doing, but her answer was completely truthful.

"And what job is that?"

She sighed, already not enjoying this line of questioning. "I'm a private investigator."

"You're not plugged into our FBI investigation, though. I would've known it."

"I have no idea what investigation you're working on." She let out a deep breath and figured she needed to provide an explanation. Maybe it would help her get away from him sooner. "I was in the woods searching for a missing girl. You may have even seen a local news story about her. Her mother recently hired me. I've been looking everywhere. I didn't see or hear anything until I felt the first bullet whiz by my ear." She was telling the truth. She had to make sure Megan wasn't in those woods tonight. It appeared that her leads had been correct. Something was going on with the Vladimir crew. And the FBI was involved. She said another silent prayer for Megan.

"Wow," he said. "You were in the wrong place at the wrong time, Ms. P.I. lady. I'm going to need to bring you in, though. Gotta take your statement. Make it official." His southern drawl was unmistakable.

"I don't think that's a good idea."

"I promise it'll be quick. You are carrying a weapon. I assume you have a permit for that and all."

No way she'd allow him to take her in, but she didn't have to tell him that. Her past struggles with the FBI were her own. Better to have the element of surprise.

"Uh, oh," he said. He jerked the wheel hard to the right sending her into his right arm. "We've got company. Hold on."

"I thought you said we were good."

"They came out of nowhere."

She turned around and saw a large dark SUV that was gaining on them. But FBI guy had some moves and was taking the curves on the dark country road with finesse as he drove toward the more populated area of town.

"Who are these people?" she asked as she clenched her fists. Were they connected to Vladimir?

"The less you know the better."

"Why don't you let me take a shot? I could probably blow out their tire."

"You're that good of a shot?" he asked with disbelief dripping from his deep voice.

"You better believe it," she said without hesitation.

He paused for a second and glanced over at her. "If you think you can, then go for it."

She was going to show this FBI guy that she was no slouch. In fact, she could probably outshoot him. All the time she'd spent at the range over the past few years had paid off. She turned around and was glad they were in a Jeep. Granted it didn't provide them with much, if any, protection, but it also meant she'd have an easier time getting off an unobstructed shot.

Steadying herself she took a deep breath, aimed, and pulled the trigger. It only took one shot, and the right front tire of the car chasing them was done for. The pursuit ended abruptly as they began to skid, the car circling in on the blown tire. "Got 'em."

"Well, Ms. P.I. lady, I'm impressed."

"You should be." Then she turned the gun toward him.

"Whoa." He lifted up his right hand at her while keeping his left on the wheel. "Just put that thing away."

Her hand was steady. "I have no reason to use this on you, but I'm not being taken in for questioning. I didn't do anything wrong."

"I never accused you of anything," he said with a raised voice. She watched as his hands tightened on the wheel.

"Take me downtown. Let me out and drive away. It's that simple."

"You're crazy, ma'am."

"No. But I'm the one with the gun right now, so I hope you don't try anything crazy."

"You're hiding something."

"It's none of your concern. Just act like you never saw me tonight."

"You know that's not possible. I'll have to write up this whole thing."

"Be creative," she countered. "Now let's get downtown. And don't try anything because I'd really hate to shoot you."

He let out a deep breath but started driving toward town as she directed. Good, she thought. She doubted that he'd let her go indefinitely. But she needed to get away and deal with this problem on her own terms. That meant not being taken in for questioning by the FBI tonight. She needed time.

When they reached the more crowded streets of downtown El Paso, she was ready to get away from him. "Slow down. Let me out. And keep on driving. Do you hear me?"

"Yes," he said in an even voice.

"Good."

He did as she asked and slowed down. She never took the gun off of him as she opened the door slowly. With the light from the streets flooding in, she could see his eyes were light blue. And questioning. "Just pretend I was never here. For your own good and mine too, okay?"

She couldn't shake the thought that she'd seen him before. She backed out of the Jeep, and he didn't say anything in response. She slammed the door shut, and he pulled away. She didn't waste any time weaving her way through the Saturday night crowd.

She was safe for now, but she had no doubt. The FBI guy would find her, and when he did, she'd be in a ton of trouble.

———

Continue reading OUT OF HIDING in Kindle Unlimited.

ATLANTA JUSTICE SERIES

DEADLY PROOF

LONE WITNESS

BREACH OF TRUST

EXCERPT FROM DEADLY PROOF

"You can't call that a settlement offer." Kate Sullivan looked directly into the dark eyes of her opposing counsel, who represented a medical device company. Jerry had just made partner and thought he could play hardball, but she wasn't going to let him get the upper hand.

"You and I both know that amount will never cut it. Come back to me when you have a number I can work with." She closed her laptop and shoved it in her bag.

"C'mon, Kate. Fifty grand is a good starting point," Jerry said. "We're done here. Call me when you're actually ready to negotiate." She stood up and walked out of the conference room before Jerry could say anything else. He wasn't taking her client's claims seriously, so she wasn't going to waste any more time playing games. He'd come to his senses soon enough. This case shouldn't go to trial, and he knew it.

Making the quick drive from downtown to Midtown Atlanta, weaving through the usual traffic, she parked in her reserved spot in the garage under a tall office building. The large office tower was home of the world-class plaintiff's firm Warren McGee.

She spent more time at her office than she did at her own home, but that was by choice. Representing innocent victims was her calling.

When she walked out of the elevator and onto the twenty third floor, her assistant, Beth Russo, greeted her warmly.

"How did it go?" Beth asked. Her fifty-five-year-old assistant had been working at the law firm for decades and knew the ins and outs of each case and every schedule. Kate would be lost without her.

"Still no settlement, but they'll cave eventually. They don't actually want to try this case."

"I hope so, because you need to get it off your docket and give your full attention to the Mason Pharmaceutical litigation. You deserve to be running that case."

Kate laughed. "Let me get on the steering committee first, Beth. Then I'll apply for lead counsel."

"Exactly. You're due in court in three hours for the hearing on the steering committee, and you've got calls piled up."

She smiled. "Thanks, Beth. I'll work through them." Calls meant business, and business was what kept her in good standing as a partner at the firm.

In the privacy of her own office, Kate stared out the large window that gave her a fantastic view of Stone Mountain in the distance. She'd earned this corner office by working hard, but she wanted more. Her goal was to be managing partner one day, and this litigation was huge.

Thousands of cases had been filed across the country against Mason Pharmaceutical Corporation, known as MPC. She was responsible for a large chunk of them, representing victims who had taken MPC's migraine drug and had died or been injured. She needed a spot on the exclusive committee of plaintiffs' lawyers that would dictate the entire direction of the case.

Her phone rang, but she let it go, knowing Beth would answer it. She had started flipping through her emails when Beth hurried into her office with a frown pulling at her lips.

"Kate, sorry to bother you, but there's a call I think you have to take."

"Who is it?" Beth's brown eyes narrowed. "She won't give me her name, but she said she has information regarding the MPC case."

Once the litigation hit the news and the firms started advertising to find clients who had taken the dangerous drug, there was a constant stream of inquiries to be fielded. The firm couldn't turn them down without hearing the person out first.

"Why don't you have one of the associates take it?"

Beth shook her head. "She says she'll only talk to you."

Kate was listed as lead counsel on hundreds of the complaints, so it made sense that this person would want to talk to her. "Okay, put her through." She waited for her line to light up red, then picked up the phone. "This is Kate Sullivan."

"I have some critical information for you, but I can't speak over the phone," a woman said, her words rushed and breathless. "Is there a place we can meet?"

Kate needed more before she dropped everything to go on what might be a wild goose chase. "And you are?"

"I don't want to say right now." Her voice was hushed.

"You can come down to my office, and we can talk here."

"No, no. That won't work," the woman said. "It's too risky. Your office is the last place I can be seen."

"Ma'am, as you can imagine, I have a lot on my plate right now. So it would be helpful if I had some idea of what this is all about."

"I have information you're going to need," the caller whispered. "Things related to your case. Things I know because of my job."

That got Kate's attention. "Are you an employee of Mason Pharmaceutical Corporation?"

"I told you, I can't have this conversation over the phone."

Kate's heartbeat sped up at the strain in the woman's voice. "All right. There's a coffee shop in Colony Square on Peachtree and Fourteenth. Can you meet me there?"

"Yes. See you in ten minutes."

Kate hung up, and her mind went into overdrive. If this woman was truly an employee of MPC, then this meeting could be huge. MPC had corporate offices in multiple states, but the company headquarters and largest office was in Atlanta.

It was likely this woman was a disgruntled employee or that she was unstable. But something about her voice tugged at Kate. Her curiosity and desire to be thorough led her to take the meeting.

She made the short walk from her office across the street and down a block to Colony Square, which housed restaurants and shops catering to the Midtown Atlanta community. It was lunchtime, and there were plenty of people out taking breaks in the warm Georgia sunshine. Since it was June, the humidity made the air thick and sticky, but it was better than being locked inside a stuffy office all day.

As Kate stepped into the coffee shop, she looked for someone who could potentially be her tipster. Not seeing anyone promising, she took a seat at the table in the back corner and waited.

After a few minutes, a woman who was probably in her mid-forties took the seat across from her. She had brown hair cut in a no-nonsense bob and wore simple wire-frame glasses that only partially obscured her bloodshot eyes.

"You're Kate Sullivan?" the woman asked in a low voice. Then she turned and looked over her shoulder. Nervous—and paranoid.

"Yes. And you are?"

"Ellie Proctor."

"Nice to meet you, Ellie. Why don't you explain to me what this is all about."

"I'm scared," Ellie said as she clenched her pale hands together in front of her.

"There's nothing to be afraid of. You're safe with me."

"No, you don't understand."

Was this lady a conspiracy theorist? Kate had no idea what she was dealing with. "Just take it one step at a time. Do you work for MPC?"

"Yes."

"And what is your job there?" Kate felt like she was conducting a deposition, trying to get information out of a witness.

"I'm one of the senior R&D scientists." Ellie shivered, but the coffee shop's air conditioning was barely functioning.

Kate pressed on. "What do you work on?"

"A variety of testing and product development for different drugs."

"And you think you know something about Celix? The drug involved in my cases." Ellie nodded. "Yeah. I did my research. I went onto the law firm websites and read all the information about the litigation."

"And what do you think?"

"It's so much bigger than what you and the other lawyers around the country are saying about Celix."

Now Ellie had Kate's undivided attention. "How so?" Celix caused brain tumors, so she wasn't sure how much bigger this could get.

Ellie looked down. Her brown eyes not making contact.

"Listen, Ellie, I can't help you if I don't know what the facts are." She needed to be patient. This woman seemed like she might go off the ledge at any minute.

"You need to dig deeper." Ellie wrapped her arms tightly

around herself as she shook. "A lot deeper, but you have to be careful."

"The case is just starting, but I'm always very thorough."

As Ellie's eyes darted back and forth, Kate began to wonder if Ellie was strung out on something. The red eyes, the shivering, the paranoia. Did this woman even work for MPC?

"The lawsuits say that MPC should have known through its testing that brain tumors were a potential side effect, but . . ."

"What?"

"I've already said too much out in the open like this, but you need to go beyond Celix. This is bigger than Celix. You have to look at other MPC drugs. Get your hands on all of the testing records for Celix and the emails about the test results. I can't provide them to you. My computer has highly restrictive security protocols. I'm hoping you'll be able to get them through your case, but I know some of the documents have already been shredded or deleted. I don't even know what's left on our servers. I think this goes up to the highest levels of the company." Ellie glanced furtively around, then leaned over the table and whispered, "I know it sounds crazy, but I'm taking a risk even coming here to meet you."

Kate looked around, and no one in the coffee shop seemed even remotely interested in what they were talking about. But even given how weird this all seemed, she couldn't just push it under the rug and walk away. "How about we set up a time and place to meet? Your choice. Somewhere you're comfortable talking openly with me, so I can gather more facts."

Ellie let out a long sigh. "Thank you. I think that's for the best. I thought I might be able to talk here, but it just doesn't feel right. Can we meet the day after tomorrow at 7:00 p.m. at the entrance of Piedmont Park?"

"Sure. I'll be there." Ellie reached across the table and gripped Kate's hand.

"Whatever you do, you can't bring my name into this. I'm

coming to you because it's the right thing to do. I can't sleep at night with all of this on my conscience." She took a deep breath.

"I'll be discreet." Kate didn't want to jeopardize Ellie's livelihood, but she definitely had to get to the bottom of this.

"I have to get back to work before my lunch break ends."

"Can I get your contact information?"

"Yes. This is my business card. I'll put my personal cell on the back." Ellie took a pen out of her small navy purse and, with a wobbly hand, wrote down her number. Then she scratched through her work contact information. "Please don't ever contact me at work."

"You did the right thing by coming to me, Ellie. I'm going to figure out what's going on here."

———

CAPITAL INTRIGUE SERIES

END GAME

BACKLASH

POWER PLAY

EXCERPT FROM END GAME

"I think they might be keeping dead bodies in their condo!"

Bailey Ryan sat beside her friends in an Arlington, Virginia, diner and took a big bite of salad as Layla Karam continued to tell her animated story.

"Bailey, Viv, I'm telling you." Layla lifted her hands. "I have to find a new place to live. My neighbors are insane. I'm not joking about the dead bodies."

Bailey laughed at her friend's ridiculous accusation.

Vivian Steele's hazel eyes glistened with excitement. "Dead bodies would be Bailey's territory. She's the hotshot FBI agent."

Bailey shook her head. "I don't think anyone has ever called me a hotshot."

Vivian laughed. "In law school they just called you the gunner."

Bailey placed a hand on her chest. "No way. Layla was the gunner."

"Lies. All lies." Layla grinned as she twisted her long black hair around her finger. "We have to decide if we're going to the five-year reunion."

"It'll depend on my schedule," Viv said. "Things are crazy at work right now." She looked down at her smart watch. "That's why we're eating dinner at ten PM." To the outside world, Viv and Layla worked at the State Department, but though Viv was a lawyer for State, in reality Layla actually worked as an analyst at the CIA. Only a very tight circle of people knew the truth about Layla's career. She and Viv were currently working on a joint project that called for some overnight assignments. "I think I'd like to go to the reunion—but only if we *all* go."

"Georgetown Law reunions are supposed to be fancy affairs," Layla said.

Bailey groaned. "Just what I need. We've stayed in touch with the people we actually liked. I'm not interested in schmoozing with anyone else."

"It's DC—everyone has an angle to play," Vivian said.

Bailey understood that point all too well. Even in her career at the FBI, she had to deal with internal and external politics and power plays. She just wanted to do her job and solve crimes.

She'd just taken the last bite of her salad when her cell phone rang. "Sorry, ladies, I have to get this."

"We know the drill," Viv said.

They had high-pressure jobs that called on them at all hours. It was another reason they got along so well. There was never any guilt over having to deal with work issues. Just the opposite —they were all very supportive of each other and stepped up to the plate to be there. To Bailey, these women were her family.

Bailey stood and answered her phone. "Agent Ryan."

"We've got one," Connor said. "Meet you at the DC morgue."

"See you soon." She had a no-nonsense but strong relation-ship with Special Agent Remy Connor. Known to everyone as Connor, he was five years her senior. They had grown very close, and he was like the big brother she'd never had.

She walked back over to her friends. "Sorry, I've got to run."

"An actual dead body this time?" Viv asked.

Bailey nodded. "Yeah."

"We should be getting to work too." Viv looked at Layla. "We're working some late nights these days. I don't think I'm cut out for the night shift. At least this assignment will be over soon."

"You'll have me there for moral support." Layla smiled.

Bailey's heart warmed watching her friends. "Be good. I'll catch up with you two later." She never asked questions about their work, but understood they were working on an important project.

She exited the restaurant and got on the Metro. Then she hopped off at L'Enfant Plaza and made the short walk to DC's Medical Examiner Office. As an agent in the Criminal Investigative Division working out of the DC field office, her days and nights were often filled with things most people would rather avoid, but she did important, fulfilling work. Much more fulfilling than taking a traditional lawyer gig at a huge firm. Although she'd had a ton of offers to do so.

Having a law degree gave her a unique perspective many of her colleagues didn't have. Most of the agents who did have JDs had chosen other divisions at FBI to work in. Not her. She thrived on the challenges that came with working violent crimes.

No stranger to the Medical Examiner Office, she flashed her badge at the security guard and made her way to Connor, who stood in the lobby.

"Thanks for waiting on me, or is it that you didn't want to visit the body alone?" She enjoyed giving Connor a hard time, but he always took it in stride.

He smiled. "You know I'm a team player."

"So what have we got?" They started walking down the hallway to the elevator that would take them to the basement morgue.

His blue eyes met hers. "DC police called us in because this is the second murder in three days with a similar MO. First murder was in Arlington, but this victim was killed in Foggy Bottom. Arlington PD and DC police stay in close communication and they put two and two together."

The elevator dinged, and they exited to see Jessie—or Doc Phillips, as she was known—as the coroner on duty. She was one of Bailey's favorite people to work with.

The short, gray-haired woman greeted them both warmly. "Good evening, agents. I'm glad you're here."

They followed her into the morgue, and Bailey was ready to jump in. "Connor tells me the victim is similar to one from just three days ago?"

"That's correct. I got the autopsy report from the Arlington ME's office. The prior victim is Michael Rogers. And while I can't say with certainty, there is a striking resemblance in what was done to the two bodies."

Doc Phillips removed the sheet covering the new victim lying on the table. The first thing that struck Bailey was the man's ultra-strong physique. Given his size and muscle tone, this made the crime all the more perplexing.

"Do you notice his build?" she said. "For someone to get the drop on him, he must have really been caught by surprise."

Connor nodded. "I'm not an expert, but from the angles of the cuts it looks like someone came up on him from behind and maybe caught him off guard." He ran his hand through his short blond hair. "Am I right, Doc?"

"You're right that the wounds were inflicted from behind." The ME pointed toward the body. "As you can see, there are multiple stab wounds. I can tell you they are in the same direction and depth as Rogers'." She walked over to her desk and picked up some papers. "Take a look for yourself. This is the report for Rogers."

Bailey and Connor both took a few moments to study the report.

"So we're possibly looking at the same killer," Bailey said flatly. "Only three days in between, same MO. No cooling-off period. This could be the makings of a serial case."

"It is my opinion that this could be the same killer, but for the rest of it, I'll leave the investigating up to the FBI." Doc Phillips looked away.

Something was up. "What are you not telling us, Doc?" Bailey asked.

Doc Phillips shifted her weight from side to side. "Well, it might not *just* be the FBI."

"What do you mean?" Connor asked.

Doc looked at him. "We ran his prints, and the results came back a bit ago."

"Who is he?" Bailey asked.

"I know exactly who he is," a deep male voice said behind her.

Bailey turned and saw a tall black-haired man standing in the doorway. He sucked all the air out of the room with his commanding presence. "And who are you?" she asked.

"Special Agent Marco Agostini, NCIS." He walked toward them.

That explained Doc's behavior. They wouldn't be working this case alone. "And that must mean he's one of yours?"

Marco's dark eyes locked onto hers. "That's need to know."

———

Marco eyed the blonde wearing the dark FBI jacket with skepticism. There was no way he was letting FBI take the lead on this case.

"You'll have to do a lot better than that, Agent Agostini," the blonde said. "We *do* have a need to know."

The ME took a few steps back. "I'm going to get some coffee while you all sort this out. I'll be a back in a few." She quickly exited, obviously not wanting to get involved in a turf war, and he couldn't blame her.

"And who are you?" Marco asked.

"FBI Special Agent Bailey Ryan, and this is Supervisory Special Agent Remy Connor."

Marco stood firm. "I know you're just trying to do your job, but so am I. NCIS is taking this case."

Bailey's bright green eyes narrowed. "We both got called down here. You know you can't waltz in and act like you own the investigation. This is the second murder of its type in less than three weeks. For all we know, this could be a serial killer, and FBI has to be involved."

Marco thought he heard Agent Connor let out a little laugh. He tried to size up the two of them, and given their titles, Bailey was the junior of the two but not by a whole lot. Regardless, he had to protect his case. "I'll say it again, ma'am. NCIS is taking charge here."

"I haven't gotten that direction from my boss." She turned to Agent Connor. "Have you, Connor?"

"Nope. Why don't I make a few calls and see if we can get some clarity on the situation?" Agent Connor stepped outside the room with his phone to his ear.

Marco took a moment to study Bailey Ryan. She had straight blonde hair that almost hit her shoulders. Her sun-kissed skin was probably a sign that she spent a lot of time outdoors. Above average height, but still stood below his six-one frame. He figured he should take the high road and try not to agitate the situation any further. "Agent Ryan, I have only the utmost respect for the FBI."

"You sure have an interesting way of showing it," she shot

back. "What happened to the directive that we should all work together for the common good?"

She had him there. "That's true, but there are still possible security issues present. I just want to be buttoned up here, and we can't afford to take any chances."

Bailey crossed her arms. "If you're worried about security clearances, I worked a joint operation with FBI counter intelligence a few months ago. I have Top Secret SCI clearance. So that shouldn't be an issue."

He appreciated her zeal, but he wasn't going to give in—it didn't matter that she seemed more than competent, not to mention pretty. In truth, he didn't have a leg to stand on with the security clearance argument. He was just trying to stall and hopefully get a grip on this situation ASAP.

Bailey stepped toward him. "As far as I can tell, this crime happened while the victim was not on duty."

"You know that doesn't preclude NCIS from taking the lead. He's still one of us. That means this is our case to run if we want it."

Bailey placed her hands on her hips but didn't say anything. Probably because she knew he was right. NCIS routinely took the lead in a felony case involving a Navy service member. Yes, they had to work with other agencies all the time, but he would like NCIS to be at the helm on this one. Everything about this scenario felt wrong to him.

His phone rang, and he looked down to see who it was. "Sorry, ma'am. This is my boss, and I need to take this."

Bailey smiled. "All right."

She was smiling because if the NCIS Director, Nadine Mercer, was calling right now, that couldn't be good. "This is Agostini."

"Agostini, it's Director Mercer."

"Yes, ma'am. How can I help you?" He dreaded what the response would be.

"You're at the ME's office, right?"

"Yes, ma'am." He swallowed hard, waiting for her to give her orders.

"I know we talked about this being an exclusive NCIS operation, but we have to play nice in the sandbox. I've gotten some pressure from my colleagues at the FBI, and they want in on this too, given the possibility that we might have a serial or spree killer on the loose and the first victim was a civilian. So this is how it's going to go. We work the case jointly, but for now NCIS is still lead."

"Why do you say 'for now,' ma'am?" He feared he already knew.

"Because you know how things could change any minute, but you need to work *with* the FBI and not against them. Am I clear, Agent Agostini?"

There was only one answer. "Crystal, ma'am."

"Agostini, I have a bad feeling about this. Get to the bottom of what's going on here ASAP."

"Roger that, ma'am." As he hung up, he saw that Connor had joined Bailey, and they were huddled up talking in the corner of the room. No doubt they'd just received the exact same message from their leadership as he'd gotten. Now he had to welcome them in. It wasn't the first time in his career he'd eaten crow, and it certainly wouldn't be the last.

He walked over to where the agents stood. He expected Bailey to rub it in, but she didn't say a word. "I'm guessing you talked to your boss too. My directive is that this is a joint investigation with NCIS taking lead. Is that your understanding?" He looked at Bailey and then Connor.

"Yes," Bailey said. "But given our resource constraints, you're going to be stuck with me. Connor will be monitoring the case but not working the day to day. We're spread very thin, as I assume you are at NCIS as well."

"Yeah, it's the reality these days for all of us. More budget cuts and hiring freezes, but the bad guys never let up." Marco prepared himself to be spending a lot more time with Bailey. He wasn't blind to the fact that she was attractive, but he also put his job first—always. That was probably why he was thirty-one and still single. "Then I guess we need to get to it. We should head to NCIS headquarters and bring in some others on my team to assist. In the meantime, I can get you up to speed on the second victim—Petty Officer First Class Sean Battle."

"What's really going on here? Why all the intense focus on a petty officer?" Bailey asked.

Marco took a deep breath. "Because this one was special. He was a Navy SEAL."

ACKNOWLEDGMENTS

Many thanks to my agent Sarah Younger and the Nancy Yost Literary Agency. Sarah—it's hard to believe we've been working together for twelve years. Thank you for always accepting me just as I am.

To my family, human and furry, thank you for always supporting my writing journey.

To my readers, you've always been a source of inspiration. I hope you will continue with me on this winding road of story-telling.

ABOUT THE AUTHOR

Rachel Dylan is an award-winning and bestselling author of legal thrillers and romantic suspense. Rachel has practiced law for almost two decades, including as a litigator at one of the nation's top law firms. Rachel lives in Michigan with her husband and three furkids—one loveable Labrador and two senior cats. Rachel loves to connect with readers. You can find Rachel at www.racheldylan.com.

instagram.com/racheldylanauthor
facebook.com/RachelDylanAuthor
x.com/dylan_rachel
bookbub.com/authors/rachel-dylan
amazon.com/author/racheldylan
goodreads.com/racheldylan
pinterest.com/racheldylanauth